PLAY
IT OFF

ALSO BY MONICA MURPHY

Lancaster Prep Next Generation

All My Kisses For You

Keep Me In Your Heart

You Were Never Not Mine

New Young Adult Series

The Liar's Club

Kings of Campus

End Game

Lancaster Prep

Things I Wanted To Say

A Million Kisses in Your Lifetime

Birthday Kisses

Promises We Meant to Keep

I'll Always Be With You

College Years

The Freshman

The Sophomore

The Junior

The Senior

Dating Series

Save the Date

Fake Date

Holidate

Hate to Date You

Rate a Date

Wedding Date

Blind Date

The Callahans

Close to Me

Falling for Her

Addicted to Him

Meant to Be

Fighting for You

The Rules

Fair Game

In the Dark

Slow Play

Safe Bet

The Fowler Sisters

Owning Violet

Stealing Rose

Taming Lily

Billionaire Bachelors Club

Crave

Torn

Savor

Intoxicated

One Week Girlfriend

One Week Girlfriend

Second Chance Boyfriend

Three Broken Promises

Drew + Fable Forever

Four Years Later

Five Days Until You

A Drew + Fable Christmas

Stand-Alone YA Titles

Daring the Bad Boy

Saving It

Pretty Dead Girls

PLAY IT OFF

MONICA MURPHY

Text copyright © 2025 by Monica Murphy Publishing
All rights reserved.

Published by Montlake, Seattle

www.apub.com

Amazon, the Amazon logo, and Montlake are trademarks of Amazon.com, Inc., or its affiliates.

EU product safety contact:
Amazon Media EU S. à r.l.
38, avenue John F. Kennedy, L-1855 Luxembourg
amazonpublishing-gpsr@amazon.com

ISBN-13: 9781662522802 (paperback)
ISBN-13: 9781662522819 (digital)

Cover design by Hang Le
Cover photography © Wander Aguiar Photography
Cover image: © Adam Vilimek / Shutterstock

Printed in the United States of America

PLAY
IT OFF

Chapter One

Sienna

Freshman year

I can't believe it—I got into a bar.

The most popular bar in Santa Mira. Charley's is where all UC Santa Mira students go to hang out. They have great drink specials. Good music—if you can hear it over the constant stream of conversation and yelling that is currently taking place. And bonus: it's where all the football players hang out.

That's my favorite part because I'm seeking a specific football player. And no, I'm not referring to my older brother. Coop is around here somewhere. I'm pretty sure he's in this very bar, and while he's totally intimidating and convinces any guy who so much as glances in my direction to keep away from me with just a look, we're close. I adore him.

Though I don't adore his overprotective ways.

"Looks like the hundred bucks I spent on the fake ID was worth it." My new roommate, Destiny, smiles, her dark-brown eyes sparkling. "How much did you spend on yours?"

"Seventy-five." I shrug when she frowns. Feels like she's always in competition with me, and I don't like it. I'm here for supportive friendships, not for constantly trying to outdo each other. She's a little weird, but she's the only roommate I've got and currently one of the only friends I've made since I came here. "My brother knows a guy."

"Speaking of your brother, where is the famous Coop?" she asks, changing the subject, her expression turning eager. She loves the fact that my brother plays for the Dolphins football team. I'm pretty sure it's the only thing she likes about me.

"I don't know. I'm sure he's here somewhere." Yet again my answer makes her frown, and I'm over it. "I need a drink."

Without waiting for her answer, I leave her where she stands, pushing my way through the crowd as I head for the bar. I'm tall—almost five ten—and as I pass guys shorter than me, they don't even bother looking in my direction. Which is fine because I've always preferred dating a tall guy. Someone who towers over me and makes me feel small, a feeling I rarely experience. I've been the tallest girl in class since kindergarten, and while there are advantages, most of the time it just means I intimidate boys.

Men.

Hmm, guess I'm more like my brother than I realize.

By the time I make it up to the bar, I'm sweating, even though I'm only wearing a pair of extremely short denim shorts and a black tube top. It's sweltering in here. If Coop saw me, he'd probably freak the hell out and escort me straight out of the bar, giving me a lecture about my clothes.

Glancing to my left, then my right, I make sure the coast is clear before I lean over the counter and give the hot bartender a solid glimpse of my ample cleavage. He notices immediately, because of course he does, and comes right to me, earning an irritated "Hey!" from the guys he was helping before he abandoned them for me.

"What's up, gorgeous?" Up close, I realize he's not as good looking as I originally thought. There's something even a little smarmy about him. Might be that knowing gleam in his pale-blue eyes or the fact that his hair hangs in near-perfect little ringlets over his forehead. He runs his fingers through said hair, pushing it out of his eyes, and I get the sudden feeling that is very much a practiced move for this dude.

"I'd like a rum and Coke, please." I flash him a smile and stand up straighter so he can't ogle my tits any longer, and his disappointment is clear.

"Coming right up." He whips out a glass and turns to grab a bottle of rum off the counter behind him. "You a transfer?"

I frown. "Excuse me?"

"I don't recognize you—and I'd definitely remember a face like yours. Figured you must've just transferred in." He scoops ice into the glass, then adds Coke before he splashes in some rum. I'd take more, but I don't want to be a jerk about it.

Oh. Right. I can't tell him I'm a freshman because I'll get kicked out of here. "Yeah, I started in the fall." That's not a lie.

"Welcome to Santa Mira." He smiles, his gaze dropping to my chest yet again as he hands over the drink. "On the house."

"Thank you." I take the drink, sip it from the narrow red straw, and realize it's stronger than I thought. All I can taste is rum. "This place is busy."

"The busiest bar in town." His gaze lingers on mine, and I can feel the frustration from other bar patrons emanating toward us as he continues to ignore them. "You come here alone tonight? Or with someone?"

"With someone—" I start, but he cuts me off with another question.

"Your boyfriend?" When I shake my head, he actually leers at me like some sort of creeper. "Perfect. I get off at midnight. Wanna go back to my place?"

I stare at him, a lump in my throat making it hard to speak. How am I supposed to turn him down? That is the last thing I want to do.

"Jesus, Sam. Stay away from this one. She's Coop's *sister*."

My heart sinks into my toes, if that's possible, because oh my God, I just got cockblocked by the hottest man alive, who only sees me as one thing.

Coop's little sister.

I can feel his presence looming directly behind me, the heat of his body seeping into mine and making me shiver. He braces one hand on the counter, caging me in on the left side, and I can't look at him. Staring into his eyes is dangerous, and I'm trying to keep my composure.

"Oh shit." The bartender's face actually pales. "Coop's sister?"

I sip as much of the drink as I possibly can because if Gavin Maddox blows my cover, I'm done for.

"Yeah. Stop flirting with her. Coop will murder you with his bare hands if you so much as touch her." Gavin pauses. "And I'll help him."

Despite his ruining my flirtation with the bartender—which I wasn't taking seriously, anyway, because the only person I want to flirt with is Gavin—I can't deny it's kind of exciting that he ran to my rescue like this.

The bartender doesn't say another word. Just switches his attention to the next customer, pasting on that faintly smarmy smile as he asks her what she wants.

"Um." I finally dare to look in Gavin's direction to find he's already watching me, his blue eyes blazing with anger. "Thanks?"

"That guy is an asshole," Gavin mutters, his frown deepening. He is so incredibly handsome that the scowl does nothing to mar his male perfection. And just like I knew would happen, I immediately become entranced with every little thing about him. "He hits on girls all the time."

"He's harmless." I say it to provoke Gavin on purpose, and it works.

"He's a slimeball. You'll end up crying your eyes out after he fucks you once and leaves you high and dry the next day, never to be heard from again. Next time you come here, he'll pretend he doesn't recognize you." Gavin scoots closer, his big, muscular body bumping into mine. "And what the hell are you doing here, anyway, Sienna? You're under—"

I rise on tiptoe and slap my hand over his mouth, silencing him. His eyes go wide, and it's almost comical, how he looks at the moment. Then I remember I'm touching him, my hand covering his beautiful mouth before he could call me out, and I can't believe I just did that.

"Don't blow my cover," I murmur, and when he nods, I reluctantly remove my hand from his face. "And how do you know so much about the sexual habits of the bartender at Charley's?"

"I might know a girl or two who had an encounter with him." He shrugs, his hand going for my arm, long fingers curling around my elbow. "Come on."

He steers me away from the bar, and we make our way through the crowd, which parts like the Red Sea because their hero, their god, is walking among them.

Gavin Maddox is the quarterback for the Santa Mira Dolphins. Halfway through his first season, the starting quarterback had a season-ending injury, and Gavin stepped in.

And he never looked back. He took them all through the playoffs—they lost the final game, never making it to the championships, but that was enough. He's been deemed the golden-boy QB of the Dolphins football team, and everyone loves him.

Even me.

It's wild to think he's only a sophomore and this season he's going to start. Wait a minute . . .

I jerk my arm out of his hold, and he reaches for me at the same time I turn around to face him.

"Hey. You're not even twenty-one," I start, and it's his turn to slap his hand over my mouth, silencing me.

I almost moan from him touching my face, it feels so good. And fills my head with all sorts of dirty fantasies of him having to keep me quiet while he fucks me into oblivion. Oh, my imagination runs wild when it comes to this man, and he doesn't even know it.

He presses his palm firmly against my lips, still not removing it, and I fleetingly wonder if he's enjoying it as much as I am. That stern expression on his face is nothing short of pure hotness, and all I can do is helplessly stare at him, getting lost in his deep-blue eyes.

"I have a fake ID," he murmurs. "Though pretty much everyone who works here knows I'm not twenty-one yet. They just choose to look the other way."

He drops his hand from my face but doesn't wait for me to answer. Just grabs hold of my hand and interlocks our fingers together as he leads me toward the edge of the bar where there are a bunch of tables and chairs. Booths line the walls, and one at the very end of the row sits empty with a little folded sign on the table that says **RESERVED**. Without hesitation he slides into the booth and drags me along with him, then lets go of my hand to rest both of his on top of the table.

"That sign says reserved," I point out, glancing around. I don't want to steal someone's table, because they're a hot commodity here. Every other one in this bar is already full of people.

"Yeah, because it's reserved for us. The football team." He lifts his arm and waves, and within seconds, a server appears. She's blond and tiny and adorable and nothing like me. I don't like how Gavin looks at her, his expression open and friendly.

I'm jealous and I hate it.

"What can I get you?" the cute server asks, her attention only for him.

"Sierra Nevada on tap." He sends me a look. "What do you want, Sienna?"

I like how he says my name. Ugh, I like every single thing this man does. "A rum and Coke, please," I tell the server.

She smiles, jotting down our orders. "Coming right up!"

I watch her bounce away, taking note of the extremely short denim skirt she's wearing and how it shows off her tanned legs. I am always pale, and anytime I'm in the sun, I burn. Or I get freckles. Lots of them.

I envy her blondness. Her shortness. Her tan skin and easy smile and how I could probably fit her in my pocket.

"Where's your brother?" Gavin asks, pulling me out of my thoughts.

"I have no idea. Hopefully not here." I love Coop, but he will ruin my night by doing Gavin one better and escorting me right out of this place the moment he sees me.

"I don't think he is. I've been here for an hour and haven't run into him."

"Any other guys from the team here? Why is no one sitting at this table?"

"Not a lot of us came to Charley's tonight. We always have two tables reserved. Nico is at the other one." Gavin inclines his head toward the other side of the bar where another row of booths is lined up, and yep, I spot Nico sitting there with a few other teammates, all of them surrounded by women.

Typical. Nico is popular with women, and with reason. The girls fall at his feet anytime he so much as smiles at them. He's extraordinarily good looking. Charming. Can talk to a wall if he has to because he will chat up anyone, and within minutes, they feel like he's their lifelong friend.

My personal opinion? I think Gavin is far better looking. With his light-brown hair and the square chin that I want to bite. That's probably not a normal urge, wanting to take a chunk out of him. I might have vampire tendencies, but it's not like I have anyone to talk about it with. I seriously need better friends because I'm afraid Destiny isn't going to cut it.

Gavin is magnetic. He walks into a room and people are instantly drawn to him, including me. He has this undeniable charisma and a beautiful smile, but he's also mysterious. Like . . . I can't figure him out. He's an excellent quarterback. Driven. He'll talk to people, but it's always surface level. He doesn't reveal much personal information, and that just makes me want to know him even more.

"Why aren't you sitting with the rest of the team?" It's a valid question. I know Gavin is a bit of a player too. At least, I think he is. He should be, because my God, look at him. He's six foot four of lean muscle and broad shoulders and long legs. He can outrun just about anyone, and when he can't find someone to throw the ball to, he does exactly that. He can definitely outthrow everybody on the team too. According to my brother, he already has NFL prospects. He'll go pro as long as he remains healthy and does well throughout the rest of his college career.

I have no doubt whatsoever he'll do that.

He's even turned into a UC Santa Mira celebrity. When I came here for orientation weekend last month, I saw banners promoting the team hanging from the light posts all over campus. The dolphin mascot in the corner and a photo of Gavin grinning with his uniform on, his hands on his hips. Larger than life and devastatingly handsome.

It's like he pops up everywhere I go, and I don't mind. Not at all. At least I have an advantage with my brother being on the team with him and one of his close friends. Not that we're close, but here I sit with him in a bar, and I can feel other women's eyes on me. On us. Probably wondering who I am and why I am sitting with their precious Gav.

"I get sick of the hangers-on. It's nice, sitting here with you." His smile is small. Almost intimate, and like a lovestruck idiot, I mentally swoon at him saying it's nice sitting with me. "Who did you come here with?"

"My roommate. We wanted to go out." I smile at him in return, loving how close we're sitting. Is he into me?

God, I hope so.

"Where is she?" He glances around, sliding his arm around the back of the booth seat at the same time, and it's almost like he's got his arm around my shoulders.

"I don't know. I kind of lost her." I feel like a jerk saying that, but I barely know her.

He laughs. "Is this the one you don't really get along with?"

I'm shocked he'd even know. "Did Coop tell you?"

"He might've mentioned it."

"My brother talks about me with you?" I sit up straighter, my shoulders bumping into his arm, and tingles spread over my skin at the contact.

"Sometimes. He's glad you're here." His gaze finds mine. "He missed having his family around last year."

"We're pretty close," I admit. Only one year separates us, and growing up, Coop and I did everything together, save for football. But I went to every game of his with my parents. I was even a cheerleader in youth league for a few years, literally cheering him on from the sidelines, but I gave that up once we got into high school. Our family lives and breathes football, which means we basically live and breathe Coop—which sounds weird, but it's true. And it was rough on all of us, not having him in the house last year. We missed him terribly. "He hasn't changed much, though—with the exception of all the tattoos."

"Pretty sure he was bored one night and somehow he ended up in a tattoo parlor. That's how it started." Gavin chuckles, leaning back against the seat, his legs sprawling out and bumping into mine. "Have you seen his latest? The one with the heart?"

"That says *Mom* in the middle of it? Our mom is going to kill him. I don't even know where he gets the money to pay for them all." The tattoos don't bother me, but my mother freaks out every time she spots a new one on Coop, which is often, considering he's gotten a bunch of them since he started here.

"He got an on-campus job and was working at a restaurant for a few months over the summer. That's how he affords them all." Gavin shrugs, averting his head so he can stare out at the crowd. "You got any?"

"Got any what?"

"Tattoos." He swings his gaze back to mine. "I don't notice any."

I have zero tattoos. "Maybe you just can't see them."

Wait. Am I flirting? I'm barely one drink in.

His lips tip up at the corner. "Interesting. Are you telling me you've got secrets, Sienna?"

"Plenty of them." My smile matches his. "How about you, Gavin? Do you have any secrets?"

"Not that I'm willing to share with you." His smile fades. "Yet."

Chapter Two

Sienna

Oh no. I am very, very . . .

Drunk.

I can't stop laughing. Everything that comes out of Gavin's mouth is funny to me, and since he won't stop talking—which is very unlike him—I can't stop giggling. I love rum. And Coke. Not the kind you snort, the kind you drink. Rum and Coke together?

Ten out of ten. Strong recommend.

Little Miss Cute Server reappears at our table yet again because Gavin basically told her about four—maybe five—rum and Cokes ago that she should keep them coming. But he silences my laughter when he makes that gesture at her like he's slicing his throat with his fingers.

"We're cutting her off." He points his thumb in my direction.

"Nooooo." I lean against him because all my inhibitions have abandoned me. I am a drunken fool who wants more, more, more. "I'm so thirsty."

"Bring her a water," Gavin advises the server.

"Will do." She takes off before I can stop her, and my disappointment runs far and deep.

"You're no fun." I let go of him and slump against the seat, crossing my arms. I'm pouting like I'm three, but I don't care.

"You'd end up crying over a toilet and puking if you keep going. You might already be at that point." He shakes his head, rubbing his jaw with his fingers. I stare at those fingers, mesmerized by the sight of them. They're long and magical. I bet he knows what to do with them, and I'm not talking about throwing a football either.

"I'm fine." I wave my hand and nearly topple over onto the seat. Gavin grabs me at the last second to keep me from falling, and I start laughing all over again. "Or maybe not."

"Definitely not." He helps me sit upright, and I beam at him.

"Thank you." I'm getting lost in his eyes again. They're beautiful swirls of varying shades of blue, and I don't ever want to look away. It's like I can't.

"You're welcome." He's still slouched in the booth seat, his big body sprawled in all directions. His arms are stretched out along either side of the back of the seat, and his legs are spread wide. Most women would call this manspreading and complain about it, but I love how much space he takes up. It's hot.

He's hot.

I'm hot too.

In fact, I'm sweating.

Over him.

"Why are you hanging out with me?" The words fall off my tongue as if I have no control, and I realize that is a correct assumption about me. I have zero control. I'm drunk, and I guess alcohol makes me bold.

He frowns. "Why wouldn't I hang out with you?"

"There are all sorts of girls out there." I waggle my fingers at the crowd, indicating all the females currently watching us—him—with hunger and longing in their eyes. "Yet you sit here with me."

Gavin watches me for a moment, and I wonder if he's having to ask himself why exactly he is with me. When he could be doing anything else. Anyone else.

Ouch. The thought of that hurts my brain. Gavin with another woman. I shove the vision out of my head as fast as I can.

"Because I like you," he eventually says, and oh, my heart.

It's currently racing. Galloping. Ready to escape from my chest and run straight out of this bar with those words.

"And I need to keep an eye on you. For Coop," he adds.

I deflate like a balloon, my heart reinserting itself into my chest, where it belongs.

"He's not even here," I mumble, hanging my head in defeat.

"Even more reason to keep watch. Especially after what Sam did." He sounds pissed, but not in my honor. More like he just knows Sam the bartender is, as he put it, a slimeball.

I am pathetic. Pitiful. This man is only here because he feels obligated to keep watch over me and not because he's infatuated with my beauty and charming personality.

Not that I'm a great beauty, nor am I particularly charming. I get why he's not into me. I'm not that attractive. Not in the traditional sense. I'm too tall and too pale, and I'm a redhead, which only a small percentage of men seem to be drawn to. I have boring brown eyes and freckles everywhere that get worse during the summer until it seems like they cover every inch of my exposed skin. And I'm a little too loud sometimes.

Okay, most of the time.

I had to be the loud one growing up because my brother is so damn quiet. Someone had to talk for the both of us, and it sure wasn't ever going to be Coop.

"Here you go!" Our adorable server is standing in front of the table, placing a giant glass of ice water in front of me. "Drink up, sweetie. Maybe take a Liquid I.V. when you get home, or else you're going to be feeling it tomorrow."

"Thanks, Vanessa." Gavin smiles at her, and it's the first time I've realized he knows her name.

"Anytime, Gav." Her eyes flash when they meet his as she hands him a glass of water, too, and I note the way her fingers brush his. How they almost tangle for a moment before she pulls away.

Oh God. I think . . .

I think he's fucked her.

The moment she's gone I'm chugging the water, then slamming the glass onto the table so hard, I worry it might smash into a bazillion pieces. Luckily for me, it stays intact.

Unlike my ego. My feelings. My head. Those all feel smashed to bits.

"I need to go," I announce, scooting in the opposite direction of the rounded booth so I can escape out the other side. "Thanks for babysitting me, Gavin."

I'm fast. I used to be in track during high school, and I can run a one-hundred-yard dash like no other, but this guy, Mr. Football himself, is on me in seconds. His fingers curling around my upper arm and holding me back before I can make my escape.

"What the hell, Sienna? Where are you going?"

I glance over my shoulder and pretend for a moment that he actually cares. That he doesn't want me to leave. That he sees me not as Coop's baby sister but as a beautiful, confident—if a little drunk—woman.

But all I detect is brotherly concern in his gaze. His grip doesn't feel possessive or intimate. He's just trying to stop me from leaving in case I'm going to hop into a car and drive drunk or whatever.

Not that anyone drives much in this town. My dorm building is literally five blocks away, max. I can walk home easily.

"I'm leaving," I tell him, lifting my chin, trying to look strong.

But then my feet seem to be on top of each other, and I stumble. Right into him.

He catches me, cradling me in his arms, and I find myself staring at his face. Into his eyes. God, he's handsome. Too handsome. It's too much. He's too much.

"I'll walk you home," he murmurs, and I swear I see amusement on his face. In his eyes. Like I'm a joke to him.

"No." I shake my head and try to disentangle myself from his grip, but he won't budge. The guy is just way too strong. "It's not a long walk. I'll find Destiny."

He frowns. "Who?"

"My roommate." I don't expect him to remember every little detail about me, but I wish he did.

"Where is she?" He looks around the front of the crowded bar, frowning.

"I don't know." A hiccup escapes me, and I cover my mouth, embarrassed. "I gotta go."

Somehow, I extract myself from his hold and turn on wobbly feet, heading for the door. I push my way through the crowd, ignoring the way Gavin calls my name. It means nothing. He's not interested, and the thought of how I basically draped myself all over him tonight is humiliating.

When I finally make it outside, I tip my head back and inhale the cool, salty air. Going to UCSM has its perks, the biggest one being that we get to live by the ocean. Which makes me think of the song "Cake by the Ocean" and how it's about going down on a girl, and all my hopes and dreams of anything remotely like that happening with Gavin are dashed completely.

"Sienna." Gavin's deep voice is full of relief, and I whirl around to find him striding toward me. "I'm walking you home."

"I don't need you to escort me. I've got this." I try to give him a thumbs-up, but it ends up being my middle finger instead.

My true feelings coming out? Most definitely.

He actually laughs, the jackass. "I think you do need my help. Come on. Which building are you in?"

"Rosewood," I mumble, dropping my arm by my side. Wishing I could give him the finger again. "It's right down the street."

"I know exactly where it is," he says with confidence.

"Snuck into a few of the dorm rooms, hmm?" I raise my brows.

Gavin frowns. "Sorry?"

"Hooked up with girls in the freshman dorms last year? Right, Gav?"

I never call him Gav. I sort of hate that nickname. But our cheeky little server called him that, and I just know—I KNOW—they've done it.

"Come on, Sienna." He loops his arm through mine and steers me down the sidewalk, heading in the direction of our campus and my dorm hall. "You need to go to bed."

The word *bed* sparks hope in my heart, which is the dumbest thing ever. "Are you going to tuck me in, Gav? Is that how you get into girls' dorm rooms? With promises of helping us go night-night?"

"Are you okay?" He sounds genuinely concerned, and I hate it. I don't want his concern. I want lust and longing and illicit touches. Desire and kissing and hot sex. Yess, sex.

Sex with Gavin would be amazing, I just know it.

For the rest of the walk, I don't speak. I never answered his question because I don't think it's necessary. He can figure out that I'm not okay just by my remaining silent, which is something I rarely do.

By the time we're in front of my dorm building, I don't want him touching me anymore. Guiding me anymore. I've got this.

"I can manage to get to my room on my own." I pull my arm from around his. "Thanks for walking with me. I appreciate your concern."

Gavin doesn't even catch the sarcasm in my tone.

"I'm taking you to your room." His voice is firm. He's not going to let me get out of this, and I accept defeat, again remaining quiet as he walks with me toward my dorm hall entrance. "I want to make sure you get in safely."

"Okay, Dad." I roll my eyes and grab my key card, waving it in front of the black pad so the doors unlock. We're inside in seconds, Gavin looking around the lobby with curiosity.

"What floor are you on?" he asks.

"Four."

We take the elevator up, me standing on the complete opposite side from Gavin because I'm sick of being close to him. I can still smell him, though. Look at him. Note the way he's checking his phone and tapping out a response to someone. I'm dying to know who it might be.

Not that I have any right to ask him. And he probably won't tell me either. It's none of my business.

The elevator doors slide open, and I dart out, turning right and heading down the hallway of endless doors. Coming to a stop when I realize my room is on the left side.

I'm an idiot.

"Wrong way," I mumble as I push past him, and he chuckles, like I'm just so amusing in my drunken state.

He follows after me but keeps his distance like he knows that's what I want. I stop in front of my door and pull the key out of my pocket, unlocking the door quickly before I open it and turn on the overhead light. "Okay, thanks, Gavin. I appreciate your help."

I'm about to shut the door in his face like a total bitch when he slaps his hand against it, forcing me to keep it open. "You alone in there?"

I frown, glancing over my shoulder to find I am, indeed, alone in here. Good. I can cry by myself, and Destiny won't be a witness to my drunk sadness. "I am."

Without a word he pushes his way inside my room, filling the tiny space with his dominating presence immediately. I shut the door and lean against it, watching as he stands in the middle of the room between the two single beds, his head turning left, then right, checking everything out.

"Looks like your standard dorm room," he observes. "Though your side is cuter than your roommate's."

Pleasure suffuses me at his compliment. "Thank you. My mom helped me set it up."

"How is she?" His gaze meets mine, and I can see the fondness there.

Everyone loves my mother. She's the quintessential football mom, meaning she's always volunteering to help out the team. Bring them snacks and water and meals. Was team mom all through the younger grades and on the board in various positions, including president of the booster club, the entirety of Coop's high school–football life. She shows up at every game with Dad, whether it's at home or away, and she cheers for everyone, not just her son.

All that love for Coop can sometimes feel like I get the leftovers, but I try not to let it bother me. I get it. Coop is the more successful sibling, while I'm just . . . me.

"She's good," I tell him, resting my hands on my hips. Desperate to ignore the way my head is spinning. I'm in full control of my body and thoughts. A little alcohol won't push me over the edge.

But then like a fool I trip over my own foot—how, I'm not sure—and I can feel myself tipping over. A little shriek escapes me, and next thing I know, Gavin is lunging toward me and we're tangled up together on top of my bed.

My stupid little twin bed that we definitely can't fit on side by side, but that doesn't seem to matter because currently I'm sprawled on top of him and he's beneath me. He's a hot, solid wall of muscle, his arms banded around me, those big hands and long fingers splayed across my back, and I lift my head, staring into his beautiful eyes, our mouths perfectly aligned.

"Sorry," I murmur, but he doesn't say anything. His gaze roves all over my face, those blue eyes darkening until they're as turbulent as a winter storm. I stare back, mute. Unable to breathe.

He lifts his head. Angles it. His lips brush over mine, and I close my eyes, shock coursing through my veins. Gavin Maddox is kissing me.

Say what?

Chapter Three

SIENNA

Gavin keeps the kiss simple at first. Almost as if he's testing me, and then I feel his tongue swipe at the seam of my lips, and that's all it takes.

My lips part. Our tongues meet. The kiss turns hot in an instant, his hands sliding down until they're covering my ass and he's pulling me in closer. Letting me feel him as he devours me. He's hard. And like the shameless drunk girl I am, I waste no time, grinding against him.

Making him groan.

The sound settles into the deepest part of my body, making me throb between my thighs. His hungry mouth never strays from mine, our tongues tangling, his hands squeezing my flesh. I mentally curse at myself for wearing denim shorts because if I had a dress on, I'd feel those hands on my bare flesh, and a shiver moves through me at the thought.

But then he makes all my wishes come true when his hands slide down, his fingers tracing over the curve of my ass cheeks, and a whimper sounds low in my throat.

"Jesus," he mutters against my lips as I basically hump him. That's all he says before he deepens the kiss, which I didn't think was possible, but oh my God, the man is good with his mouth. Oh, and his hands, which isn't a surprise, considering how well he plays football.

I straddle him, my thighs on either side of his hips, my pussy directly against that thick bulge beneath his jeans. He is as hard as a rock, and a tiny thrill buzzes through my veins. That's because of me. I did that to him.

Little ol' me.

He pulls away from my still-seeking lips to kiss a burning trail down my neck. "You smell fucking incredible."

My entire body aches. God, I want him. I want to take his clothes off and feel his skin on mine. I want to touch him everywhere I can reach, and I would give anything, everything I've got, to see this man naked. Have him naked beneath me.

He removes one of his hands from my butt, and I'm sad. But then he cups the side of my face, his fingers sliding into my hair as he angles my head just so, his mouth back on mine, and I am melting. Oh, I love it when a man touches my face, not that any ever have before. Not even my high school boyfriend. I've seen it in movies, though, and it's the most romantic gesture ever.

We kiss and kiss, and I try to touch him everywhere I can, but my reach is limited. I can't get enough of him. And it's like he can't get enough of me, either, those fingers of his slipping beneath my denim shorts to skim across my flesh, dipping lower until they're dangerously close to where I want them.

And when they brush against my pussy, dipping into my creamy flesh, a shudder racks my body. I could come if he keeps this up. I'm already primed, completely on edge, and when his fingers slide deeper, I end our kiss, desperate to catch my breath.

"So fucking wet," he murmurs as he begins to stroke me, and I can't speak. A strangled sound leaves me, and I return my mouth to his, never wanting this moment to end.

Who knew it could be like this? I think of my ex-boyfriend and all the things we did together, but none of those moments compare to this.

He fucks me with his fingers, and I move with them, unsure how he's managing this thanks to the barrier that is my denim shorts, but I can't worry about logistics. I lift my hips, his fingers streaking over my clit, and I moan into his mouth, my orgasm getting closer—

"Oh my God! You should've left a scrunchie on the door to let me know you had a guy in here!" Destiny screams the moment she opens the door.

I leap off Gavin so fast my head is spinning. Destiny slams the door shut, and I can hear her footsteps as she scurries away. Swallowing hard, I turn to look at my bed, taking a mental picture so I can store this memory away forever.

Gavin lying across the bed, filling every inch of space. There's a tent in the front of his black shorts, and his T-shirt is shoved up, revealing his six-pack abs. Did I do that? I must've.

He looks like he's in shock. Unable to move or even speak. Slowly he lifts himself up on his elbows, staring at me for a moment before he finally says something.

"Your roommate?" The quiet rumble of his voice settles in a low throb between my legs, and I can't even believe I had him beneath me only moments ago. That I had been on the verge of coming thanks to his magical fingers.

Stupid Destiny. Her timing is for shit.

"Yeah." I nod, brushing my hair away from my face. I'm fairly certain he had his hands in it at one point, or am I just imagining that?

He tugs his T-shirt down and hauls himself off my pitiful bed, and that's it. The spell is broken. The mood ruined. Pretty sure I had my hand beneath his shirt right before Destiny opened the door. The distinct, smooth texture of his abdomen still burns my fingertips, and the regret that is currently flooding my bloodstream is overwhelming.

I am painfully sober, watching as he makes his way to the door. I'm also painfully quiet. What do I say? Please don't leave? Come back to my bed so we can continue what we were doing? He might laugh. He might regret it. Maybe he didn't mean for it to happen or, worse, he kissed me and had his fingers between my legs because he somehow felt sorry for me.

Oh, that is the worst thought of them all.

"Are you okay?" His voice is gentle, and when I dare to look into his eyes, I see the sympathy there. He feels bad about . . . something. Maybe all of it?

"Yeah." I nod, wishing he would at the very least hug me and reassure me that everything is going to be okay.

But he does none of that. Instead, he says, "See you around," and walks out of my room.

Chapter Four

SIENNA

Junior year

I arrive at my brother's house armed with a case of High Noons because Coop and his friends always forget to stock the good stuff at their place. I don't bother knocking on the door either. I just barge right in to find the living room already filled with a variety of men, most of them tall, hulking beasts who play for the Santa Mira Dolphins.

Ignoring all of them, I shut the door with my foot, scanning the area in search of my brother. He's not hard to spot. Over the last few years, he's somehow bulked up even more, and both his arms are covered in tattoos. He's intimidating as fuck and never lets anyone forget who he is or what he might do to them if they ever wrong me.

In other words, he's a menace to society and destroys my dating game all the time. Hence me having to keep any interactions with men a secret.

"Hey. There you are." Coop appears out of nowhere, taking the case of High Noons from me like the gentleman he is. Yes, my feelings for my brother are contradictory, and no, I can't help it. He truly is a teddy bear once you get to know him, and our parents raised him right, but his overprotectiveness will be the death of my social life.

Scratch that—it already is. Mostly.

"Hi." I follow him into the kitchen, noting how clean it is. Hmm. That is suspicious. Did they hire someone to clean this place up? I know they've only lived here a few days, but they're self-proclaimed slobs. "I can't believe you guys are having a party already."

They don't do it often. More when they were younger, but now that they're seniors, whenever they invite a bunch of people over, it turns into chaos. They're just too popular, too revered on campus. Everyone wants a piece of the football team, a chance at being able to say, *I know that guy* or *We're friends* or *I gave so-and-so a blow job in his bathroom last night.*

Trust me. We've witnessed it all. Heard it all.

"We're keeping it low key tonight. Nothing big." Coop shrugs his massive shoulders, glancing toward the living room when a loud bang sounds. "What the hell was that?"

"Your low-key, nothing-big party kicking into high gear." I reach for the case of High Noons and tear it open, pulling out one that's watermelon flavored. My favorite. I don't hesitate cracking that baby open and taking a long pull. "Want me to check?"

"Nah. I'll do it." He mutters a string of curse words as he strides out of the kitchen, and I'm amused for all of about two-point-five seconds when I hear what I think is a familiar deep voice ring out in greeting.

But I realize quickly that isn't who I think it is, and relieved, I take another long drink from the can, savoring it. Enjoying the languid sensation of the alcohol flowing through my veins. I can always feel it course through my body, and people call bullshit when I say that, but it's true.

And tonight, I need lots of alcohol if I'm going to get through this party.

My brother reenters the kitchen wearing a grim expression, reaching for the beer he left behind and taking a big swig.

"What happened?"

"Someone was fucking with the PlayStation." He shakes his head. "I told Nico not to invite the freshmen."

Nico is my brother's roommate and the star wide receiver on the team. He's become even more handsome to the point of distraction, and he's still a complete player. The worst out of all their friend group, and with reason. His smile dissolves panties campus-wide. I found myself falling under his sway more than once but always knew it would be dangerous. Besides . . .

I already tried something once with my brother's teammate, and it bombed big time. I'm not going there again.

"You can't discriminate against the freshmen," I remind my brother. "Maybe you guys should've put away the PlayStation."

"Good call. We'll do that next time." Coop turns so he's facing me fully, blocking my view from the living room completely. "There's something I want to tell you."

The grave tone of his voice has me immediately filled with concern. "What's wrong?"

"Nothing's wrong. We have a new roommate." He pauses. "Her name is Everleigh."

"Her?" I'm stunned. "What happened to your other roommate? Sampson?"

"That asshole bailed out on us. Said rent was too expensive. We were talking about it at the café earlier over breakfast, and this girl— Everleigh—overheard us and said she was looking for a roommate, and well . . . now she's moved in," Coop explains.

"Where is she?" I start to head for the living room, but Coop grabs my wrist, stopping me. "I want to meet her."

"I'll introduce you if I get the chance. But don't be afraid to approach her if you see her. She's about yay high." He holds his hand up to the middle of his chest, indicating she's short. "And she looks nervous all the time."

"Aw, Coop. That's so mean." I laugh, though not at his new roomie. "You guys probably make her nervous."

"You're right. I think we do." He rubs a hand across his cheek. "She doesn't know we're football players. Well, she knows, but I don't think she realizes just how . . ."

His voice drifts, and I fill in the rest of the sentence for him. "What a big deal that you guys are?"

"I didn't want to say it." He shrugs. "I sound like an asshole."

"You're an asshole who speaks the truth." I pat him on the shoulder. Extra hard, like a sister should. "I'll let her know what she's dealing with. Give her a warning."

Coop's brows shoot up. "What do you mean by that?"

"I have to warn her about all of you. Dollar." Coop and Nico's other roommate and teammate is Frank Dollar, and while he's a sweet guy, he can also be a little pushy. As in, if he zeroes in on a woman who he believes he has a chance with, he won't let up. He's rather determined.

Hmm, sounds awfully familiar, but I push that nagging little thought out of my brain.

"Yeah, about Dollar." Coop grimaces. "He's already started in with Everleigh."

"Oh, the poor girl." I rest my hand against my chest.

"He means well."

"But he always takes it too far. I wish he could find someone who's completely into him." Frank is really a decent guy. He just needs to find someone who loves as hard as he does. Who'll shower him with all the attention that he deserves. "I'll talk to her. I'm going to warn her about Nico too."

"Yeah, you better," Coop mutters, shaking his head. "They're sharing a bathroom, by the way. Nico and Everleigh."

"Seriously? Well, that ought to be interesting."

We hear the front door open, and a bunch of female voices fill the space, their excitement obvious. I lean back and see who's entered the house—a group of women that I know, some better than others. All of them are hot for a football player. Any football player. They don't discriminate.

"I'll go talk to them," I tell my brother, who practically sags with relief. I polish off one High Noon and grab another, this one pineapple flavored. Within seconds I'm standing with the girls, listening to them all talk animatedly about their class schedule, who the hottest guy is in the house, on the team, blah, blah, blah. I nod and smile, taking a sip. One after the other. Fortifying myself to get through this conversation, yet never really adding to it.

Here's my issue: I don't have a lot of close girlfriends in Santa Mira, and so much of that is because I don't trust people when they try to get to know me. I've been burned multiple times by other women who were friendly merely because they wanted an in with the football team. And my roommate? We're not close at all. I still live with Destiny—we just moved into a two-bedroom apartment, and we each get our own bedroom and bathroom—but we don't really hang out. She's a private person and a little grumpy—okay, fine, she's a lot grumpy. It's like she merely tolerates me, and I know sometimes I annoy her. Which is fine because she annoys me too.

But we're good together as roommates. We leave each other alone and stay out of each other's business. Better to tolerate someone you know versus finding a new roommate who might not work out is my philosophy. After seeming into them at first, now Destiny has zero interest in getting to know the football team, which works for me. Though I do wish we were closer . . .

We may go to a big school with a huge campus, but the social circles are small. The ones around the football team? Impossibly tight. I'm rather protective of my brother and his bonehead friends and teammates. They're like family to me.

Knowing there is a potential new member of the family—and another female—is exciting. But I don't want to get my hopes up. What if she doesn't like me? What if she's weird or rude or downright cruel? I mean, who knows what she's like? Right now she'll be on her best behavior.

Eventually Nico ambles over, that charming smile plastered on his face, his dark eyes flashing. He is sinfully handsome, and worse? He knows it—and uses it to his advantage whenever possible.

"How's it goin', ladies?" His voice is a smooth, low drawl, and they all giggle while I roll my eyes.

"Nico! I've missed you." One of them pulls away from the others, launching herself at him, wrapping her arms around his neck while she clings to him like a lifeline. He has to push her away from himself to detach her, his expression slightly panicked.

"Yeah. Missed you too." I can tell by his casual tone that he most likely has no idea who she is or what her name might be. He even sends me a helpless look, like I might offer assistance, and I smile at him, wagging my fingers in a tiny wave.

"See you later!" I take off, and not a single one of the women cares, though I can feel Nico's gaze on me as I make my escape. Poor dude. I bet he wishes he was leaving with me.

Oh well. He deserves this.

I'm opening my third High Noon when I'm approached by Dollar, who is currently holding a nervous-looking woman's hand. She must be the new roomie, and already he's territorial.

"Hey, Sienna, have you met our new roommate, Everleigh?" Frank asks.

I'm smiling as I study this poor woman, who is now removing her hand from Frank's. "Not yet, but I've heard all about her from Coop. Hiiiii." I pull her in for a big hug, clinging to her for a moment, and I love that she doesn't try to pull away. I'm the one to do it first, keeping my grip on her upper arms so I can examine her. "I'm so glad you moved in with them. Now I have a friend to hang out with here beyond my brother and his annoying roommates."

"Hey," Frank protests, but I laugh, slipping my arm around her shoulders and keeping her next to me.

"Don't be so sensitive, Frankie. Now go hang out with your bros and let me and Everleigh get to know each other. Alone." I shoo him away with a flick of my fingers.

"Nico is right behind you," Frank points out.

"Oh, please." I shake my head. "He's flirting with the blondes. He's not paying attention to us."

Frank reluctantly walks away, that hangdog expression on his face that tells me he's feeling left out. Once he's gone and I'm positive he won't hear me, I lean in closer to Everleigh, lowering my voice. "Is he flirting with you?"

"Who?" Everleigh looks confused.

"Frank. He's a sweetheart and he means well, but he's desperate to find a girlfriend. All the guys give him endless shit about it too. Poor dude." My gaze shifts to Frank, who is currently sitting on the couch next to my brother. Watching us, though he looks away quickly when I catch him. "I saw the way he was holding your hand."

"It was nothing." Everleigh smiles and shrugs. I feel the need to warn her.

"Not to him it wasn't. That's his problem. If he could learn how to play it cool for once, he'd have women chasing after him instead of the other way around. I mean, look at Nico." I make a halfhearted gesture in his direction.

"Right," Everleigh says, her voice weak, her gaze stuck on him.

Hmmm. "He's hot, isn't he. And I hear you two are sharing a bathroom?"

The concern on her face is obvious. "Who told you that?"

"Cooper. He tells me everything. Well, mostly everything." She appears a tad horrified by that revelation. "By the way, if you catch Nico coming out of his bathroom naked, please, for the love of God, take a pic and send it to me. I hear his dick is ginormous."

I burst out laughing at her shocked expression, and I feel a little guilty for trying to shock her, but it's like I can't help myself. Am I testing her to see if she's cool? Definitely. And I can't help the way I talk—I sound like all the guys, but I do spend a lot of time with them. They're rubbing off on me, and probably not in the best way.

"Oh my God." Everleigh's face is bright pink with embarrassment. "I really hope I never see his—dick."

Why do I not believe her? I know I wouldn't mind catching a glimpse, though I'm not interested in him like that. A girl's allowed to be curious.

We keep chatting, and I get her to share bits of information with me. She's a nutrition major and agreed to cook the guys meals in order to save money on rent. I made sure they weren't taking advantage of her because I don't necessarily trust these guys, even my own brother. And then I proceed to warn her off Nico again and even Gavin.

I've got my own selfish motives to keep her away from Gavin. Like the fact that we've been doing this delicate dance with each other over the last couple of years where we pretend that moment in my dorm room never happened. I've never discussed it with anyone. Not a single soul. The only person who's aware of that interaction is Destiny, and luckily she's kept her mouth shut.

At the moment Nico is giving me grief about my red hair, which he hasn't done for years, but really, I think he's trying to catch Everleigh's attention when the front door swings open and in walks my own personal nightmare.

Or absolute dream of a man. Take your pick.

Shouts of "QB!" fill the room, and Gavin stands there, looking pleased with himself. A proper reception for the king of the team, no doubt.

"There's Gavin," I whisper to Everleigh, who's openly staring at him. I can't fault her for it. He's stupidly handsome.

One of the blondes Nico was chatting with earlier runs over to Gavin, then throws her arms around his neck and kisses his cheek. I burn with jealousy, wishing I could do the same, but he would never allow it. He's afraid of my brother, the rest of the team, and whoever else and what they might think of the two of us together.

The coward.

He sets the blonde away from him, his gaze going to mine, and I see the apology in his blue eyes. Or what I think might be an apology. Who knows? I can't read this guy, and I've avoided him more than talked to him ever since our incident. But being the polite person that I am, I offer him a wan smile and wish I could disappear.

Instead, I just stand here and take it. Fighting my feelings for a man who struggles with knowing what he wants. Even though I'm standing in front of him, willing and able.

Seriously. Men are the worst.

Chapter Five

GAVIN

Football is my life. It keeps me going when times are tough, and the game exhilarates me like nothing else. I feel whole out on the field, playing with my teammates, guys I know and love and trust. We're like family, and I count on them more than even my actual family, though that's not saying much. I'm an only child and have a strained relationship with my parents. My dad has controlled me my entire life, and he hates that he can't tell me what to do any longer, though he knows just what to say to get into my head and stay there.

The miserable son of a bitch still has the power to make my life a living hell. My mother does nothing to stop him either. She doesn't say much at all. He keeps her under his thumb just like he's done to me until I got into college. Escaping our house helped me breathe easier, but he still has the power to get into my mind and fuck with my self-esteem. I've gotten better at shutting him out over the years, but he still sneaks in here and there. And I hate it.

Otherwise, I've got my head on straight. My focus is 100 percent football. Okay, 95 percent football and 5 percent school. I want to play professionally. I'm a business major, but I chose that because it's easy. I'm good at math—I'm interested in economics and all that shit—but that isn't what I really want to do.

Football. That's my plan. The NFL. I can see it in my dreams. Can practically taste it, I'm so close, but things could change. For all I know, we could have a shit season—

No. I can't let any negative thoughts crowd my brain. I need to stay focused. Manifest that shit and make it happen.

But there's only one distraction. One person I'd consider tossing everything aside for if we could guarantee we'd run away together and no one else would have to know. And it's the statuesque redhead standing within ten feet of me, wearing a pair of denim cutoffs that are criminally short and a tank top that shows off the perfect curve of her amazing tits.

Sienna Cooper.

I grimace the moment I think of her last name because that's what her older brother goes by. Everyone calls him Coop. Even his parents and sister. Hell, most of the time I don't even remember what his first name is. Only when I see the official team roster do I ever recall.

She briefly glances in my direction, looking away the moment our gazes lock. I stare at her, those long legs and those damn denim shorts. All the memories come back when I see them. Of her draped over me and my hands all over her. Inside her. The scent of her pussy still lingers in my mind because I was a sick fuck who didn't wash his hands for hours after our singular hot encounter.

The hottest moment of my life, and we didn't even fuck. I figured I'd idealized the moment in my brain and I feel that way because we never did the actual deed. It could've been awful. She could've turned into a nightmare. A lousy fuck turned into an overpossessive woman who might try to control my life. I don't need it.

Who am I kidding? I know Sienna well enough that I'm confident she wouldn't act like that. I just tell myself those kinds of things to make me feel better.

But damn it, she haunts my dreams and makes me crazy with lust. I can't remember the last time I fucked some random chick. It's been forever, and most of the time the ones I do choose don't resemble her at all because I don't want the reminder. And look, I have sex with other women on occasion while I assume she has sex with other men, because we're not together. We never have been and most likely never will be. Pretty sure she's still interested in me, though she always keeps her distance.

I'm interested in her too. It's like I can't help myself.

I come from a fucked-up family that Sienna doesn't need to be subjected to. While she comes from a set of dream parents who are supportive and wonderful. They're always there for their kids, while I'm over here still trying to get out from underneath my father's thumb. His kind of attention isn't what I want. Even my mom avoids him as much as possible, and she married the man.

"Who's the chick with Sienna?" I ask Coop once he calls me over and hands me a beer. I settle into the couch next to him, not surprised at all when it's our friend Frank Dollar who informs me who she is.

"Our new roommate, Everleigh," he announces proudly.

Coop and I share a look, and I get what my friend is trying to tell me while not speaking a word. "You into her, Dollar?"

"Sort of." Frank shrugs, trying to play it off while Coop coughs the word *bullshit* into his hand.

"Is she cool?" I am specifically addressing Coop because I don't trust Frank's assessment of her. He's into her; it's obvious.

"I don't think she realizes who we are exactly—" Coop starts, but Frank interrupts him.

"She knows we play football."

"But I don't think she gets what we're about," Coop continues. "Damn, I sound like a conceited asshole. I already said all this to Sienna, but she agreed with me."

"I agree with you too." I like that Sienna and I think the same. Jesus, I feel like I have a middle school crush. "She doesn't realize the impact we have on campus, right?"

"Right." Coop nods.

As in, she doesn't understand that we're the most popular football team UC Santa Mira has ever had in the history of the school. We're not just popular—we're also national champions. Minus last year, damn it. We're winning it this year. We have to. The coaches, the team, my fucking father—they expect nothing less.

"You don't think she'll be a problem?" I don't know who let the chicks who are currently roaming around into the house because we all know them—or of them, at the very least. They're fans. Groupies. Whatever you want to call them. Women who are willing to toss all self-esteem aside and give their all to snag one of us for good.

I'm not interested. I don't think any of us are, save for Nico, who's currently laying on the charm with one of them. But that asshole—he's one of my best friends; I'm allowed to call him that—flirts with any female he meets. It's an issue.

"Nah. She seems cool." Coop inclines his head toward his sister and new roommate. "Sienna likes her."

"Sienna likes everyone," I grumble, because it's true. With the exception of me.

"She doesn't like you much." Coop slaps the back of my head, and that's all it takes. I leap to my feet, giving him the finger before I head for the kitchen.

I'm starving, and I have a feeling I can find something to eat. At the very least, find some chips or crackers, and then we can order a couple of pizzas. Though that's the last thing we should be eating as we get ready for football season. I need to watch what I eat if I want to get shredded.

Ah, fuck it. We only live once.

I'm rummaging around in the pantry when I feel a presence behind me. More like I smell her. I'd recognize that scent anywhere. I used to think it was her perfume, but I realized that it's her shampoo. She smells like a tropical beach.

"What are you doing?" Her soft voice wraps around me, and I pause in my search, glancing over my shoulder to find Sienna standing there, watching me with an unreadable expression on her face.

"Looking for something to eat." I snag a box of Cheez-Its and turn to face her, popping the top of the box open and grabbing a handful of crackers before I shove them into my mouth.

She makes a face like I disgust her, which—not gonna lie—kinda hurts. "Cheez-Its for dinner, Gavin? That's a poor choice."

"I agree. Definitely need a full-blown meal. Want to order pizza for everyone?" I ask after I swallow.

She slowly shakes her head. "Shouldn't you be eating lean fish or chicken or whatever? No fats, no carbs, nothing but protein?"

Sienna is absolutely correct. "That's boring."

I exit the pantry with the box still in my hand, and she follows after me, standing on the other side of the kitchen island like she needs the distance, which makes sense, considering we've been keeping our distance from each other for a long time. Almost two entire years, which is wild to think.

Don't get me wrong, we've talked to each other. Our group is so small, we can't always avoid each other. I'm polite to her and she's polite to me, but I always felt something . . . simmering between us. Each time we get close. Like now, for instance. I can feel it. I'm drawn to her. Eager to stare at her face and listen to her voice. Watch her mouth move, her eyes light up.

Chemistry. That's what we've got. The air is charged every time we're in the same room together. I set the cracker box on the counter, then curl my fingers into my palms. Reminding myself that I'm wasting my time. This woman isn't interested in me. Not like that.

She remains quiet, watching me shovel crackers in my mouth, her gaze still disapproving. The sound of her long-suffering sigh is what pushes me over the edge.

"Is there something you wanted to talk about?" I ask her, my voice weary. Because damn it, I am weary. Our situation exhausts me. I don't know what she wants, but then again, I don't know exactly what I want either.

Meaning whichever direction we take, we're fucked.

"I've been thinking about it, and Gavin . . . I'm tired of trying to avoid you all the time." Her voice is soft, and she keeps her gaze downcast, as if she's afraid to look at me.

"You are?" I sound like an idiot.

Sienna nods, her thick auburn hair sliding past her shoulders. She has soft hair. Silky. And it smells like heaven. "I've been mean to you for . . . years."

I snort, reach for my beer, and take a couple of swallows. Wishing I had something stronger to drink. "You aren't that mean, Freckles."

She jerks her head up, her mouth turned downward. "What did you call me?"

"Freckles." I shrug, wondering if I stepped too far. "You've got a lot of them. It's an obvious nickname."

That frown doesn't budge. "You guys usually call me Annie."

Annie. For Little Orphan Annie, which I always thought was dumb. Someone came up with the nickname—I don't know who—but Nico ran with it. Though I haven't heard him say that in a while.

"I don't think I've ever called you Annie in my life," I tell her.

"You're right." The frown fades, replaced with the tiniest smile. "You haven't."

Pushing the cracker box out of the way, I lean across the island like I'm trying to get closer to her, and hey, maybe I am. "You've been busy, Sienna."

"I have." She nods.

"And I've been busy too. I never thought you were purposely ignoring me." Lies. All lies. Since that night in her dorm room when she was a sweet little drunk freshman and I kissed her and touched her like I wanted to fuck her—news flash, I did—I've tried to stay away from her out of respect for her feelings. I'm not outwardly rude, because I like the girl far too much, but I did my best to keep my distance because, damn it, I'm a gentleman.

Despite the fact that all I can think about is defiling her in every way possible every time I'm near her, I am a gentleman who stays away. I'm not about to corrupt her with a few nights of hot and heavy sex because, knowing me, that's as long as it'll last. I can't commit. I'm that asshole who refuses to be in a relationship. The ones I've witnessed—mainly my parents'—are a mess. It's better to be alone. I don't need anyone.

Not really.

"Oh. Well, I definitely thought you were ignoring me." Her voice is like a song, and her smile is extra sweet. "But that's okay. I was ignoring you too. It's just . . ."

"Easier?" I offer when she doesn't finish the sentence.

"Yes." She nods. "Easier."

"I say we call a truce."

"Were we ever fighting, Gavin?"

I like it when she says my name. Everyone calls me Gav or QB or Captain, and I don't mind. But Sienna never really calls me anything but Gavin. With the exception of that night when she got so drunk and started calling me Gav. There had been sarcasm in her tone, though. Almost as if she hated calling me that.

I don't know. My biggest issue with Sienna is I can never quite figure her out. She's like a puzzle I can't solve—no matter how many times I try to, all I want is more.

More time with her. More time talking to her. Looking at her. If I finally gave in to my urges, would I figure her out? Would my curiosity be satiated and I could move on? I want to believe that's all it would take, but I don't know. There's something about her that's . . .

Addicting.

"No, we weren't fighting," I answer when I realize I haven't said anything. "But I think we could stand a do-over."

"A restart?" she suggests.

"Exactly." I stretch my arm out. "Shake on it?"

She drops her gaze to my hand before looking at me again, those velvety brown eyes drinking me in. Her face is striking. I remember what those lush lips tasted like. How soft her cheeks were. How soft she was everywhere. The subtle freckles that are sprinkled across her nose and how more appear during the summer.

"I don't know, Gavin." Her voice is cautious. "Sometimes it's easier for me to pretend that you don't exist."

The pain her statement brings me is crushing. I drop my hand and push away from the island, curling my arms in front of me and going into pure defensive mode. I hate acting like an asshole, and I try my best to be the good guy in all situations, but sometimes my true nature comes barreling out as if I can't help myself.

"We can keep up the pretense, then, if you'd like," I snap, feeling like a dick the moment that the words leave my mouth.

Another pained sigh leaves her, and she rounds the island until she's standing in front of me, holding out her hand. "Fine. Let's be friends."

Her voice is like a dare. A challenge that I'm eager to accept.

We shake on it, and I keep my grip gentle while she tries to strangle my hand with her fingers. Her touch is electric, even when she's trying to hurt me. I can't help but want to keep holding her hand, but she breaks free of my grip, taking a step back like she needs the space, and I notice the way her chest rises and falls rapidly. Like she's out of breath. And when I lift my gaze to find her almost glaring at me, I can't help but smile. She probably regrets making this agreement with me. I know I do.

"Don't think you can try anything with me, Gavin. Just because we're friends now doesn't mean I want to be president of your fan club," she retorts.

I burst out laughing. "That's too bad. I had a T-shirt made for you and everything. It says Gavin's number one fan across the front. What do you think? Would you wear it for me on game day?"

She gives me the finger and exits the kitchen without another word, her head held high.

This girl—no, this *woman*—is a bit of a menace. But only when it comes to me.

Chapter Six

SIENNA

Calling a truce. Restarting our relationship—no scratch that, our *friendship*. Oh, that word is funny to me. I don't want to be Gavin's friend. I want to fuck his brains out and witness him coming completely apart. I want to ride him like I'm a cowgirl and he's my favorite horse. I want to feel him wrap his arms around me from behind and nuzzle my neck, his mouth on my skin. I want to see his eyes go soft when he first sees me, like I'm the only thing that matters to him. I want it alllll, and instead I settle for friendship.

Am I purposely trying to torture myself by allowing Gavin back into my life?

Not like he ever fully left it. How could he? He's one of my brother's best friends. They spend a lot of time together, and not just during football season either. They have genuine affection for each other, and Coop runs everything by his besties—mostly Nico, and even Frank.

And considering I spend a lot of time around Coop and all his teammates, that means Gavin is always around. Lingering nearby. Popping off with some silly comment or laughing at something I say, though he rarely says anything back. He's kept his distance as if he knew that's what I preferred, and he's right. He's 100 percent right.

I suppose I only have myself to blame for approaching him and having that conversation. Why did I do that again? I wasn't even drunk, so I can't say it was too much alcohol.

I am frustrating. Even to myself.

Currently, I'm wandering around campus during a huge break in between classes. Three hours, as a matter of fact. I don't know what I was thinking when I created my schedule and gave myself so much time in between these two classes, but it's too early in the quarter to use this time wisely. I don't have any major homework or projects due. Yet.

I'm about to leave campus and come back later—always dangerous because I rarely come back later; I end up skipping class—when I hear someone call my name. A familiar male voice that sends shivers down my spine every time I hear it. I don't even need to turn around to know who it is.

Gavin.

"Hey." He's walking beside me in seconds, and I know he ran to catch up, though he's not out of breath. He does this sort of thing—run—on a regular basis, and he's in peak condition. Nothing fazes this man. "How are you?"

I'm stunned that he approached me, but we have new rules now. Guess I shouldn't be that surprised after all. "I'm—bored."

Gavin frowns, readjusting his backpack strap on his shoulder. "Bored? We're too early in the quarter for that."

"I have a three-hour break in between classes." I make a face. "That's too long."

"Yeah, it is," he agrees, glancing around campus. The cool breeze coming off the nearby ocean ruffles his dark hair, and oh, he's gorgeous. I could stare at that chiseled jaw and square chin all day long if he'd let me.

But then I'd look like a total creeper, and that's not cool. I tear my eyes away from the perfection that's his face and stare straight ahead while I keep walking. "I'm headed back to my apartment."

"Coop mentioned you live pretty close to campus." He says this casually. Too casually. Did he ask about me? Does he bring me up in conversation with my brother? Coop's never mentioned it, but he rarely offers up much info when he talks, so why would he?

"I do," I agree, though I give him zero details. Let him ask for them.

"Who are you living with?"

"Um . . . Destiny."

He comes to a stop in the middle of the sidewalk. I do too. "Destiny, as in your roommate in the dorms Destiny?"

I nod, coming to a stop as well. "Yep."

"I thought you hated her."

That he remembers me griping about her that long ago touches my heart when it shouldn't. "I still kind of do." Well, that's extreme. I don't hate Destiny. I just . . . don't know what to think about her most of the time.

"Why do you live with her then?"

"It's not like we don't get along. I stay out of her way and she stays out of mine." Well, this sounds familiar—like my relationship with Gavin. "I don't see her often, because she's either in school or at work or with her girlfriend. She's not a bad roommate," I admit. "We lived together in the dorms for two years, and we agreed we should try to find an apartment together. At least now I have my own room and bathroom."

I reference my own bedroom to remind him of what happened between us when we were in that dorm room. On my bed. I still can't forget it.

"Wild." He rubs his chin, a little habit of his that he does often. "And she has a girlfriend?"

"Yeah. Her name is Lizzie, and she's the sweetest. I think she makes Destiny a little nicer." It's not that Destiny is a complete bitch, but she always seemed on edge, especially when we were in the dorms. Then she met Lizzie and became nicer. This is her first relationship with a woman, and when I asked her what the difference was versus being with a man, Destiny said, "I never have to explain my moods or why I'm acting the way I am. She just gets it."

Makes total sense.

"Whatever works, right?"

I appreciate how Gavin accepts my answers, and when he does question me, it's because he's genuinely curious. That's what it feels like, at least.

"I don't live too far from campus either," Gavin continues. "And I was just headed home."

"Oh."

"Want to walk together?"

"You walked to campus?"

"Always. Nico is the only one who's so lazy he drives to campus when it takes him, like, less than five minutes." Gavin grins and I smile too.

Nico enjoys driving his truck everywhere. Plus, whenever anyone needs something he's the first one to offer to go get it. He drives the guys home from practice when they're dog tired since the stadium is on the farthest end of campus. That walk can be daunting, depending on the circumstances.

"Their new roommate has a car," I tell him. "And she said Nico gave up his spot in the driveway so she wouldn't have to park on the street. Her car got broken into the day she moved in with them, and now she has nothing."

Poor thing. I felt so bad for her when she told me about it.

"Dollar mentioned that to me. He also said you offered some of your stuff to her." He sends me a look I can't decipher. "That was nice of you."

Him saying that reminds me I need to go through my clothes that I was going to get rid of and put aside stuff that might work for Everleigh, though there might not be much. We're not exactly the same size. "I can be a nice person when I want to be. We're supposed to meet up later."

"You and Everleigh?"

"Yeah. She's really nice." I hope we can be friends. I miss having someone around I can gossip with. Commiserate with. Just being able to have girl time with her will be nice. Growing up, at one point I wanted to be my brother. And if I couldn't be him, I wanted to chase after him and spend all my time with his friends.' They tolerated me because, as one of them told me a long time ago, I wasn't too girly.

I was a tomboy at heart and in spirit until around eleven, when I realized some of Coop's friends were cute. I didn't stop hanging around them after the realization, though. Instead, I took advantage of having a bunch of football players around me all the time and even dated a few in high school. The relationships all fizzled out, save for one during my senior year, and he was my first and has been pretty much the only serious boyfriend I've had.

Marc was cute and popular, and at the end of it all, he turned out to be a complete cheater. I gave him my heart and my virginity. He was my senior prom date, and we walked together at graduation, and at a grad party one of our friends was having, I found him and said friend making out in her bathroom. I was devastated. I eventually got over it and was glad to start college single and ready to get my party on.

Then my crush on Gavin came to complete fruition and sort of ruined my life. Well, that's dramatic, but still. I've dated guys. Even had sex with a couple of them, but ultimately, I only want one man and he's unattainable.

Despite walking with him back to our respective apartments, everything about this man screams off limits—and those limits are ones I set for myself.

"She seems nice enough." Gavin shrugs. "I think Nico is into her."

"Oh God. I worried about that." I rest my hand against my chest, shaking my head. Nico is a great guy, but he is far from boyfriend material. The man walking beside me is the same, but he doesn't publicly go through an endless stream of women.

Or maybe Gavin is more discreet. I'm not sure. He is Mr. Mysterious, after all.

"It's only because she's new. And he has to see her every day, so he's tempted. He'll get over it." His nonchalant words make me wonder if that's what he did with me. Was he only interested because I was new, but then he got over me quick?

Can't think about it, won't think about it. If I concentrate on that theory too much, I'll get mad. And then tell him to shove it. When I'm supposed to be his friend.

This is more difficult than I thought it would be.

We come to a stop at an intersection, waiting for the light to change, and this is the moment when we could possibly separate. I need to go right, but he might cross the street and keep heading for the endless row of apartments that is on the other side. They're newer. Nicer. Whereas my apartment complex has seen better days.

"I turn here," I tell him, and he squints in the direction I point.

"I keep going." He inclines his head to point across the street, just as I suspected.

"Well, thanks for walking with me." I smile at him, ready to take off when he asks me a question.

"Want to see my apartment?"

Chapter Seven

GAVIN

I am playing with fire. Temptation. Whatever you want to call it, I shouldn't be inviting Sienna to my apartment. I live by myself, meaning we'll be all alone, and that's dangerous. The last time I was alone with Sienna, I basically mauled her and had my hands all over her juicy ass—and other places.

My gaze drops to said juicy ass, and I stare at it for a moment too long. Meaning she catches me, and when I look up, there's a satisfied glow in her eyes that wasn't there before.

She is feeling it too. That makes this even more dangerous.

"I'll come check out your apartment, Gavin." The moment the light turns green, she's walking across the street, and I keep up with her, startled she agreed so easily. "Can't lie—I've been curious about your domain."

"My domain?"

"Your private space. You've always lived alone, you know. And you rarely invite anyone over."

"I lived in the dorms my freshman year, and I had a roommate." It's required that all incoming freshmen are in the dorms their first year of school at UC Santa Mira.

"Oh, right. I wasn't here then." She smiles up at me, and if I was a more dramatic person, I'd clutch my chest and stagger backward because, damn, that's a beautiful smile. "You've been living alone since I arrived in Santa Mira, and I never hear about anyone hanging out with you."

"That's not true." I have the occasional girl over, but I always give them the boot before the sun starts rising. Not that I'll mention that to Sienna. "Your brother comes over sometimes."

"He does?" She's surprised.

"And Nico. Some of the other guys." It's boring at my place because it's just me. I use it for what it is—somewhere to eat, sleep, and shower. I don't like being by myself for too long, and I'm rarely there.

"You've never invited me over."

"Because you avoided me like I had a contagious disease."

She laughs, tilting her head back, and her auburn hair catches the light. The temptation to sink my fingers into the silky strands and give them a tug is strong, but I restrain myself. "True. Don't forget you avoided me too."

"And look at us now. Spending time together." I give in and reach out, tugging on the end of a strand of her hair. "We're making progress."

"I guess we are." She dodges away from me like she wants me to stop, and maybe she does. Why do I lose all sense of boundaries when I'm around her?

We make small talk until we arrive at my apartment complex, and I lead her down the walkway toward my building. She takes everything in, her eyes wide. "This is really nice. Is it brand new?"

"They remodeled the entire complex a few years ago. I guess it was in bad shape. They opened back up my freshman year, and my father got in on the wait list." He's all about appearances, and he wanted his son to stay in the best apartment complex near campus. Considering most of the complexes are old and not in the best condition, he got lucky. Even though he grumbles over how much everything costs in this town.

The only reason they can command these sorts of prices is because of their location on the coast.

The old man loves to complain, even if he has more money than God.

She turns to face me fully. "Are you close with your father?"

I want to laugh. I want to blurt out *Fuck no*, but that would be rude. Instead, I say, "Not really."

And I leave it at that.

"Oh." She waits, like I might say more, but when I remain silent, she falls into step beside me as I keep walking, heading for my building. It's in the back, on the far right, and my patio butts up against the police station. Meaning it stays relatively quiet around here because no crime is happening that close to the cops.

I walk past her and go to the front door, opening it for her and letting her walk inside first. She stops in the middle of the living area and does a slow circle, taking everything in, which isn't much.

"You don't have a lot of furniture," she observes.

"It's enough." I shrug. There's a couch and a coffee table and an end table with a lamp on it. A big-screen TV hangs on the wall, with a gaming console on the floor, the controllers sitting neatly on top of it and the cords wrapped around them. I don't have a dining table, even though there's space for it, but I do have a couple of barstools tucked under the kitchen counter.

"One bedroom or two?" she asks as she glances toward the hallway.

"One. I don't need two." She looks back at me. "You can go check out my bedroom if you want."

Her curiosity is practically vibrating off her body, and I've got nothing to hide.

Sienna doesn't even hesitate—she heads for my bedroom, then pushes the door open and peeks inside before she fully enters the room. I give her a moment, let her look her fill, and then I walk in, looming behind her as she examines the giant poster on the wall that hangs above my dresser.

It's a photo of the three of us—me, Nico, and Coop—after our team won the national championship our sophomore year. It was an epic season, an epic moment, and the campus store actually sold this poster at the beginning of our junior year. I bought one immediately and had it framed.

"This is a great photo," she murmurs as she studies it.

"It's my favorite. I'm grateful the photographer captured the moment."

"You all look so happy."

"We were."

"Especially you." She aims that potent smile straight at me, and I feel it all the way down to my soul. "I don't think you've ever looked this happy."

"Oh yeah?" I stand next to her and examine the photo closely, trying to see what she sees. I do look happy. That was the most triumphant I'd ever felt. Like I hit the pinnacle of my college football career, and I was only a sophomore. I haven't felt that high since. "There are no posters of us this year."

"You can't beat yourself up over the loss, Gavin. You'll get it this year." Her voice is confident, and I wish I felt as positive as she sounds.

"You think so?" The doubt creeps in, which is rare. I'm a confident person. In my position, I have to be. I've been at this long enough that I believe in myself and my abilities. I am a solid quarterback who is only made better by the team that surrounds me. Together, we feel unstoppable.

But last year a couple of our key players were taken out during the season with major injuries that required lots of recovery time. The other teams got serious and studied our film, figuring out what we were doing. And just like that, we were taken down a peg or ten.

Outwardly I chalked it up to bad luck, but deep inside, I was devastated. Humiliated. I wanted to crawl into a hole and hide for the rest of the school year, but my friends and teammates wouldn't let me, especially Coop.

"My brother thinks you're going all the way this season, and when he says stuff like that, I tend to believe him." She glances up at me at the same time I look down at her. She's tall, but I've still got her beat. "You've got this."

"From your lips to the football gods' ears," I joke, realizing my mistake when I say the word *lips* out loud. It's all I can do. Stare at them. Her lips.

They're the perfect shape, her upper lip as full as the bottom, and this close to her, I can see she has an actual freckle on her bottom lip. That's the cutest fucking thing I've ever seen, but I know if I bring it up, she'll get defensive because her freckles seem to be her greatest insecurity.

"I should probably go." Her voice breaks the spell, and she takes a step back, creating some distance between us, but I take a step closer, addicted to her scent. The warmth emanating from her body. She goes completely still, lifting her head to meet my gaze, and I realize we're closer than I thought.

Running on pure instinct, I reach for her, and she doesn't flinch or push me away. She lets me touch her cheek. Streak my fingers along her soft skin as I shift even closer, our chests brushing. I slip my other arm around her waist, tugging her into me, and again, she doesn't protest or struggle to get out of my hold. I'd stop if she asked me to.

But I don't stop. And she doesn't ask me to.

Dipping my head, I brush my mouth against hers. Her lips are soft and plump and perfect, and when I kiss her again, I hear her sigh. I shouldn't do this. Coop would kill me. I'm not ready for a relationship, and Sienna is a relationship-type woman. It's what she deserves, and trust me when I say this woman deserves the entire world.

Am I the one who can give it to her? Doubtful. I've been on this planet for nearly twenty-three years, and I haven't figured out how to be selfless yet. At least when it comes to a woman.

I tip my head to the side, eager to deepen the kiss, when I feel her hands rest on my chest and gently push me away. I stumble backward, my eyes flying open to find her watching me with such a sad expression on her face, my heart actually hurts.

"Sienna . . . ," I start, but I don't know what else to say.

She slowly shakes her head, and I know I've disappointed her. Typical.

"I should go," she murmurs. I hear a stomach growl, and at first, I think it's mine, but then I realize from Sienna's suddenly pink cheeks that it must've been hers. "Apparently I need lunch."

I'm tempted to offer to take her somewhere, but I don't. She'd probably tell me no, anyway. I never should've kissed her, though I can't deny that I don't regret it.

Not at all.

Instead, I walk her to the door and tell her goodbye, thanking her for stopping by my place. "You're the first girl who's been here in a while," I admit, and just from the faintly disgusted look on her face, I know I've blown it.

"Gee. What an honor," she mutters as she walks away. I half expect her to flip me off, but she doesn't. I breathe a sigh of relief.

And berate myself for the rest of the afternoon for inserting my foot into my mouth around Sienna yet again.

"Okay, fuckers." Nico rubs his gloved hands together, the noise they make grating on my already tired nerves. "We need to kick our asses into gear. No more lagging on the field. We have our first game in a week. Shit's turning serious real fast."

Me, Nico, and Coop are standing in front of the team, supposedly giving them an inspirational speech. Our coaching staff is having an unexpected meeting, and they left us in charge.

Dangerous.

"Are you trying to scare the hell out of them or what?" Coop shakes his head. "Coach said to motivate, not terrorize them."

"You speak then." Nico waves his hands at Coop, knowing full well that won't happen.

"He's not the speech type and you know it." I stand in front of the both of them, cutting them off as I start speaking, giving the most rousing speech I can come up with. Talking about the season and how much this year means to me and my closest friends since we're seniors. Our futures are on the line, and every single game counts.

"Every single one," I tell them, my hands on my hips and my voice heated. Even Nico and Coop appear enthralled with what I'm saying. "But we can't do this alone. We need to rely on each other. Not make stupid mistakes, especially during practice. If we make one wrong move and one of us ends up injured? We're done for." I pause for effect. "The season is over."

The entire team is quiet. I can even hear the water crashing against the surf on the other side of the stadium and the shrill call of the seagulls as they fly overhead. And this is exactly what I want. Driving in my feelings, my worry, my need for this season to be the best that it's ever been. I want this.

Fuck, I need it.

"Let's go out there and make shit happen. We need to practice today like we're playing an actual game. No fuckups. No mistakes. Just pure, clean game play while we get everything dialed in. What do you say?"

A collective "Yes!" sounds, their deep voices rising.

"Then, let's do this!" I clap my hands together, Nico and Coop seeming to know exactly when to join in and clap along with me. "Get into position!"

Everyone scrambles out onto the field, and I'm about to jog out there and join them when Nico calls my name. I stop and wait for him.

"Bro, you do that way better than I do," he says.

"Do what?"

"Inspire people. The team." He slaps me on the shoulder. "You got them all rowdy. Even me."

We jog out onto the field together, and I think about what he said. Being the quarterback is always a leadership role with the team. It's something I've done for years, and I guess it just comes naturally. I'm sure as shit I didn't get any inspiration from my father. That guy may lead a multimillion-dollar company, but he's never shown me any type of leadership while I was growing up. Unless when you refer to leadership you mean your dad is constantly yelling in your face how you're not good enough, you need to toughen up. Do you really want to give your position up to some other asshole? Do you want to end up a loser?

That's what my father would say to me. I remember him yelling at me like that after a youth-league game. I was ten. And I wasn't allowed to cry.

No, I owe any leadership skills I've acquired to the coaches who've taught me and my teammates. That's it. Dear old Dad gets zero credit.

None.

I'm about to get into position when my gaze snags on a figure sitting in the bleachers. I stand taller, squinting in the sun, and yep, that's Sienna. I'd recognize that beautiful red hair anywhere.

She raises her hand to shade her eyes, staring back at me, and even from this distance, I feel a jolt. Her lips curve into a small smile, and I smile back like a goof, knowing she isn't here to watch me but pretending she is anyway. And I proceed to play my fucking heart out, showing off for her. Hoping that she's impressed because, deep down, that's all I want.

To impress Sienna.

Chapter Eight

Sienna

We're going to Charley's. You should join us.

I stare in shock at the text I received from Gavin, who I haven't spoken to since that kiss. He actually invited me to their favorite hangout. My brother has done this before, and that's no big deal. Even Nico has done this. Oh, and Frank. Along with a handful of other football players over the last couple of years. After I was silently rejected by Gavin my freshman year, I set my sights on other men—all of them football players, which looking back on it now, was kind of shitty of me. But they were all men who weren't afraid to show their feelings and were willing to be seen with me. I even dated a few somewhat steadily.

One turned into a possessive asshole I had to dump after two months. Plus, the sex wasn't that spectacular because he was always drunk and couldn't get it up. He eventually got kicked off the team because he partied too much.

The other one was sweet but too wishy-washy in bed. Meaning he cared too much about my supposed tender feelings. I realized after I broke up with him that I want someone who takes charge. Who likes to be in command and boss me around in bed. The type who tells me what to do and slaps my ass and all the delicious things that come along with that. But I also want him to be an alpha male who respects me and won't act like a complete douche when we're in public. Does that sort of guy exist, or is he a complete unicorn?

I'm not too sure.

I wait for approximately ten minutes to respond to him because I'm not above playing the game, and at about seven minutes in, I receive another text.

Gavin: ???

This man isn't above ditching the game to gain his answer quickly. I appreciate that. Biting my lip, I type out a response, going for nonchalant.

Me: Oh sorry, I just saw this! When are you going to be there?

He doesn't hesitate with his answer.

Gavin: I'm headed to Charley's right now. A bunch of guys from the team are there already.

Hmm. I hope he doesn't try to set me up with someone else. I mean, we've come to an agreement that we're just friends now. But would he do that? Is he that blind? I have zero interest in any of the guys, even though some of the new recruits are really cute. But they're like eighteen or nineteen years old, and just . . . I don't mind a younger guy, but they're not serious enough for me at the moment. Not that I'm looking for anything *serious*.

Wait a minute. I don't know what I'm looking for. Not really. I'm just letting things happen and seeing where I end up. Probably not the best way to plan my life, but it's all I've got at the moment.

Me: I'll be there soon. Give me fifteen minutes.

Gavin: I'll be waiting.

I stare at his response, wondering if I'm reading too much into it. I'm sure I am. He's just being nice. Gavin is a nice guy. A little oblivious when it comes to women, but nice. He's also got that charisma going on. People have always been drawn to him, and not just women. He's easy to talk to. Has a beautiful smile and a commanding presence. People want to be around him.

Like me.

I go to my room and comb through my closet, pushing aside every option I've got. None of it works. I don't want to wear any of it, and it's not like I can go shopping. First, I don't have the time. Second, I don't have any money to spare. I need to get a job, but I've been lazy and living off grant money since I came back here.

Guess I'm sticking with wearing something tried and true.

I find a simple black T-shirt dress, and I pair it with strappy black flat sandals. I slick my hair back into a sleek ponytail, then add some thin silver hoops to my ears. I keep my makeup understated. A little blush on my cheeks and mascara coating my eyelashes. The freckles on my nose have become more prominent thanks to me spending more time outside lately, but there's nothing I can do about it. Maybe Gavin thinks they're cute. He did call me Freckles . . .

Deciding my outfit is good enough, I grab my phone and head out to Charley's.

"Yo, Sienna!" My brother throws his arm into the air when he spots me entering the bar, and I head in his direction, shocked that he screamed my name. That's so unlike Coop, but when I get closer, I can tell he's already had a few beers by the twinkle in his eyes.

Someone is feeling good tonight.

"Coop." I hug him because I always do when I see him, and he returns it with extra enthusiasm, squeezing me tight. When my brother drinks, he's affectionate. "How many drinks have you had?"

"Two." He holds up three fingers, chuckling as he drops them. "It's the pretty waitress's fault."

"We don't call them waitresses anymore," I remind him. "She's a server."

"Whatever. She's hot. Won't flirt with me, though." He mock pouts, something I don't think I've ever seen him do before in my life. "I don't even know her name."

Frank appears at Coop's side, a full mug of beer in his hand. He sets it on the table in front of him. "Here ya go, buddy."

"You think that's a good idea?" I ask Dollar.

He shrugs. "You know how it is. I give your brother what he wants, no question."

"Just don't get him too drunk." I look around, trying to spot this server my brother is supposedly flirting with. "In fact, after this one, maybe you should cut him off."

"You're no fuckin' fun, Sienna," Cooper mumbles, making me laugh.

"You'll be fine, Coop." I pat him on the shoulder before I turn and run smack into a solid wall of man flesh.

He's warm and muscular, and I'd recognize that scent anywhere. His hands curl around my upper arms, steadying me, and I tilt my head back, smiling up at him. "Hey, Gavin."

"Freckles." He doesn't let go of me. "Looking cute tonight."

Cute. I sort of wished for beautiful or stunning, but I guess I'll settle for it. "You're looking good too."

Gavin is wearing a white polo shirt that offsets his tanned skin and a pair of black shorts. He looks ready to hit the golf course, which is something he does on occasion with "the boys," meaning Coop, Nico, and Dollar. They claim golf relaxes them, which I think is a lie. More like they bet each other on every round and end up throwing back a few at the clubhouse before they head home. One of them always remains sober, and that's usually Coop.

"I need to do laundry. I only had a couple of clean shirts," Gavin admits, releasing one of my arms so he can tug on the collar of his shirt. "You want something to drink?"

"Please." I sound breathless. I feel breathless, which is dumb. It's just Gavin. Nothing is going to happen. It doesn't matter that he wanted me to come out tonight. He's just my friend. I can't read too much into this.

But my brain is going into overdrive, and I stand there proudly by Gavin's side like a goddamned girlfriend while we wait at the counter for the bartender to see us. Sam eventually takes our order—yes, he still works here—and he won't even look in my direction as Gavin tells him what I want: a rum and Coke. It shouldn't make me feel good that he remembers what I like to drink, but it does. Once Sam takes off to make our drinks, Gavin's shoulders seem to relax, and he turns to face me.

"Can't believe he still bartends here," I marvel.

"Oh, I can. What the hell else is that guy going to do for a living? He loves it here. It's like he's going to one big party for work, every night."

Valid observation. "Do you still hate him?"

Gavin glances over at me, frowning. "When did I ever say I hate Sam?"

"You were pretty pissed at him two years ago when he tried to hit on me that one night," I remind him.

He says nothing at first. Just looks at me for a moment, and I realize this is the first time I've ever referenced that night between us. The best night of my life.

Sometimes I wonder. Was it so good between us because it lasted for such a short amount of time? If we'd turned into something real, would he have ended up disappointing me? Would we hate each other and never speak again? The possibility is there, and I doubt if I'll ever figure it out either.

"There was no trying. The asshole was legitimately hitting on you," Gavin bites out, his narrowed gaze going to Sam. "I guess I do still hate him."

"Aw, that's so sweet. And in my defense too." I pat Gavin's massive biceps, wishing I could press and squeeze into the hard muscle. It's like the man is made out of stone.

"You were so young." There's regret in his voice. In his eyes. "And you still ended up letting an asshole take advantage of you."

We stare at each other, unspoken words passing between us, and realization hits me like a punch to the gut.

He's referring to himself. And that night. While I made a tentative attempt at referencing the past, Gavin just plunged right in and went for it.

Typical.

"There was no taking advantage of anyone that night." My voice is low, and I don't know how he hears me, but he does. I can tell by the dip of his head. He's trying to get closer to me. "I was a willing participant."

He jerks away from me as if I burned him, and he's blinking profusely.

Uh-oh. I think I just shocked him. The unflappable Gavin Maddox is flustered. His face is turning red, and there is panic flaring in his eyes.

"You've gotta be kid—"

"Here ya go." Sam slams our drinks onto the counter in front of us, his voice curt. "You want me to start you a tab?"

"Uh, sure." Gavin doesn't even look in his direction when he answers him.

I grab my drink and take a sip, my lips tight around the skinny straw while Gavin stares at me, baffled. Taking a swallow, I tell him, "You should grab your drink."

He does what I suggest and starts walking, as do I. We head back toward the table the guys are sitting at, but Gavin keeps going until he's at a table for two, then settles into a chair, his expression expectant as he watches me. I pass the table, ignoring the strange looks from my brother and the rest of the guys, sit down across from Gavin, and take another needed sip from my drink. There's a lot of alcohol in this glass, and I bless Sam for the heavy pour.

We sit in silence for a few seconds, the tension building between us until it appears Gavin can't take it any longer.

"What you just said earlier . . . did you mean it?" He's frowning. There's a crease between his eyebrows like he's thinking way too hard, and I wish I could reach out and brush my finger over that wrinkle to ease it. This man.

"I wouldn't have said it if I didn't mean it" is my reply.

He averts his head, staring out at the crowded room. There are people streaming in, the front door seeming to stay permanently open as they enter, and I'm glad we snagged this table. I'm also excited that he wants to talk about this, though I tell myself not to get my hopes up. I've been down this road before, and Gavin is a tease.

"I've been beating myself up over that night for years," he finally murmurs, the agony in his voice obvious. "I felt like a shithead for doing what I did."

"Do you remember what you did?"

He whips his head to face me so fast, I'm surprised he didn't hurt himself. "Of course I do."

"Okay. Do you remember what *I* did?"

The frown deepens. "What do you mean?"

"You say you've been beating yourself up over that night, but that makes me think you don't recall how I reacted." I lean over the table, trying to get as close to him as I can. His scent wafts toward me, that mouthwateringly delicious cologne he wears doing things to me. Like making my pussy throb. "I liked it."

"You did no—"

"I loved it," I say, interrupting him. "I wanted more. Until stupid Destiny showed up and ruined everything."

Gavin slowly shakes his head. "I can't believe you still live with her."

Now I'm frowning. Is that really what he has to say about all this? The fact that Destiny is still my roommate? Such an odd response, but then again, Gavin has never done or said what I expected, so this is on track for his behavior.

Ignoring what he said, I forge on. "We had something going on between us that night."

He remains quiet, just watching me.

"You couldn't feel the vibe between us? I mean, it was a couple of years ago, but I haven't forgotten." I finish off my drink just as he grabs his glass and drains it, smacking his lips when he's done.

A server who's wandering around the bar chooses that moment to appear at our table, her attention only for Gavin. "You want another drink, Gav?"

I roll my eyes at her familiar tone and the obnoxious way she says *Gav*. Doesn't help that she's staring at him like he's a tasty little snack and she's starving. She even licks her lips—ew.

He doesn't notice, though. Just rattles off what he wants before settling that heavy gaze on me. "You want another one, Freckles?"

My heart flutters at the nickname, and when I check on the server, she appears annoyed by it, which gives me a little thrill. "Another rum and Coke, please."

"Coming right up." She's gone in an instant, and I rattle my glass, shaking the ice. Wishing it wasn't devoid of liquor.

"You're freaking me out, Sienna."

"I am?" Oh, my tone is nonchalant, and I'm proud of myself. Does it feel like I have the upper hand for once in my life when it comes to Gavin? Yes, yes it does.

"Like I said, I thought I took things too far." He clears his throat. Shakes his head. Readjusts himself in his seat like he's uncomfortable, and it hits me that he *is* uncomfortable.

Oops.

I decide to be completely honest and reveal my feelings. "We were interrupted, Gavin. I didn't push you away or ask you to stop. I didn't want it to ever stop. And let's not forget the kiss we shared at your apartment."

"Right." He says the word slowly. "You ended that one first, though."

"Does it really matter? It happened again. And again—" I lower my voice. "I liked it."

His gaze drops to my mouth, and I wonder if he's remembering what it was like. Kissing me. You can't tell me he didn't enjoy our last kiss or especially that moment we shared in my dorm room. He had an erection, for the love of God. His hands were all over me, and so was his mouth, his tongue . . .

"Here you go!" The server returns to our table in record time, setting our glasses in front of us. I reach for my drink, tempted to chug it, but I restrain myself and use the straw, cursing the fact that it's so damn skinny. I need more liquor in my system ASAP.

"Thanks," Gavin mutters, not even bothering to look at her this time around, and she flounces away with an irritated huff, which makes me smile.

Hey, I need to get my thrills where I can.

Chapter Nine

GAVIN

This girl. This gorgeous, sexy-as-fuck woman is blowing my mind tonight, and I don't know what to say. Or how to react.

That's a lie. I know what I want to do—lunge across the table and kiss the shit out of her—but her brother is sitting mere feet away from us, and I'm not about to cause a riot in Charley's tonight.

Instead, I try my best to remain calm. I shift my hands under the table so she won't see how they're curled into fists, resting on my thighs. I have to keep them like that. Otherwise, I'd be reaching for her. Pulling her into my lap and wrapping my arms around her waist. Staking my claim.

I am a possessive motherfucker. I've known this about myself since I was younger, and I'd get so pissed when I'd like a girl and she'd already have a boyfriend. Or worse—when she seemed into me and then I'd catch her flirting with someone else. I had a girlfriend in high school— great girl, really sweet. Too sweet because she was kind to everyone, and that made me jealous as fuck.

It's a flaw. I know it is. That's another reason why I'm not interested in anything serious. As long as I don't grow feelings for someone, I can keep things casual with a woman. Once the jealous feelings start, forget it. I act like an asshole.

And then there's the relationship I witnessed between my parents while growing up. It was an utter catastrophe and the worst example ever. I'm not a good boyfriend. Sometimes I worry I'm too much like my dad—and he's not a good person. He's possessive, too, over all his things. And his things include his wife and son. We're objects to him, not actual human beings, and I worry I would do the same to a woman.

That's why I don't get close, I don't catch feelings. The only woman I genuinely care about is sitting across the table from me, and she's off limits.

I drain half my fresh beer in one long swallow and set the glass down with a loud thunk, lifting my gaze to Sienna's. She's watching me with those dark eyes, and I can tell she's excited. By our conversation and what she admitted. I'm still blown away that she had been into it that night—into me. Originally, I believed she was, but after it all happened, when she constantly avoided me, I wrote it off that I'd offended her and left her alone. I'm not about to chase after a woman who's not interested.

I'm not about to chase after any woman. That's not my style. I remain distant until it becomes convenient.

Meaning I am a callous prick. I shouldn't even be allowed to be this woman's friend. And she's still looking at me with an expectant glow in her eyes, when all I'm going to do is break her heart.

Jesus, I should be locked up for what I'm about to say because it's positively criminal.

"You know the deal between us," I murmur.

"What deal?" She's frowning. Confused.

I'm quiet for a moment, letting it stretch out for as long as possible for maximum effect. "We can only be friends, Freckles."

She sits up straighter, which causes her chest to thrust out, and my gaze automatically drops. Lingering there. Remembering how for one hot second two years ago, I had my fingers barely in her wet pussy before we were rudely interrupted by her roommate.

"What did you just say?" She sips on that damn straw. Her lips pursed around it remind me of other things. Moments I've fantasized about over the years. Like Sienna kneeling before me completely naked, waiting for me to tell her what to do. And what do I want? First, I would request a blow job, which she'd give eagerly. Her enthusiasm shines in everything she does, and I don't doubt for an instant she'd do it well.

But I destroy all my secret sexual fantasies starring Sienna with the next sentence that leaves my mouth.

"Friends, Sienna. That's all we can be, you know? A relationship between us wouldn't work out. Don't you agree with me?" If I get her to say that she agrees, I'll feel better. This wouldn't be all my decision. No, we'd share it equally.

"Why wouldn't a relationship work between us?"

I want to groan. Should've known she'd question me. And I don't feel like boring her with all my personal, fucked-up family trauma. "Your brother, for one."

It's an excuse, mentioning her brother. Yes, I don't want to piss him off because, knowing me, I'd end up hurting her, and he'd come for me in her defense. Coop is a good guy. They have a close relationship.

"Coop doesn't care."

He might not, but I do. And I think she's lying. Coop would totally care.

That's not the only reason I shouldn't pursue anything with Sienna. Despite how much I like her, I know I'll mess it up somehow. Mess us up. And I can't stand the thought of not having her in my life, especially now that we're on friendly terms.

I'm such a selfish asshole. How am I going to be able to resist her? In my eyes, she's the perfect woman.

"We spend a lot of time together. All of us." I wave my hand toward the table where my best friends sit. "You included. If we attempt . . . something, it could end spectacularly and ruin friendships."

Her expression turns void. Any happiness she might've been feeling moments ago is gone, just like that. Just like I knew would happen. "Like with my brother?"

I nod. "I value him. He's not just a teammate to me. He's also one of my best friends." And I don't have a lot of those.

It's her turn to remain silent, and I want to squirm in my seat for how long she lets it go on. I'm this close to saying I might've made a mistake when she finally speaks.

"Apparently you value him more than me." Blowing out an irritated breath, she plucks the straw out of her drink and downs it until there's nothing left but ice. "You're an idiot, Gavin. You have a willing woman sitting directly in front of you, yet you're pushing me away because you're scared. You're nothing but a scared little boy who never commits to any woman because . . . why? You don't want to tie yourself down? Are you afraid something better might come along if you do?"

"That's not it at all—"

She talks right over me. "You're an idiot, Gavin Maddox. Worse than that, you're blind. I think we're perfect for each other, but you can't see it. And that's a damn shame."

I watch in silence as she grabs her phone off the table and jumps to her feet, then turns her head, her attention seeming to zero in on something. Someone. I glance over my shoulder, but all I see is an endless crowd of people.

"There's Everleigh. Oh, look at that. She walked in with Nico, of all people. If anyone is afraid of commitment, it's that guy, so I'd love to hear what's going on between those two." She starts walking but stops right next to my chair, and I tilt my head back. She's sneering at me like I disgust her, and I assume I do. "Thanks for the drinks, *Gav*. Hope you have a great night."

She leans down and kisses me. Right on the lips. It's far too brief, and my hand automatically reaches for her as if I have no control, but she's gone before I can touch her. Strutting away from me and leaving behind a fucking mess.

Me.

Finishing off my beer, I stand and head over to join the rest of my teammates, sliding into the booth and sitting on the edge of it since it's already crowded. Coop seems to be having the time of his life, which is not normal. Not that he doesn't know how to have fun, but he's not one to drink when we go out. Usually he sits there and watches over everyone like he's our dad, making sure we don't do anything too outrageous.

Did he spot me and Sienna sitting together? Did he witness his sister kissing me before she walked out? Fuck, I hope not.

"What's your problem?"

I glance up to find Nico standing in front of me, a full-blown scowl on his face. "What do you mean?"

"You look like someone ran over your dog." He jabs his thumb at me. "Scoot over."

"I'm already sitting on the edge and about to fall out of this fucking booth." I stand, glancing over at the table I abandoned only a few minutes ago to find it's occupied.

By Sienna and Everleigh.

"Those two are looking cozy," I mutter, annoyed. More at myself than anyone else.

Nico turns his head, watching Sienna and Everleigh, and a fond smile stretches across his face. "I think it's great. Everleigh doesn't really know anyone here, and Sienna is always complaining there aren't enough girls in our friend group. I'm glad they seem to get along."

I stay quiet. Mulling over everything Sienna said to me, her words on repeat in my brain. And I definitely can't forget the way her lips felt on mine, even though the kiss was way too quick. Those sexy lips were plump and soft, and I immediately wanted to grab her. Pull her down into my lap and devour her. Didn't care if we had an audience—my impulsive nature was ready to get it on.

Clearly, my impulsive nature is also a total jackass.

"You have a problem with them getting close?" Nico asks, his irritated voice invading my thoughts.

"What? No, of course not. Why would I have a problem with them being friends?" I chuckle, but it doesn't sound right, so I shut up.

"I don't know. You've always been kind of weird when it comes to Sienna." Nico's gaze narrows. "And she's weird about you too."

That's just fucking great. I thought no one noticed our interactions, but I guess we're more obvious than I thought. "We're friends."

"Uh-huh." The doubt in Nico's voice is strong. If he had suspicions about us, why didn't he ever bring it up to me before? "She says the same thing."

"Then we're in agreement." I need to change the subject, and fast. "What about you and the new roomie, hmm? You liking her?"

"Sure." He shrugs, playing it off as his gaze goes right back to her, lingering. Shit, I'd recognize that look anywhere. The dumb fucker probably likes her. "She's nice. A little bossy."

"Bossy? Like how?"

"She's trying to get us to eat better, for one thing." Part of their agreement with Everleigh was that she would cook them meals and they would reduce her share of the rent.

"And that's a problem why? Coach would love that." Our entire coaching staff would praise her for trying to fix our bad eating habits. We try to do good, but look at us. Currently drinking beer when we should be watching our calorie intake. We suck.

"She can't tell me what to do," Nico mutters, making me laugh.

"You sound like you're five."

"When I'm around her, sometimes I feel like I'm five." Nico shakes his head. "She's fine. I just need to get used to living with her. It's different, having a woman there."

"I'm sure it is." I decide to poke the bear. "She's pretty."

Nico jerks his gaze to mine. "You really think so?"

"Definitely." I rub my chin, contemplating both women sitting at the table, but really only looking at Sienna. "She's gorgeous." I'm not talking about Everleigh when I say that. My words, my feelings are all for Sienna.

But I blew it with her, and there's no going back now. That woman was willing and eager only a few minutes ago, and I turned her down. Meaning I am exactly what she said—a complete idiot.

"Back off," Nico practically snarls, which makes me laugh all over again. The moment I do, Sienna's gaze levels on me, and I stare right back. She doesn't look mad or even disappointed. No, she looks fucking sad.

And that's ten times worse than any other emotion I want to see.

"I'm not interested in your new roommate, Nico. You can have her."

"Oh gee, you're so generous. Thanks, QB." Nico nudges me in the ribs, and I step away from him, annoyed. I am a big motherfucker, but Nico is bigger. And then there's Coop, who's the biggest of us all.

"You're fucking welcome, Valente. If you're interested in her, let it happen. Have a little fun."

"No way. With my luck, I'll do something stupid, and she'll end up hating my guts. Then we'll have to live together until we graduate. Fuck that. I'm not about to start something that will most likely go down in flames," Nico says.

I understand. I'm in the same predicament with Sienna.

"You're probably right," I tell him, clapping him on the back. "Best to stay away from her."

"Like you need to stay away from Sienna?" he taunts.

"Exactly."

Chapter Ten

SIENNA

It's Saturday afternoon. Game day—the first one of the football season, and we're playing at home. The stadium is packed to the brim. The UCSM band is out on the field, playing a rousing version of some Metallica song I recognize, but I don't remember the name of it. Everleigh is sitting next to me, her face fully painted with the team colors and Nico's and Coop's numbers on each cheek, thanks to me. My face-paint artistry has improved over the years, and I now consider myself an expert. I even painted a pretty cool dolphin on my own cheek for the game. Not sure what I might do once my brother and the rest of his friends—ahem, Gavin—graduate. Will I come to games next year?

I'm not sure.

"The air is positively electric," Everleigh says as our team runs out onto the field to the roar of the crowd. She's rubbing her arms, and I notice the goose bumps dotting her skin.

"It's really just the best time ever. I have so much fun at games." Even sitting in the friends-and-family seats.

My first year, I tried sticking to the student section, but I didn't have many friends, and honestly? I didn't want to reveal to anyone that my brother was out on that field. Though my first year, Coop was benched most of that season only because they had such a strong offensive line. Right before playoffs, Coop got to go in, and he wowed everyone with his brute strength. My brother has zero hesitation out on that field. He will mow someone over with his big, burly body and make it look easy.

He makes me proud. They all do.

Even stupid Gavin. Gav. Just to irritate myself I should only think of him as Gav because oh, how I loathe that nickname. I don't know why. Maybe because all the women that surround him call him that, thinking somehow it sounds more intimate.

While I'm the complete opposite. I feel it sounds far more intimate if I call him Gavin. Who else ever calls him by his full name? He has so many nicknames, and he answers to all of them. Some of his teammates even call him Mad Dog, and I'm like . . . what? Why?

Okay, I need to get over myself.

After I gave up on sitting with my fellow students, I found my people in the friends-and-family section. Parents and siblings and girlfriends and wives all sit here, and last season, I was great friends with the wife of one of the players. They got married when they were barely twenty, and while I thought they were rushing things, they were high school sweethearts. And he was stunningly gorgeous. Like maybe even better looking than Gavin?

Nah.

Anyway, she had to lock that boy down, and I don't blame her. He was recruited by the Broncos, and now they live in Denver. Her life has been so busy; we've sort of lost touch these last few months. I should text her.

Everleigh and I make small talk before I get up to go grab some popcorn. I'm PMSing big time, and I've got the munchies, so I need something to continuously snack on. Plus—and I'd never admit this to anyone—I'm full of nervous energy over this game. I don't know why. These guys do so well, I shouldn't be worried.

But I am. It feels like so much is on the line, and I want them to do well. I want the team to succeed and go all the way. Not just for my brother, though he's the most important member on that team to me, but I also want it for . . .

Gavin.

Stupid Gavin and his charming smiles and broad shoulders and dark hair I want to run my fingers through. Who says the silliest shit I've ever heard in my life. Like how we can only be friends, though I know I stunned him when I admitted that I was into our brief encounter we had oh-so long ago.

Men are clueless. I don't know what else to think.

I'm about to be first in line when a typical clueless man is about to walk right past me and then stops, his gaze zeroed in on me.

"Sienna?" His smile is friendly, and okay, yes. He's very cute. A little on the small side but still cute.

"Yeah?" I don't recognize him at all.

"Hey." He approaches, stopping directly in front of me. Pretty sure I'm taller than him but not by too much. An inch, maybe two. "We went to high school together."

I frown. "We did?"

"We definitely did. Sienna Cooper. Your brother plays for the Dolphins. He's a senior. I graduated with him."

I am racking my brain trying to remember this guy. He's got darkish-blond hair that's a little long on top and floppy, but not in a bad way. No, more like in an attractive way. He has a nice face. Friendly. And when he smiles, he goes from cute to handsome in an instant.

"Ryland. Ryland Hartwig."

Oh.

Oh.

I remember him. He was even shorter back in high school, and heavier too. Much heavier. Back when Coop was on the wrestling team in middle school and then his freshman year in high school, Ryland was too.

"I've lost some weight since then," he says sheepishly, a self-deprecating laugh leaving him as he dips his head. "I understand if you don't remember me."

"I totally remember you." His head lifts, and his eyes sparkle. They're hazel, a swirl of varying colors. "You were on the wrestling team with Coop in high school."

"I was, though he left after freshman year. Football took all of his time up, which I get." He keeps pace with me as the line inches forward, and now I'm next to order. "How is Coop? Looks like he's doing well."

"He's doing great. Have you been here since freshman year?"

"Nah, I took a year off school after I graduated and fucked around." He snaps his lips shut, seemingly embarrassed. "Eventually got my act together and went to community college. Transferred here this year. I'll graduate next year."

"Me too. What's your major?"

"Environmental science. I want to be a park ranger." Again he seems a little embarrassed, though I don't know why. "I like spending time outside and figured I may as well find a job where I can do that all the time."

"That's so cool." I send him an apologetic look when the lady at the concession stand barks at me. "Hold on, okay?"

I go up to the counter to order a large popcorn and pay for it, taking the giant bucket from her before I turn, fully expecting Ryland to have disappeared, but nope. He's still standing there waiting for me with a hopeful expression on his face.

Hmm. I think my expectations in regard to men are terribly low thanks to the jerks I usually deal with.

"Do you come to all the games?" I ask him.

"Yeah, most of them. I'm here with some friends today. We're in the student section since tickets are cheap," he explains. "I assume you go to all of them."

"Definitely." I nod, holding the popcorn bucket toward him in offering, but he shakes his head no.

"You're with friends too? A boyfriend?"

Oh, he's fishing. I sort of love this for me. Even though I swore when I was fifteen that I would never date a man who's shorter than I am, I might reconsider breaking that rule.

"I'm here with a friend." I smile. "And there's no boyfriend."

"Oh yeah? Cool." He shoves his hands into his pockets, trying to look nonchalant, but I can tell he's pleased with this information. "Maybe we could, uh, get together sometime. Catch up on the hometown gossip."

"That sounds nice. Want me to give you my number?"

Ryland seems startled by my offer. "Yeah. Yeah, that would be great."

He opens up his text messages and starts a new one while I rattle off my phone number. Within seconds I receive a message that says, this is Ryland. He included a smiley face emoji.

How cute.

"It was great to see you after so many years," I tell him once he pockets his phone. I lift my bucket of popcorn up. "I should head back. The game will be starting soon."

"It was really great running into you, Sienna." He takes a few backward steps, lifting his hand up in a wave. "I'll text you. Maybe we could get together next week?"

I am beaming. "That sounds perfect."

Rylan smiles and nods, then turns and walks away while I just stand there, watching him. That was a different experience, having a guy seek me out versus me always either (a) chasing after him or (b) avoiding him like he's trash.

For once, a man approached *me*. One who seems sweet and kind, and he's attractive. He's not Gavin Maddox status, but I am most likely aiming too high and wasting my time with guys like that. I need to find a normal man. One who seems into me and isn't afraid to talk to me.

Like Ryland.

Chapter Eleven

SIENNA

It got a little sticky at one point, but eventually the Dolphins win the game, and all is good in our little world. Everleigh and I even waited for the guys to come out of the locker room after the game, which is what I usually do. Always hoping for a glimpse of Gavin even while I avoided him over the last couple of seasons.

This season? I should be still avoiding him after our conversation at Charley's a few nights ago, but screw it. There's a newfound confidence in me thanks to possibly going on a date with Ryland, and at the moment I feel unstoppable.

When the guys exit the locker room and we start heading out to go celebrate, I have no qualms walking right up to Gavin. "Great game today."

He does a double take, startled by my approach. "Uh, thanks."

"You looked good out there, QB." My voice hopefully rings with sincerity. I want him to know that I am truly proud of him. "I mean it."

"I appreciate that, Sienna." He sends a soft smile my way, and I do my best to steel my heart, but it's no use.

Seeing that smile melts me.

"You came to the game with Everleigh?" he asks, trying to keep up our conversation.

"I did. She's really sweet. Did you know she's never been to a football game before?"

He seems shocked. "Not even in high school?"

I shake my head. "Can you believe it?"

"No, I can't. My entire life has been around football."

"Same," I murmur, thinking of all the youth-league games we went to when we were younger. By the time I was in high school, I gave up on cheer and wanted to do something on my own. I was on the volleyball team my freshman year, and while I had the height, I was awkward with the ball. I shifted to track that spring and never looked back, participating in it all four years of high school.

Decided not to pursue it in college, though. I was over it. My athlete years are done.

"You coming with us to Charley's or heading home?" Gavin asks me.

"Going to Charley's. I mean, what else am I going to do on a Saturday night?" I shrug.

"Don't have a date?"

Oh, now look who's fishing. This is such an interesting turn of events. Not just one man is asking me if I'm seeing anyone; now there are two. And considering the second man knows pretty much everything I'm doing at all times, he has to also realize that I am not dating anyone in particular. Though that could all change thanks to Ryland.

Life is so weird sometimes.

"Gav, baby. You of all people should know that I'm not seeing anyone." I keep my tone light and flirtatious, hoping I sound like every other starstruck girl who tries to talk to him.

"Right." He nods, kicking a small rock on the sidewalk and sending it skittering into the street. "And did you really just call me *Gav baby?*"

I burst out laughing, the tension easing from my body at his question. At the way he's looking at me. Smiling at me. I forget all about my potential with Ryland, my focus entirely on the man walking beside me. Towering over me and making me feel small and delicate. And not small in a bad way. More like small in a feminine, *I'm just a girl* way.

Sometimes a strong woman wants to feel like she's "just a girl," and there's nothing wrong with that.

"I did," I finally say. "I'm trying to be like all of those girls who come around."

Gavin grimaces. "Seriously? That's the reason we like having you around, Sienna. Because you're not one of those girls who's trying to get with us."

I'm oddly touched by his appreciation for me. "Not that you've tried to spend any time with me over the last couple of years."

"Not that you've been warm and welcoming toward me either," he throws back.

"True." I shrug. No point in arguing with him about that. "Are we finally at peace with each other?"

"Are you still pissed at me?"

Why is it suddenly so hard to stay mad at him? I did a pretty fair job of it before, though I was never really mad. More like I was hurt and positive that I'd done something to turn him off. God, he made me feel insecure about everything, and I hated it. That's why I stayed away from him.

"Not really," I admit, glancing over at him to find he's already watching me. "Even though I probably should be."

"Look." A ragged exhale leaves him. "I'm not always good with my words, especially with women."

"I'll say."

"And I know I keep saying dumb shit that makes you angry."

"Uh-huh."

"I don't mean to." His gaze is dark and heavy. Full of sincerity. "I'm sorry, Freckles."

I wish he didn't call me that, but then again, I would miss it if he stopped. "It's okay, Gavin."

We're quiet as we walk side by side along the sidewalk through campus, surrounded by everyone else's chatter. I can hear Nico grumbling to my brother behind us. I watch Frank walking with Everleigh and notice how she's listening to every word he says, which I know he appreciates because he loves an audience. And speaking of an audience, I notice that there are a lot of people joining us as we walk through campus. And that they're trying to ask us questions.

"Hey! Who's the girl?" someone asks, and I know exactly who he's referring to. The team's fellow students and fans are used to seeing me around the guys. Everyone knows I'm Coop's sister, but they don't recognize Everleigh, and they're curious.

Increasing my pace, I come up on Everleigh's right side and hook my arm through hers. "She's my friend."

"Oh, come on. I heard she lives with Cooper and Valente," someone else says, their tone almost taunting.

Everleigh and I share a look, her gaze filled with worry. She's not used to this sort of attention, and what exactly are they trying to imply, anyway? That Nico and my brother have some sort of throuple relationship going on with Ever?

Please.

"She's our roommate," Coop says, and I can tell by the sound of his voice that he's irritated. "Nothing more, nothing less."

The crowd explodes after that, people shouting questions at the guys one after another, their voices getting higher and higher. Concerned, I let go of Everleigh's arm and go over to Gavin. "You should call security," I tell him.

He doesn't even hesitate and has his phone to his ear in seconds, making a few quietly said commands before he glances over at me. "Done."

"We need security," Nico says as he runs past us to insert himself in between Frank and Everleigh.

"Already on it," Gavin says. "They'll be here soon."

He sends me a reassuring smile, and like the dumbstruck woman I am, I smile back, grateful that he listens to me.

The bar is packed, but they reserved a bunch of tables for the team like they always do, and that's where we're currently sitting. There are only a few women celebrating with the guys tonight. A couple of girlfriends. Everleigh. Me.

I'm sitting right next to Gavin because he slid into the booth seat beside me when the server brought us to the tables, his thigh pressed firmly against mine. An almost painful reminder that distracts me. I can't concentrate on what people are saying because I'm too wrapped up in the sensation of his very bulky and very firm thigh nestled right next to mine. How he leans into me when he speaks to the guy sitting on the other side of me. I don't even remember that guy's name, though his face is familiar. And at this point, I can't be bothered to try to figure it out.

Instead, I remain where I'm seated and revel in being this close to Gavin. His delicious scent, the warmth of his body, the deep rumble of his voice. The way he speaks to his teammates, always giving them so much credit while they go over the highlights of the game as they're always wont to do. They enjoy reliving their glory moments, and I don't blame them. It was a great game, and especially for the seniors on the team; this is their last season. They want it to be epic—the very best games they've ever played.

The thought of Gavin graduating leaves me melancholy, and I wallow in my sad feelings for a moment, until that little nagging reminder deep inside my brain tells me I need to get over it and enjoy this time with him rather than think about the future and how he'll be gone.

"Want another drink?" Gavin asks, and I smile at him, nodding. He lifts his hand, signaling the server who's at the other table taking orders, and once she walks over, he puts on the Maddox charm.

The smile he levels upon the woman could slay a thousand dragons dead, and of course she falls for it. I watch the tension bleed from the stiff lines of her shoulders, and her entire expression goes soft. "Whatcha need, QB?"

He rattles off a few requests, and I realize he must've asked everyone at the table if they wanted something else. He even orders two large plates of nachos, which have my stomach growling just at the thought of them.

Once the server is gone, he leans against the back of the booth seat, his shoulder brushing against mine. "I was starving. Nachos aren't the best choice, but fuck it."

"Yes. Fuck it." I giggle. Oops. I think I'm buzzin'.

He appears amused at my little giggle. "Someone's probably had too much to drink."

"Do not cut me off, Gavin Maddox. I probably just need something to eat. Like nachos." I had popcorn and ate a hot dog during halftime at the game, but that was hours ago. I'm definitely hungry.

"I would never." He rests his hand against his chest, that fond smile on his face doing things to my insides. Like twisting them into knots. "You know what I like about you, Sienna?"

I sit up straighter at the sincerity in his voice—and, of course, at the words he said. "What?"

"How loyal you are. You're always there for Coop."

"He's always there for me." Don't get me wrong—we argue. We've even gone through stages when we seriously disliked each other, but that's all in the past. Now I consider my brother one of my best friends.

One of my best friends who I keep a few secrets from, but we won't focus on that at the moment.

"And you're always here for the team too. We appreciate you." He pauses. "I appreciate you."

A lump lodges in my throat, making it difficult to speak. Taking a deep breath, I lean into him, pressing my shoulder against his. "Thank you, Gavin."

He wraps his arm around my shoulders and drops a kiss to my temple, making me freeze. Making him freeze too. Did he really just do that? Did anyone see him? Us? I've never witnessed him be affectionate toward any woman before, and that was completely out of character for him.

Not that I mind. It's what I want. What I crave more than anything, and I press myself into him as much as I dare, knowing this moment is going to end far too quickly.

He slowly removes his arm from my shoulders and shifts away from me, though he can't go far. I'm not offended. And truly? He appears rattled, and I get it. That was mind blowing, what he just did. And how natural it felt between us.

Eventually the server brings us our drinks and nachos, and I stuff my face, not even caring if I look like a pig. Everyone is gorging themselves on food, and it doesn't really matter. I sip my drink, trying to pace myself. I'm feeling good, but I don't need to get trashed. I notice Gavin has stopped drinking and switched to water.

Hmm.

By the time it's past midnight, most of the crowd at our tables has dissipated, though the bar is busier than ever. I see a few of the players among the people still here, even my brother, but Gavin remains seated by me. Quiet. Downright contemplative. I'm mostly silent, too, enjoying being with him and even a little sad that these moments are slipping away from me. One by one, game by game, until the season is over and there will be no reason for us to see each other beyond a friendly *Hi* or *Bye* in passing.

It's devastating to think about, which shocks me. We've gotten close in a short amount of time after mostly avoiding each other for two years. I wonder if he feels the same way . . .

"You good?"

I glance up to find Gavin watching me carefully. There is no one else in the booth seat with us, yet we're still planted right next to each other. "A little tired," I admit, unsure of what to say.

"Want to get out of here?" he asks, his voice a low, sexy rumble.

I lean in closer, certain I misheard him. "Excuse me?"

"I asked if you wanted to leave." He looks deep into my eyes, as if he can see into the depths of my soul. "With me."

I blink at him, thrown by the question. "You want to leave with me?"

Gavin shakes his head, averting his gaze and staring off into the distance. "Don't question it too much, Sienna. I might take it all back."

That is the only prompt I need to hear. I scoot out of the booth and stand. "Let's go."

Chapter Twelve

GAVIN

What. The. Hell. Am I doing?

I leave Charley's through the back entrance with Sienna, her just behind me, our hands linked. *Linked.*

She doesn't say a word. Neither do I. We walked to Charley's, and we are just as capable of walking back to my apartment, where there is no one to disturb us. No roommates around either. We'll be all alone.

And fuck me, I don't know if I'll be able to control myself. Maybe I don't want to.

Yeah. I definitely don't want to.

The entire night at Charley's was torture. The moment I see Sienna, I want to be around her. She's so damn sweet, so giving, and after the blistering conversation I had with my father earlier, I'm still feeling raw. Needy. He had some harsh criticism for me as usual, reminding me of all the mistakes I made, which always messes with my head. This might be the dumbest idea of my life, but here I am, desperate to be alone with her and making it happen.

Fuck it. I'm tired of holding back. She wants me. I want her. What's the harm in it? I haven't had sex in months. Mostly because no one appeals to me, with the exception of Sienna. She seems to understand me like no other woman I've ever met, and I just . . .

I need someone tonight. I need her.

We're back at my apartment within five minutes, and I unlock the door via the keypad, pushing it open and holding it for her to let her in. She walks past me, her body brushing against mine, my skin catching fire from the contact, and I slowly close the door. Lock it. Press my forehead to it for a moment and take a deep breath.

"Why did you invite me back here?"

Damn, she would ask the tough questions.

"I just want to talk." I turn and face her, noting the skepticism on her face.

"Okay." She rests her hands on her hips, looking ready to challenge me. She's so damn hot in the Dolphins T-shirt and jeans. She washed off the face paint at the bar, but I still see a few specks of white and blue on her skin. "Let's talk."

"Not in here."

"Then where?"

"My room?"

Sienna goes quiet, her teeth sinking into her lower lip and looking sexy as fuck. "Gavin. What exactly are you asking me to do?"

"I'm tired, Freckles. I need to relax. And I couldn't do that back at Charley's. It was too busy. I just—need someone." I swallow hard. Wonder if she knows that took a lot for me to admit.

"Just someone? Anyone?" Her brows lift. She's going to make me say it.

"I need you," I murmur.

Her expression barely changes at my confession. I spot a flicker of something in her eyes, but that's it. "Let's go to your room then."

She follows me into my bedroom, and I don't bother turning on the light. I just shed my clothes until I'm standing there in only my boxer briefs, feeling exposed. Even a little raw. This isn't how I operate, telling a woman that I need her. I've gone through most of my life acting like I need no one. I believed I could do everything, gain anything I wanted on my own.

I've come to realize that I need a team. Not just with football because, yeah, that's the fucking point. But in my life too. I need people I look up to like Coach and the rest of the staff. My friends—my best friends. I depend on those guys. They're like family to me.

And then there's Sienna. Right now, I need her the most. I like having her as a friend, but there's more to it. More to us. She's inserted herself into my life, and I allowed it to happen. I wanted it.

I want her.

I've been a selfish motherfucker for most of my life, but I'm always careful around her. I don't want to ruin it. Ruin her. Ruin my friendship with Coop. I'm tired of holding back and not giving in to my feelings. This girl . . . means a lot to me. I care about her. And I know she cares about me too.

I don't want to mess this up.

Sienna doesn't say a word while she watches me strip, and I have to admit, having her appreciative gaze on me is a boost to my ego, which is feeling battered tonight. Not that I've told anyone why.

Tugging back the comforter, I crawl into bed and then pat the empty space beside me. "You should join me."

"Gavin . . ." Her voice is filled with caution, and I see the look on her face.

She's terrified. And I did that to her. All the back-and-forth over the years has come to this.

"Please?"

That single word sets her into motion. She's toeing off her shoes and shimmying out of her jeans, kicking them aside. She keeps on the Dolphins T-shirt, and for a brief moment, I imagine her wearing my jersey. My number. That familiar possessive feeling rises within me, growing with every second that passes, and I tell myself to calm the fuck down.

She joins me in bed, sliding under the comforter and pulling it over her body. She rolls over onto her side, facing me, and I do the same, facing her. It's dark in my room, though the blinds are cracked, letting in streams of light from the full moon outside. I stare at her face, drinking in her striking features, and I wonder what the hell is wrong with me that I won't make a serious move on her.

"What's bothering you?" she asks. I part my lips, ready to tell her, but she speaks right over me. "And don't say it's nothing, because it's fairly obvious something is eating at you."

For someone who avoided me for years, she certainly knows me well. "I spoke to my father earlier. He called me."

Sienna frowns. "When?"

"Right after the game, when we were in the locker room. The conversation—didn't go well." It never does.

She remains quiet, and I have a feeling she's trying to choose her words carefully. "What in the world did he say to you besides 'good job' and 'congrats on winning the game'?"

"Nothing positive." I release a ragged breath. "He told me I played like shit today."

"That's not true." She sounds indignant on my behalf, which is exactly what I was seeking from her. I need that blind loyalty of hers tonight. Maybe it'll ease the sting from my father's criticisms. "Did he not watch the game? You were great out on that field!"

"Maybe," I hedge. I'm full of doubt, thanks to that phone conversation with dear old Dad. He lit into me from the moment I said hello, and I couldn't even tell you why. Maybe because he lost control of my life a long time ago and it still pisses him off to this day? The man acts like he holds a serious grudge against me, and I don't know what the hell I ever did to him to make him feel this way. Maybe it's because I was born?

Jesus.

"Hey." She grabs hold of my face, her fingers pressing into my skin as she stares into my eyes. "Don't listen to him. Coop has mentioned you don't have the best relationship with your father, but don't let his words get in your head."

I nod once, trying to absorb what she's saying, but it's difficult. I can't block out what he says, no matter how hard I try.

"Seriously." She gives my head a little shake, like she can rattle out the years of negativity my father has spewed at me. "Don't let him ruin your confidence. You're Gavin fucking Maddox. One of the best college quarterbacks to ever play."

A smile curls my lips. "I don't know about the 'to ever play' part."

"You know what I mean." She cups my cheeks, her touch turning gentle. "You shouldn't ever doubt yourself, Gavin. That'll only make everything worse. Whenever Coop gets too in his head, he does terrible. It messes with his game, and he's created a ritual where he puts in his AirPods and tunes out the world before every single game."

She's right. He does do that, and we all leave him alone. Maybe I should start something like that, too, but my team needs me. I'm their leader. Coop is a team captain, too, but it's different when you're the QB. And I want people to look up to me, to seek me out so I can give them advice. I dole out the positivity because it feels good. Something I learned from my dad, who was too hard on me. Eventually that shit eats you alive.

"You need to stay confident and believe in yourself," she adds. "You're a great quarterback, Gavin, and your team needs you just as much as you need them. You've got this. I know you do."

I nod, savoring the feel of her hands on my skin. How she's completely focused on me and nothing else. "You make it sound easy."

"I know it's not." Her voice softens. "But I have faith in you."

"At least someone does," I mutter.

Her face falls a little, the sympathy flaring in her eyes. "I hate to see you suffering."

"I'll get over it. I always do."

She drops her hands from my face, and I immediately miss her touch. Until she slides her fingers into my hair, her fingernails lightly scratching my scalp. "Has he always been this hard on you?"

"My entire life." I close my eyes and exhale softly, enjoying the head massage she gives me. I could get used to treatment like this. Couldn't I?

"He's a dick." She goes still, and I crack open my eyes to see her peering up at me, her expression full of guilt. "I'm sorry. I probably shouldn't have said that about your dad."

"Why not? You're only speaking the truth."

She removes her hand from my hair and rolls over so she's lying on her back, staring up at the ceiling. "This entire moment is surreal."

"What do you mean?"

Her head swivels to the right, her gaze meeting mine once more. "I'm in Gavin Maddox's bed on a Saturday night trying to give him a pep talk. Like, what is this life?"

"I'm not that big of a deal."

"Oh, but you are. You're just downplaying it." She sighs, her focus returning to the ceiling. "Why did you ask me to come back here again?"

"I needed someone to talk to. Someone I can trust." I keep my attention fixed on her, admiring her profile. The gentle slope of her nose. Her full lips. Her smooth, soft skin dotted with freckles, and I'm tempted to reach out and touch her, but I keep my hands to myself.

"You have plenty of friends you can trust. Why me?"

"I can't tell them my doubts and insecurities."

"Not even to my brother?"

I hate that she brought up Coop. He's the last person I want to think about while I have his little sister in my bed. "I don't want to ruin his good time. They're all on a high from the win, and they don't need to deal with my shit. My dad isn't their problem. He's mine."

She turns her head, her dark eyes locked with mine once again. "They would be there for you and listen no matter what. You're one of Coop's best friends."

"I know. You're right." I blow out a harsh breath. "I'm being a pussy."

"No, you're not. You're allowed to have feelings, Gavin. And we all want our parents' approval. It's okay to feel this way. You don't have to be emotionless all the time."

"You think I'm emotionless?"

"I think you try to hold back your emotions, yes."

"I trained myself to not show any after a while so I wouldn't trigger my dad. It's like he looks for signs that I'm weak and attacks me."

"That's awful," she murmurs, sounding horrified.

"It is. But I just learned how to deal, you know? My parents aren't anything like yours. They support you guys no matter what you want."

"I don't know about that."

Her tone—and her words—startle me. "What do you mean by that?"

She returns her focus to the ceiling yet again. "My parents have focused all of their attention on Coop my entire life. I love my brother and I'm proud of him, but sometimes I feel like I'm an afterthought to my family."

Her confession is shocking. From the outside, the Coopers look like a supportive, loving family. I've never seen Sienna act like she doesn't want to be around her parents. They've always seemed really close.

But I suppose I get what she's saying. I don't have siblings to fight for attention from my parents. It might've been nice, to have a brother or sister. They could've taken the heat off me for a moment.

"That's tough," I murmur. "I didn't know you felt that way."

"I've never told anyone because why should I make this about me? Coop is the star of the family. I don't mind standing in the shadows."

I don't believe her. I can hear it in her voice. She wants to shine like her brother, and she deserves to.

"If you didn't have to live in your brother's shadow, what would you do, Sienna? Have any secret dreams about your life? Your future?" Has anyone ever asked her those questions before? I'm guessing no.

"I don't know," she starts, but I reach for her, pressing my finger against her plump lips, silencing her.

"That's a lie and you know it." I keep my voice low and my finger on her mouth, sending her a meaningful look. "Be real with me." I drop my hand from her face and wait for her to speak.

She licks her lips, and I stifle the groan that wants to escape at seeing her pink tongue. "I've always wanted to start my own business."

"Doing what?" I ask.

A soft sigh leaves her, and she keeps her gaze fixed on the ceiling. Like she can't face me when she says it. "I want to run my own ice cream stand."

Seriously? I almost say the word out loud, but I don't want to offend her. That just feels like a . . . small goal in the scheme of life, but what do I know? If this is what she wants, then she should go for it. And why should I shit on her secret dreams, anyway? I feel like this is a big deal, that she'd admit this to me.

"It's dumb, right?" she asks after I remain silent.

"No, it's not dumb if that's what you want to do," I say, choosing my words carefully. "What inspired you to want an ice cream stand?"

"It's a little silly, but I saw this teenage boy out on the beach last year, and he had his own ice cream stand. Like one of those freezers on wheels you can push around? He had a nice little setup with a cute fringed umbrella keeping him in the shade and a colorful sign on the front of the freezer listing all of the ice cream he carried. I kept tabs on him, and he had this endless line the entire time I was out there, and I couldn't stop watching him. He always had a smile on his face, and so did everyone who was buying his ice cream. He was bringing joy to those people, and I realized that's exactly what I want to do. Bring joy to people. And what better way to do that but hang out on the beach all day and sell ice cream? Everyone loves ice cream," she explains.

"Not anyone who's lactose intolerant," I can't help but point out.

She sends me a vaguely irritated look. "You know what I mean. And there are plenty of nondairy options out there."

"Well, if you want to do that, you should."

"How? There will be expenses, and I don't have a lot of money. I looked into an ice cream cart like the guy had on the beach, and that's around two thousand dollars. I don't have that kind of money right now. I'm still trying to find a part-time job to get me through college."

I'd offer to loan her the money, but I know she'd turn me down, so I stay quiet.

"I'll need to invest in the freezer and all the ice cream. That can't be cheap. And it's a pretty limited job, don't you think? I'd only be able to do it during the summer. Besides, I'll be graduating soon, and I should probably focus on getting a job where I can use my degree."

She sounds defeated, but she shouldn't be.

"Not if you do it here in Santa Mira. The weather is pretty good year round. Maybe you could do an ice cream truck. That might be an easier option." There are food trucks all over the coast, but I don't know if I've seen one around here that sells just ice cream, beyond the vans that cruise through the neighborhoods during the summer when the little kids are out in force. There is one food truck that creates specialty shakes that I see around on the weekends, but that's different than what Sienna wants to do.

"That sounds even more expensive. My parents can't help out. They don't have a lot of money either," she mumbles. "And it's a silly idea. No one wants a career selling ice cream. I guess I had dreams of hanging out on the beach all day, though I'd probably get sunburned and turn into a walking freckle."

"Sienna." She turns her head to look at me. "It's not silly. Nothing you ever do or think is silly. Though the idea of you turning into a walking freckle . . . that's kind of silly."

I'm teasing her with the last line. I meant every word I said.

Her smile is faint and she reaches for me, her hand landing on my neck, warm and comforting. "You know just what to say to make me believe in myself, even when my ideas are bonkers. Thank you, Gavin."

We stare into each other's eyes for far too long, and she scoots closer, her hand never straying from my neck. I shift closer to her too.

Until our bodies are next to each other and her body heat is seeping into me. We don't have much clothing on, and when her legs tangle with mine, I give in.

Grabbing hold of her slender waist, I haul her into me and kiss her.

She doesn't fight me. No, she gives in beautifully, her lips parting automatically for my tongue, her hands winding around my neck, her fingers sliding into my hair. I wrap my arms around her even tighter, jerking her forward, wanting her as close as I can get her, and she moans into my mouth.

The soft, sexy sound does something to me. Kicks my urges into overdrive, and I roll her over so she's lying beneath me and I've got her pinned to the mattress. I search her mouth with my tongue, run my hand up and down the side of her body, and when I finally break the kiss, I lift away from her, staring at her beautiful face.

Her breaths come fast, and there's so much fear in her eyes. Like she's afraid I'm going to push her away right now, which is what I usually do.

I'm such an asshole.

But I don't push her away. I keep my eyes on her as I reach in between us, my fingers curling around the hem of her T-shirt before I lift it up slowly. Glancing down, I watch as I expose the tops of her thighs. The little red panties she has on—damn, they're barely covering her. The soft, pale skin of her stomach above said tiny panties. I stop when just the underside of her breasts are exposed, and I release a ragged exhale, staring at her perfectly shaped tits.

I shouldn't do this. I'm a selfish bastard who just wants a look. Maybe even a taste. I won't take it any further. I promise.

"I promise," I murmur as I slide down her body, my mouth landing right above the waistband of her panties. I breathe deeply, inhaling her familiar scent. The musky scent of her pussy. Right. I won't take it any further.

I'm lying to myself.

"What are you promising, Gavin?" she asks, her voice raspy, her breaths coming in soft little pants.

She doesn't want to know that I was promising to myself that I wouldn't take this too far, but that's not true. I want to take it as far as I can get with her. As far as she'll allow me. My mouth literally waters as her scent intensifies, and I drop my head. Press tiny kisses along the waistband of her panties, overcome with the need to tear them off.

I'm desperate to taste her. Just once.

Chapter Thirteen

Sienna

My hands automatically go to the top of Gavin's head, holding him in place. My entire body is on fire because I didn't expect him to do this. Here we are playing True Confessions in his bed, and then he's got his mouth right above my panties, like he's ready to go down on me.

Okay then. Let's go. *Finally.*

He slides his hands up along the outside of my thighs, causing sparks to fly everywhere he touches, and I remain as still as possible, fearing I'll break the spell and he'll come to his senses. I hold my breath when he curls his fingers around the sides of my panties and slowly pulls them down, completely exposing me.

I close my eyes as he tugs the thin red fabric down my thighs until they're around my knees and I can't move my legs. He pulls my panties tighter with one hand, trapping me while he touches me with the other, his fingers tracing a barely there line through the strip of pubic hair I have neatly waxed every three to four weeks, which gets expensive to maintain but is now totally worth it, considering what is happening at this very moment.

"Red. Just like your hair," he murmurs, and I open my eyes to find he's staring at my pussy like he's completely fascinated by it.

"Did you ever doubt I'm a natural redhead?" I ask, my voice faint. Every part of my body is throbbing in anticipation of what Gavin might do next. I don't even know how I formed words to ask him that question, I'm strung so tight.

"Never," he murmurs as he slides up my body to kiss me on the mouth. He devours me, really. I push past the disappointment because I had his mouth so close to the spot where I'd love it the most, but having his lips on mine is also good.

No, they're great. The man hasn't lost his ability to kiss, not that I thought he had. He might even be better, though that might have to do with how long I've craved another moment between us like this. And this one is even better than the last. His mostly naked body pressed against mine, all that firm, hot muscle settling on top of me carefully so he doesn't crush me as he searches my mouth with his tongue. I wrap my arms around him and stroke my hands up and down his smooth back, dragging my nails across his skin and making him shiver. He pulls away slightly, and fear locks tight around my throat, ceasing my ability to breathe.

"We need to take this off" is what he says, tugging on my T-shirt, and the relief that floods me is overwhelming. I thought he was going to back away. Tell me he couldn't do this, that we're just friends.

Please. This man is not my *friend*, not in the traditional sense. I want him too badly, and I think he feels the same way.

I lift my arms to help him pull the shirt off, and he whips it over my head, tossing it on the floor and leaving me mostly naked. I kick off the panties tangled around my calves, and somehow we end up sitting in the middle of the mattress, me in Gavin's lap, my legs wound around his hips, his erection nudging me. God, I wish he didn't have the boxer briefs on. I'd sink right on top of him, taking him inside me. I'm in the perfect position to do just that, and I rub against him, my breath catching.

Gavin grabs hold of my hair, clutching it in his fist and jerking on it gently, my head tilting back. I open my eyes to find him watching me, a fiercely sexy expression on his face, his eyes blazing with hunger. "You're a tease."

"No. You're the tease." I angle my hips just so, rubbing against him once more. His fingers tighten around my hair, and he pulls it a little harder. "You've still got clothes on."

"The moment I strip, I'll be fucking you. Hard." His mouth lands on my neck, and he sucks the sensitive skin, nibbling on it with his teeth. His words shock me, making my core throb even harder, if that's possible, and I cling to him, gasping when his mouth finds mine in a filthy, messy kiss.

We sit like this for deliciously long minutes, our mouths connected, his hands wandering all over me once he lets go of my hair. He cups my breasts, strumming his thumbs across my nipples, and I want to die from the pleasure of it all. His mouth and hands and hard body and even harder dick. His soft hair and hot skin and the stubble lining his cheeks. I want to feel those cheeks between my thighs, want to feel his mouth on my pussy, his tongue on my clit.

"You're so fucking wet, you're soaking my boxers," he murmurs against my lips, sounding pleased. "Teasing my cock with your sopping cunt."

Whoa. I didn't expect the extra-dirty talk from Gavin, but then again, I shouldn't be surprised. The man has always been a mystery, and I am loving this side of him.

Feels like I love every side of Gavin—except for when he rejects me.

I refuse to think about that, though. Instead, I concentrate on the rhythm of his tongue and maintain the same rhythm with my hips, rubbing back and forth across the head of his dick, bathing his boxer briefs with my juices. I let go of all my inhibitions because this is the most monumental moment of my life. Wrapped around Gavin, naked. Knowing we're going to have sex.

My entire body tingles with anticipation.

His hands fall to my waist, and he lifts me away from him with ease, ignoring my whimpering protests. He drops me on the mattress and crawls off it, shucking his boxers off as he stands beside the bed and kicking them aside before he opens the nightstand drawer and pulls out an unopened box of condoms.

I swallow hard, watching him as I push my hair out of my eyes. He tears open the box and pulls out a wrapped condom, setting it on top of the nightstand before he rejoins me on the bed, his focus only for me.

"I don't know if I want to fuck you or eat you first."

"Eat me?" I say it as a question, but he takes it as a suggestion because the next thing I know, I'm pinned to the bed and he's slowly making his way down my body, leaving devastatingly sweet, hot kisses all over my skin. He lingers over my chest, licking and sucking my nipples, eventually shifting lower, streaking his mouth across my belly until he's lying between my legs. He grabs both my thighs and drapes each of them over his shoulders, and I watch him, nearly wanting to die when he lifts his gaze to mine.

Oh, he looks good between my legs. Just like I knew he would. He doesn't take his gaze off me as he slowly lowers his head, his tongue sneaking out to tease at my clit. I hold my breath, dying for more, and he turns his head at the last second, pressing his mouth on the inside of my right thigh before he does the same thing to my left.

I am a quivering mess. My clit is pulsating, my entire body strung tight with the need to come, but I also don't want it to happen yet. I want to draw out this moment, revel in it forever because what's going to happen when this night is over? Will we go back to being so-called friends? Or worse, will he ignore me?

I cannot stand either option.

"Gavin," I choke out as he continues to press lazy kisses to the inside of my thigh.

"Yes, Freckles?" He sounds calm and in control of the entire situation, and I sort of want to hit him.

I also want to beg him to keep doing what he's doing because, oh my God, it feels amazing.

"Wh-what are you doing?"

"Kissing every freckle that I find." He turns his attention to the other thigh, kissing it everywhere because I have a lot of freckles.

"That'll take all night."

"I've got time."

That confident tone of his is going to be my downfall. He is truly the sexiest man alive, and I still can't believe I've got him between my legs. That his mouth is so close to my pussy. That it's already been on my pussy. And I want it back there right now.

"Ummm . . ." I stop talking when he takes a swipe at my slit with his tongue. There and gone in the blink of an eye. "Oh God."

"You close, baby?"

Him calling me baby in that growly voice has me melting. Am I even a functioning human anymore? I don't think so. "Yessssss."

His mouth is on me. All over me. He spreads me wide with his fingers, his flat tongue touching me everywhere, and I lift my hips, seeking more. Needing more. He slides a thick finger inside me, filling me, and I go still, moaning when he slowly withdraws it only to plunge back in. Over and over he does this, his lips finding my clit and sucking it hard. Tonguing it while he fucks me with his fingers.

Yes, his fingers, because he added another, and I appreciate the way he doesn't hold back. It's like the dam broke and he's unleashing all his want and need and desire all over me. I spread my thighs wider, lift my hips as much as I can, and basically mash the lower half of his face with my pussy, and he lets me, encouraging me as he hums against my flesh, and then I'm coming. All over his mouth and chin.

Panting and screaming and coming hard. I'm shaking as wave after wave hits me, and he never lets up. Keeps licking and sucking and fucking me with his fingers, and I swear another orgasm builds, this one smaller but still so, so good.

Eventually I can't take it any longer, and I push him away, my skin too sensitive. I crack open my eyes to watch as he settles back on his haunches, licking the fingers that were just inside my body. Another jolt hits me, maybe even yet another, tinier orgasm, and when our gazes lock, he smiles, the sight of it devastating. Obliterating all my brain cells and leaving me a complete idiot.

Over this man and no one else.

"Freckles, you are the sexiest woman alive," he murmurs, licking his fingers clean. "The way you just came right now . . ."

"I was a hot mess," I finish for him, staring at his face because the lower half of it is currently covered in my juices.

"More like hot." He moves over me, dipping his head, and I kiss him, the musky taste of my own pussy on his lips. "Clean my face with your tongue, baby. Taste what I just tasted."

Oh. He keeps saying things like that, and I don't know if I can take much more of it.

I do as he says, gently lapping at his face with my tongue, tasting myself all over him. He cups the side of my face, guiding my lips to his, and the searing kiss he delivers lights me back up like I never experienced those delicious orgasms he gave me. My body is already needy and eager and desperate.

"I need a condom," he murmurs against my lips at one point, and all I can do is nod.

Yes. Yes, he does. I need to feel him inside me. I want him to fuck me hard, just like he promised.

I reach for him, my fingers curling around his hard cock, and I start to stroke, making him growl. There is nothing awkward about this moment, when normally, I'm a bit of a fumbling mess. It's not that I've had bad sex or terrible partners; it's just never easy for me. More like it's always awkward and weird, and I get too in my head over it.

Not with Gavin. It just flows between us, and when he lifts away from me, I am sad. Bereft at the loss of his body on top of mine. I roll over on my side and watch as he opens the wrapper and rolls the condom over the tip of his dick until it's fully sheathed. His gaze lifts, his fingers curled around the base of his erection, and this is a moment I never want to forget. I take a mental photo and store it away in my memory bank, saving it for later.

Reaching out, he tugs my body closer to him as if I don't weigh a thing, until I'm lying beneath him and he's hovering above me. Slowly he dips his head, his mouth finding mine in a sweet, tongue-filled kiss as he positions himself, the head of his cock brushing my pussy.

Oh God. This is it. The moment I've been waiting for since I was a drunk freshman. We have grown and changed over the last two years, but my feelings for this man have only intensified. I don't care about anyone else. Want anyone else.

Just Gavin.

He slides inside me slowly, inch by excruciatingly thick inch, filling me up. I hold my breath and close my eyes, my body still, my brain shifting into overdrive. The significance of the moment, one I've been waiting for so long to happen, hits me hard, and I think I might . . .

Oh God, I am crying.

The tears well in my eyes, and I squeeze them tight, trying to keep the tears from falling, but they do. Leaking out of the corners of my eyes and sliding down my face, and Gavin pauses, his cock inside me, his hands braced on either side of my head.

"Sienna," he whispers, and I can't look at him. This is . . . this is embarrassing. Overwhelming. I'm being silly, reacting like this. I need to keep it together and focus on the hot sex we're about to have. The delicious, toe-curling orgasm he's going to give me because I meant what I said to him earlier—I have faith that Gavin is capable of doing allll the things.

Including making me come while he's inside me.

"Sienna." He repeats my name, louder this time, his fingers drifting across my cheek, and I open my eyes, my vision blurry thanks to the sheen of tears currently covering them. I blink, sending the fresh tears cascading down my face, and I notice his furrowed brow. The concern filling his beautiful eyes. "Baby. You're crying. What's wrong? Do you want me to sto—"

I cut him off. "No. Please don't stop."

"Why are you crying?" He dabs his thumb in one of my tears, absorbing it into his skin. He brushes the rest of them away, dipping his head to kiss me before he murmurs, "My dick is too big, huh? Am I hurting you? I'll go slow, baby. I promise."

I burst out laughing. I hope that was his intent because, oh my God, the confidence filling his voice at calling himself too big was . . . a tad comical. "You're not too big, Gavin. And you're not hurting me. It feels good, having you inside of me. *You* feel good. I'm just—this moment. It's emotional for me."

"I don't know if I've ever made a woman cry before when having sex with her. This is definitely a first." He starts to move, taking his time as he fucks me slowly. Our bodies getting used to each other as we find our rhythm.

We stop talking. There's no need for words as he increases his speed, his cock plunging faster inside me. Harder. He grunts with every thrust, not holding back, and I match his movements, wrapping my legs around his waist, sending him deeper. Making him groan. Making me whimper.

He nudges something deep inside me that sends a scattering of tingles all over my body, settling in my core. He does it again, and I cling to him, whispering my encouragement.

"Oh my God. Just like that," I murmur close to his ear.

Gavin wraps his arm around my back, lifting me off the mattress as he holds me firm and fucks me hard. I keep my legs tightly wrapped around his lean hips, shocked breaths leaving me with his every push inside my body. He keeps hitting that spot, over and over, and I close my eyes. Bury my face against his neck right as the tremors take over my body.

"Oh, fuck, Sienna," he groans right before his own orgasm sweeps over him. His body shudders against mine, and I hold on tight. Reveling in the experience of feeling Gavin Maddox come apart in my arms.

This night, this moment, has completely transformed me. And I don't think I'll ever be the same.

Chapter Fourteen

SIENNA

I wake up slowly, my body aching from being in a prone position for too long. The spot between my thighs aching for a different reason . . .

Shifting my legs, I knock my feet into something.

Someone.

My eyes pop open, and I realize I'm tangled up in Gavin's arms. In his bed. He's fast asleep, his lips slightly parted, his eyes closed. There's a massive amount of dark stubble on his cheeks, and there are faint shadows under his eyes.

He's still devastatingly handsome. How can he not be?

My movements are slow as I try to pull out of his embrace, but I wake him up anyway. His eyelids slowly lift, revealing his hazy gaze, and a furrow appears between his eyebrows when he sees me. That furrow sends me into a panic spiral, making me fear he regrets everything that happened. But that slow, sexy smile stretches across his face, and he leans in, trying to kiss me.

I block him with my hand, turning my head away.

"What the fuck, Freckles?" he murmurs against my palm, and I almost want to laugh.

"Morning breath, Gavin." I slowly drop my hand, hoping the look on my face is a warning. "You do not want to kiss me right now."

"Bullshit." He leans in and does it anyway, and his lips linger, soft and persuasive.

Nope. I end the kiss before he deepens it, trying to roll away from him, but his grip on me tightens before I can slip out of bed. He pulls me back in, my back to his front.

"Where do you think you're going?" Oh, that low, rough murmur is hot. The way he trails his lips along the back of my neck and shoulder is even hotter. And I can feel his erection poking against my ass.

"To brush my teeth?" I say hopefully.

"You don't have a toothbrush here." He licks at the spot between my neck and shoulder, making me shiver.

"You have mouthwash?"

"Probably."

"You don't know?"

"I don't really care." His hands come around my front, cupping my breasts. "You really want to talk about mouthwash right now?"

No. No, I do not. Deciding I shouldn't speak at all, I remain quiet as he touches me all over my body. Those deliciously rough hands roam, lingering on all the good spots. And when he slides his fingers between my legs, I bite back a moan, spreading my thighs to give him better access.

"You always wake up this wet?" he asks before he gently bites the side of my neck.

"Do you always wake up this hard and horny?" I return.

He pinches my clit between his fingers at my response, making me gasp. "Such a smart mouth."

"You like it." Oh, I am breathless when that pinch turns into a caress. Tight little circles that ratchet up the flame burning inside me.

"I like everything about you." He thrusts his hips against my butt, letting me feel him, and I swear a fresh gush of wetness floods my pussy. He removes his fingers and brushes them against my parted lips. "Taste."

I do as he asks, sucking his fingers deep into my mouth. I haven't given him a blow job yet, and I'm dying to, but he never gives me the chance. Always fucking me instead. Like he's about to now.

"You're right," he says once he's pulled his fingers from between my lips. "I do like that sexy mouth of yours."

I hum my pleasure at his words, arching against him. He grabs my hips, holding me in place as he pushes inside me, and I moan when he fills me completely. Morning sex. I've never been a fan. Always worried about the bad breath thing or how I might look. I have a feeling there is leftover makeup smeared all over my face, along with traces of paint, but he doesn't seem bothered by it. No, he's too intent on fucking me to oblivion, his cock feeling deeper like this. More intense.

When I lift my arms and circle them around his neck from behind, he begins to move in earnest, our skin slapping, our moans filling the air. I'm on the verge of orgasm already, my tired body coming alive, and when he settles his fingers over my clit and begins to rub, he sends me straight over the edge.

It's too good. Overwhelming me in the best possible way, and for a moment, I black out. Lose all train of thought and consciousness. His hands return to my hips, keeping me in place as he plunges inside me, and I come back down to earth, whispering, "Pull out."

"What?" he rasps.

"Pull out. You're not wearing a condom."

He does as I ask with a groan, and I feel that first splatter of semen on my back. My butt. He comes and comes, and I lie there, shocked when I feel it trickle all over my back, dripping down the crack of my ass. I can't believe he—we—lost all control and had sex without a condom. I mean, it felt amazing. But oh my God.

That was close.

"Fuck, your ass looks pretty with my come all over it," he mutters, swiping his fingers through the mess he left.

I clench my thighs together at his rough, dirty words. Gasp in surprise when he grabs hold of my shoulder and flips me over so I'm facing him, thrusting his fingers in between my lips so I have no choice.

"Lick them clean, baby. Show me how much you like it," he demands, and I do. Licking his fingers as if my life depended on it, earning his smile of approval. This man is filthy and I love it. No one has talked to me like this before. Treated me like this before. I didn't know I liked this sort of thing, but apparently I do.

Gavin finally removes his fingers from my mouth, and we lie there facing each other, staring into each other's eyes, our breaths still labored, my body aching from all the delicious abuse it's endured since last night. A swirl of emotions rises within me, the most prominent one being panic, though I try to remain calm on the outside.

But seriously—he almost came inside me. I haven't paid much attention to my period app like I do when I'm actively having sex, and I know I should be starting my period in about two weeks so . . .

Yikes. I am probably fertile as fuck right now. Oh my God. This is not good. In fact, this is downright terrifying.

I drink in the most handsome man on earth, who is currently naked and smiling at me while we're in his bed, and I mentally tell myself to stop freaking out. It's time to shove my worry aside and put on a brave face.

"Good morning," I singsong, keeping my voice soft.

"Mornin'." He bends down and kisses me, still completely unaffected by the possibility of morning breath.

"That was . . . nice." Oh, and that was awkward, how I phrased what we just did. It wasn't *nice*—it was absolutely earth shattering. The man can rock my world like no other.

"Nice?" He tilts his head and drifts his mouth along the length of my neck. "I'd use stronger words for what we just experienced, but if you wanna say nice, I can go with that too."

"What words would you use to describe it?" My stomach jumps with nerves, and I have no idea why. Maybe because we just had unprotected sex? Yeah, that would do it.

"Mind blowing." He brushes the hair away from my face. "Spectacular. Fucking phenomenal."

I blink at him, surprised by the high praise, though I feel the same exact way. Still a little freaked out, though. "Those are pretty strong words."

"Well, I have pretty strong opinions about last night and this morning so . . ." He delivers another kiss, this time on the tip of my nose, before he lets go of me and rolls over on his side, facing me. "Want some breakfast?"

I slowly shake my head, turning to look at him. "I don't like to eat much in the morning."

"I do." He reaches for me, cupping my pussy. "I'll take some of this."

My sensitive skin practically quivers when his fingers slide along my folds. "With bacon?" I am teasing. Bacon? I sound ridiculous.

But Gavin goes right along with it, a grin spreading across his face as he removes his hand from between my thighs.

"Nah, baby. With sausage." He grabs hold of his cock, his fingers circling the base, and I burst out laughing all over again. "That was cheesy as fuck."

"I'll say."

Once our laughter dies, he's reaching for me again, pulling me into his arms, his gaze steady on mine. "Hey."

"Hey," I whisper, my fingers crawling up his firm chest. He is somehow so hard yet soft at the same time, and I wonder if he'll let me explore my fill of him someday. I'd love to kiss him everywhere. Stroke him everywhere. Do whatever I want to him while he has to lie there and just take it. Hopefully he'd return the favor and do the same to me.

Mmm. Sounds like my every dream come true.

"I'm sorry." His voice is solemn, as is his expression.

I frown. "What are you apologizing for?"

"That I fucked you without a condom."

Oh. Right. He definitely did do that.

"I kinda lost control of myself," he continues. "I wasn't thinking. And I'm always thinking. Always careful. I don't have sex with a woman without protection, meaning condoms. Ever."

I stare at him, not surprised at his admission, but then again, I *am* surprised because what he's implying is that I'm the only one who makes him lose all control.

Me.

"And I'm not saying all that just to reassure you, Sienna. I'm telling you the truth. You can trust me," Gavin says when I still haven't spoken. "I got tested over the summer, and I'm all clear. I've never fucked around without a rubber. I'm not about to put myself in a stupid position."

Like getting someone pregnant. Ugh.

This conversation, while necessary, is making me uncomfortable. First, I'm not one to talk so freely about sex with the guy I'm having sex with. And second, I do not like talking about him having sex with other women. I'm being a complete hypocrite because I've had sex with other guys after our little interaction two years ago. I mean, what was I supposed to do? Wait for this man to get his head out of his ass while he's off having sex with other people?

Not that the sex I had with only a handful of guys—okay, two— was as good as it is with Gavin. The man knows what he's doing, which tells me he's done it a lot. But I don't need my face rubbed in it.

"Okay." I nod. "I trust you."

I trust that you'll stop talking about all of this, I think to myself. The last thing I want to deal with is listening to him ramble on about his active sex life.

"I can't even remember the last time I had sex with someone," he admits.

Wait a minute. Did he really just say that?

"You don't have to lie to me to make me feel better," I reassure him, patting him on the chest. "You had a life before me."

And you'll have one after me, I almost say, but I clamp my lips shut before I can.

"Well yeah, but I'm serious, Sienna. I haven't fucked someone in . . . an embarrassingly long time." He ducks his head so I can't see his eyes. "I've been too caught up."

"Too caught up in what? Football?"

"Football. School. Practice. My life." He lifts his head. "You."

The air between us crackles with tension at his admission, and I just—come on.

"Stop it," I whisper. "You don't mean that."

"I do. I—I've been fighting my feelings. For you." His gaze is almost pleading when it locks with mine. "You had to know that."

"No. No, I really didn't." I'm in complete shock. What is he trying to tell me?

"And I know the timing isn't the best. Us having sex right now. At the beginning of the season," he continues, averting his head.

Uh-oh. "What's that got to do with anything?"

His gaze finds mine once again. "I need to concentrate, Sienna. Everything is on the line this season. My future. Other people's futures, like your brother's. I can't slip. Can't get distracted." He touches my hair. "And you are by far the biggest distraction I've ever had."

He says that like I should take it as a compliment, but I don't. More like it's an insult, and I am so sick of being put on the back burner in everyone's life. Didn't I just tell him that? Didn't I make my big confession to him last night? Look at how easily he forgets. I can't trust him for shit.

He's like everyone else. I deserve to be someone's priority. I refuse to settle for pitiful slices of his life. I deserve the entire fucking pie.

I pull away from him. Roll right out of his bed, jump to my feet, and bend down to snatch my discarded T-shirt off the floor and hurriedly pull it on. Oh, I'm pissed. Furious. "What exactly was this about, huh? Did you try to sweet-talk your way into my panties and see if you could fuck me out of your system, and oops, it didn't work?"

He sits up to watch me, the comforter pooling in his lap. Ugh, I am cursing him a thousand times in my head, but he looks mouthwateringly delicious with the mussed-up hair and the stubble all over his face. The muscular, broad chest and washboard stomach, and I am almost positive I can see his erection poking against the thin comforter in his lap.

I'm tempted. Tempted to jump right on him and have sex with him yet again, but that would be a major mistake. The man is sitting here trying to give me a speech about why we shouldn't be together because I'm too much of a *distraction*. He's got more important things to take care of first.

I pride myself on being a patient person. I understand football and its importance to this man probably more than any other woman at this university. I've witnessed it firsthand growing up with my brother. But I'm not going to sit around and wait for him to get his head out of his ass. I've had it.

"You know I like you. We've always been drawn to each other, and this—I didn't expect for this to happen." His lips curve into a gentle smile, like that's going to soften the blow of his shitty words.

"Uh-huh." I give up on trying to find my panties, and I grab my jeans and tug them on. They feel extra tight for some reason, and I work to pull them over my hips, wincing when I jerk the zipper into place and button them. I do not like wearing jeans without undies, and oh, I regret not finding those little red ones. Though maybe it's a good thing that I'm leaving them behind. A nice souvenir for Gavin to come across later. Maybe he'll even use them to jerk off with because he wants to keep up the fantasy with me long after the reality of me is gone.

That'll serve him right.

"Are you mad?" He sounds incredulous.

I throw my hands up in the air. "What do you think?"

Not bothering to wait for his answer, I flee his bedroom, racing to the front door, and I hear heavy footsteps behind me. Feel his long fingers curl around my arm as he stops me from escaping. I whip around to face him, coming to a halt when I find him standing there completely naked, and my gaze drops to his dick because, Lord have mercy, it is beautiful.

And I don't think dicks are beautiful. They definitely have their uses and are pretty freaking amazing, but Gavin's penis is museum quality.

Clearly, I have lost all common sense after having sex with this man.

"Don't be angry with me. I'm just—I'm asking you to be patient with me." The pleading expression on his face is almost my undoing.

But not quite.

Steeling my spine, I glare at him, forcing myself to keep my gaze on his face and not his dick. "What do you think I've been doing for the last *two years*? Patiently waiting for you to notice me, Gavin. Patiently waiting for you to realize that we have potential. That we could be great together. And lo and behold, I was right. Last night was freaking amazing."

His smile is faint. "You're right. It was."

"And then you had to go and ruin everything this morning by opening your mouth and saying dumb things." I reach for the front door and undo the lock before opening it. "Have a great day, *Gav*."

I slam the door in his face, cutting off his response.

Chapter Fifteen

SIENNA

I wake up to the sound of my phone ringing, the tone indicating it's a FaceTime call. It's Sunday afternoon, and I know exactly who it is.

My mother.

Groaning, I roll over and blindly reach for my phone, knocking it off my nightstand. The ringing stops. Blissful silence reigns. I close my eyes, eager to drift back off to sleep and do my best to forget the last twenty-four hours ever happened, when the ringing starts up again. She won't stop until I pick up, and if I don't, she'll probably call Coop and ask him to come check on me. Make sure I'm alive.

No way do I want that to happen. How would I explain myself to my brother?

Oh hey, yeah. I'm devastated because I just had the best sex of my life with your best friend, and now he's telling me I need to wait for him and . . . no. Fuck that guy.

I don't think Coop would understand.

"Shit." I hang over the edge of my bed and pluck my phone off the floor; then I sit up and brush the hair out of my face before I answer. "Hey, Mom."

"Sienna!" Her normal enthusiastic greeting shifts into motherly concern when she sees me. "Sweetheart. Are you all right?"

I can't tell her what happened. I refuse to bring Gavin into the conversation with my mother for fear she'll tell Coop and then shit will hit the fan and Coop will go after him. Give him a talking to or, worse, warn him away from me. Then Gavin will hate me forever, but I sort of hate him at the moment, so we'd at least be on equal terms.

Okay, I'm being completely dramatic, but Coop knowing about what happened between me and his bestie would definitely cause problems, and while I'm frustrated and angry with Gavin, I'm not about to ruin friendships. I'd rather remain quiet and keep the peace.

"I'm just tired." I offer her a smile, but it feels forced and fake. I let it fall and yawn, covering my mouth with my hand. "Maybe I'm coming down with something."

"You look like you've been crying." She's frowning at me, and I study her face, seeing much of my own reflected back at me. While Coop took after Dad, I definitely look like our mother, though she's much shorter. But we've got red hair—hers is a little brighter—and matching brown eyes. If that's what I'm going to look like in my late forties, I'm not too worried. Mom has still got it going on.

"I haven't been crying," I reassure her, lying through my teeth. I was crying in bed earlier, before I finally fell into an exhausted, dreamless sleep. This is what happens when you stay up all night getting thoroughly fucked by the love of your life. Also known as the biggest idiot in the world.

Who does he think he is, telling me to wait for him? To be patient? Haven't I done that enough already? Doesn't he get that I know how to handle myself around football players and that I understand the pressure they're under? I feel like everything he said to me was some sort of secret code for *I don't want anyone to know about us.*

And while I find that hurtful—is he embarrassed of me?—I also do get it. To an extent. Announcing a relationship with a man of his status is monumental and extremely public. Lots of questions will pop up, and I don't think either of us is ready to answer them.

He should've approached it better, is what I'm saying.

"Are you sure?" My mama knows me too well, and so I smile again, trying to make it look as real as possible.

"I'm positive. What did you think of the game yesterday?"

"They played amazing. Oh, I wish we had been there to watch." Mom shakes her head, her disappointment clear. They try their best to never miss a game and do pretty well, but this weekend they had plans. A couple they've known for years was celebrating their twenty-fifth wedding anniversary, and the party was last night. There was no way they couldn't go, and while both my mom and dad stressed about it, Coop assured them it was fine. And he meant it too.

"It was a good game," I agree.

"You went?"

"Of course," I retort. "When do I ever not go?"

"You're such a good sister, Sienna. Barb was asking about you last night." Barb is the woman who had the party. "She wanted to know what your plans were once you graduated from college."

Hmm. Something my parents haven't asked me, yet good ol' Aunt Barb—she asked us to call her that a long time ago—just did.

"I couldn't answer her because I don't know." Her gaze is filled with sadness. "That made me feel like a bad mother."

"Aw, Mom . . ."

"No, don't start defending me or whatever it is you wanted to say. I called you today because I wanted to apologize to you. And for your father. We get so caught up in your brother and everything he's doing, we sometimes forget to check in on you."

Her timing couldn't be better. It's like her mother's intuition kicked in and she picked up on the vibes I was giving out last night when I complained about them to Gavin.

"Yeah, you do kind of forget about me sometimes." It's better to agree with her than deny it, because where will that get us?

"I'm sorry about that. I really am. And there's no excuse for us doing that. Barb's question has made me aware of our bad behavior. So tell me." Mom sits up straighter, resting her arms on the dining table in front of her. She must have her phone sitting in one of those stands so she can remain hands-free. "What are your plans after you graduate?"

"I don't know," I admit, my voice barely above a whisper.

She frowns. "You don't know what to do? Don't have any plans? Any idea of what sort of industry you'd like to work in?"

No, no, and no is what I want to tell her, but that's not entirely true. I have an idea . . .

"I was thinking about starting my own business."

Her entire face lights up. "Oh really? Doing what?"

It took a lot of bravery for me to confess my interest to Gavin last night, and I was thankful he didn't laugh at me. Oh, he made the lactose-intolerance joke, but that was funny. *He's* funny, and I love that about him. He was supportive and said all the right things. Even better, he sounded sincere. Like he really believes in me, and I don't get that much. From anyone.

Too bad I'm still annoyed by our earlier conversation. I came home so preoccupied by it all, I never even took a shower. Just collapsed into bed and cried, grateful Destiny was over at her girlfriend Lizzie's house.

Tucking my head into my shoulder, I can still smell him. On my shirt. My skin.

"Sienna?" Mom's tone is questioning, and I realize I've taken too long to respond to her.

"Ummm, I was thinking an—ice cream stand. Or an ice cream truck where I can serve specialty ice creams? I'm not talking about the little white van with the ice cream man driving around the neighborhood. I'm thinking something cooler. Edgier." Mom remains quiet for like two seconds, and I keep talking to fill the silence. "I know it sounds like a stupid idea, and it probably is, but I thought it might be fun—"

"It doesn't sound stupid. Not at all," Mom says, interrupting my defensive ramble. "I happen to love ice cream. Your father does too. Don't you, Jerry?"

I hear my dad yell back at her. "What are you asking me, Joy?"

"You love ice cream, right?"

"Always have." Mom switches the camera, and there's my dad, sitting in his recliner. He waves at me. "Miss you, Sisi."

"Miss you, too, Dad." I wave at him, and Mom switches the camera back to her. I swallow past the sudden lump in my throat. "You think it's a good idea?"

"Sienna, honey, we'll support you in whatever you want to do. You want to have an ice cream truck, I bet your dad will come down there and help you set it up. I bet he'll even drive it around for you."

"You gotta pay me in ice cream. That's it," he says, still yelling from his chair.

I smile, my heart swelling at their unwavering support. She didn't even hesitate, immediately saying it was a good idea.

Why did I think people would hate on this again?

"I'm sure there's a lot involved in this, and you'd probably need to take out a loan? We don't have much money or else we could contribute, but whatever you need from us, honey, we'll help you," Mom says, Dad agreeing with her in the background. "Are you sure that's what you want to do?"

"I can't stand the idea of working at an office every day," I admit. "I like being outside. Doing my own thing."

"You'd have to be disciplined with your work schedule. A self-motivator."

"I can do that." I hope I can.

"Have you looked into something like this at all? Done a little research? Like, how much a food truck might cost? You'd really only need a freezer in it and a fridge. You won't need a stove or anything like that. I bet that would save you some money," Mom says.

"You're right. I've looked into prices some, but I kept stopping because I worried this entire plan was a dumb idea," I say. "And I was really thinking only about a freezer cart." I tell her about the boy I saw selling ice cream at the beach and how he inspired me. "A friend suggested a food truck."

"That's a smart friend. I think that's a better way to go. I see all the food trucks that show up in the parking lot and on the street around the stadium," Mom says. "That would be a great way to make money, with those big crowds that come for every game."

We talk about other things. My classes. I tell her about my new friend, Everleigh, though she already knew about her since she lives with Coop.

"I'm glad you like her and you're becoming friends." Here comes that concerned-mom look on her face again. "I always worry about you. You don't have enough of them, save for all the boys on the team."

And there I go again, thinking about Gavin. I decide to change the subject.

"I need to go find a part-time job," I tell her. "Now that I've got my schedule figured out and I'm settled in, I need to make some money."

"You should go on the job hunt tomorrow," she suggests. "Maybe you could work at an ice cream shop!"

"Maybe," I hedge. I don't know what I want to do, but I need to occupy my time so I don't sit around and think about Gavin as much. What better way to handle that than go to work somewhere. "You're right. I'll go on the job hunt first thing in the morning."

"That's my girl. I'm sure you'll find a job easily!"

I smile, grateful for her. For both my parents. They might not show it as much since the bulk of their attention is for my big brother, but at least they always support me in everything I want to do. Unlike some people's parents—such as Gavin's.

My anger has eased some, and I know we need to talk, but I need a little more time away from Gavin before I seek him out. I don't want to blow up at him again. I need to keep a level head when we talk about us. Whatever *us* means.

Ugh. Men. They make me want to bang my head against the wall.

I get up bright and early Monday morning to go on my job hunt and decide a good place to start would be downtown Santa Mira. I'm sure there will be a few help wanted signs hanging in the business windows, but as I walk down the streets and even check the side streets, I find there isn't much. Actually, I don't really see any at all, which fills me with utter defeat.

That's all on me. I'm late in my job-search adventure. I should've been doing this in August when I first moved back to Santa Mira, but I was feeling lazy and believed I could stretch out the grant money I received last quarter. Now that funds are drying up, I'm left with no choice.

I need to work.

Entering a cute clothing store, I wander around and look through the racks, sinking my teeth into my lower lip when I see the prices. This place is expensive. I don't think I could afford shopping here even if I had a full-time job.

"Excuse me? Do you need some help? Looking for anything in particular today?"

I turn at the friendly-sounding voice, smiling at the woman who approached me. "I'm okay. Just looking."

"Okay." The woman nods. I'd guess she's around my age, maybe a little older. "Let me know if you need anything."

She's walking away from me when I speak. "Actually, I do need something."

"What can I do to help you?" She turns to face me with a wide smile, her expression open and welcoming.

"I was wondering if you're . . . hiring at the moment?" I wince. "It's okay if you're not. Just thought I'd ask."

Her expression turns contemplative, and she taps her index finger against her pursed lips. "As a matter of fact, Myra is always looking for more sales associates. You want an application?"

Myra must be the owner or manager. I would love to get on Myra's good side. "Yes, please." I follow the sales associate to the counter where the cash register is, and she slips behind it, bending down to search the shelves before she pops back up, an application clutched in her hand.

"Here you go. I'd apply quickly if I were you. Someone stopped by earlier and turned in her application and résumé. She already spoke to Myra too." She gives the application to me, and I take it, already defeated. "Tell her Jamie sent you. I'll put in a good word. What's your name?"

"Sienna." I scan the application, mentally kicking myself for not printing out a couple of résumés before I left the apartment.

"Right. I knew it was you. You're Coop's sister, right." Jamie grins. "It's so good to meet you! I love the Dolphins football team. Do you know Gavin Maddox?"

My heart sinks to my toes at her question. Now I'm being recognized thanks to my affiliation with the team? Is that why she wants me to work here? "Yeah. I know him." *I was in his bed Saturday night* is what I'm dying to tell her, but that would be rude. Plus, it's none of her business.

"You're so lucky! Oh my God, do you think he'd come into the store? Oh, do you think he'd invite me to the parties they have? I'll tell Myra she has no choice. She has to hire you." Her eyes are sparkling at all the possibilities.

And that is the last thing I want—being used for my connection to the Dolphins football team. No thank you.

"I'm not sure." I hold up the application. "Thank you for this."

"Come back after two. Myra should be here by then. I'll let her know a Santa Mira celebrity wants to work here!" Jamie waves enthusiastically when I exit the store, and I wave back at her through the window as I pass by, rounding the building before I lean against it with a sigh, pressing the back of my head against the rough brick wall.

Well, that was a complete waste of time. No way am I going to apply there. While they'd probably hire me on the spot, they'd only do it thanks to my connection to Coop—and Gavin. Plus, they'll also have certain expectations, and all of them will have to do with the team.

And Jamie probably wants a shot at Gavin too. She's pretty. Would he be interested in her? It doesn't even matter that we had sex two nights ago. All my old insecurities come flooding back, and I shove them out of my brain, mad at Jamie and Myra and Gavin.

Definitely at Gavin.

I haven't reached out to him, and he hasn't reached out to me either. We're both playing a dumb game, and if I keep this up, I'm definitely going to be the loser.

Yeah, taking this job would be a disaster. I'm not about to set myself up for failure. For pain and suffering. I want to work, but not that bad.

I go into a few more stores and ask for applications, but none of the people I spoke to could tell me if their place of employment was hiring or not. I end up at Back Yard Bowl, a locally owned smoothie-and-acai-bowl place, feeling down in the dumps as I order a berry bowl, ready to hand over my debit card to make my purchase when I spot the tiny sign taped on the back of the register.

NOW HIRING! QUESTIONS? ASK FOR MATTY.

"You're hiring?" I ask the cashier, who is a tiny thing I could probably squash like a bug. She looks terribly young too. Like maybe she's still in high school or just graduated.

"We are." She smiles and shifts the card reader closer to me. "Go ahead and tap."

I do as she says and add a small tip because I'm feeling generous—and she did make me that bowl. "Can I ask you an honest question?"

She's frowning. "Sure?"

"Do you like working here?"

Her frown fades and she's smiling again. "Oh yeah. The hours are great. We're currently only open until seven, even on weekends, and after Labor Day, we'll reduce it to five. It can get pretty busy here in the morning and around lunch, but our manager always schedules enough people, and it never feels too stressful, you know?"

121

"How long have you worked here?" I'm glad there's no one behind me in line, which gives me the time to ask these questions.

"A couple of months. I started in June right after I graduated from high school."

Hmm, I was right. "Do you go to UC Santa Mira?" I ask.

She nods. "I just started, but I love it."

"I'm a junior there," I tell her. "And I really need a job."

"You want to talk to Matty? He's the manager."

"He's here?"

"He is. Go eat your bowl, and I'll let him know you're interested." She adds a pile of napkins and a fork to my tray.

"Should I fill out an application?"

"Nah. He's pretty informal. Just have a sparkling personality and a willingness to work pretty much anytime, and he'll probably hire you on the spot."

I actually salute her like a dork. "I can manage that."

We both laugh, and I take the tray to an empty table, feeling lighter than I have in days. Maybe even weeks. Hopefully things are going to work out for me after all—at least job-wise.

Chapter Sixteen

GAVIN

Practice is rough all week. The coaching staff have kicked up the intensity every single day as we prepare for a stretch of away games. Their expectations are high, and their demands are getting to everyone.

A sophomore second-string lineman collapsed on the field near the end of practice this afternoon because he was dehydrated, and that was on him. We were all aware he was partying at his frat last night since he posted it to his stories for everyone to see. Coach Porter wasn't amused, especially when he specifically requested that we watch what we eat and drink the next few weeks. Nothing but protein and water, and carb loading before practice and the game. No junk food, no alcohol. They want us lean, mean fighting machines.

And we're all keeping up with it, save for the younger guys. They don't take it as seriously as the rest of us, and unfortunately, that means we're all punished for their slipups. I've never run around the track as much since I was a freshman. I've lost five pounds over the last week, and I'm pretty sure I've shed it thanks to sweat. Doesn't help that the temperatures have been warmer here lately. Fall is actually the warmest season in Santa Mira since we get so much fog here during the summer.

"Fuck me running, I'm exhausted," Nico complains to me in the locker room.

"Same," Coop mutters, stripping off his cleats and then his sweaty-ass socks. A pungent odor immediately fills the air, and Nico starts bitching.

"Damn, Coop. Your feet should be fucking illegal." He pinches his nose and waves a hand in front of his face like he's eight and just smelled a fart. "What the hell is wrong with them?"

"Nothing." Coop grabs one of his smelly shoes and threatens to throw it at Nico, who dodges behind me, using me as a human shield. Chuckling, Coop drops the shoe in the bottom of his locker.

"Bro. You should take that shoe home and wash it. That's what I'd do," I tell him, keeping my voice low. Trying to show our friend a little respect, unlike Nico.

"Good call." Coop dumps his shoes in his bag, glaring at Nico like he's daring him to complain. Surprisingly enough, Nico remains quiet.

They're roommates and love to give each other constant shit. It's part of their relationship, and I suppose I'm used to it. Still bugs me sometimes, though. I don't like it when someone gives me shit.

At all.

Does that make me a sensitive little flower? Perhaps. That's what my dad used to call me when I was younger, and that would piss me off like nothing else. God, my father was a dick. He still is.

He's tried calling me over the last few days, but I've ignored him every single time, letting the calls go to voicemail. I don't need his negativity getting in my head and ruining my game play. Screw that.

"You coming to yoga tonight?" Dollar asks me as he approaches.

Nico makes a dismissive noise, and I ignore him. He's sexually frustrated because his cute roommate is hosting yoga sessions in their backyard for some of us guys on the team. I finally went to one a few days ago. It was great. Just what I needed after a rough practice. Helped me stretch my aching muscles and clear my head. I call that a win.

Of course, I also stepped in it after the yoga session. Sienna was there, and I was trying my best to ignore her while we were in the backyard and she was right next to me. But fuck me, she looked extra hot in her workout gear, showing off her curvy body in a pink sports bra and matching tight shorts where her ass cheeks were hanging out. Ass cheeks I've cupped in my hands. Ass cheeks I came all over last Sunday morning. It took every ounce of strength inside me not to look, but come on.

I looked. And I wanted another go at it—at her. The woman was obviously trying to get my attention. Or *someone's* attention, and that thought filled me with jealousy. That's what set me off, my irrational reaction to her possibly trying to get with someone else, which I know wasn't her intent. She's into me, even though I'm sure she's still pissed. But I overreacted and ended up calling Everleigh *wifey material*. Which only pissed off Sienna, and she left when we were all going to have dinner made by Everleigh together—hence the wifey comment. That made Nico angry at me too.

He got over it, though. He can never stay mad at me for too long, and I feel the same way about him. Sienna, though?

Pretty sure she's still pissed. Not that I've heard from her. And not that I've sought her out. I've been too busy. Between school, practice, extra weight training in the morning, and yoga sessions in the evening, I'm beat. By the time I get home at night, I take a quick shower, jerk off, and collapse into bed, where I also might jerk off. I haven't washed the pillowcase Sienna used yet. I can still smell the scent of her shampoo on it. Oh, and I found the red panties crumpled in a wad under my bed last night. They distinctly smelled like her pretty little cunt. Did I use those to jerk off?

Not yet, but I probably will. Which means I'm a sick fuck.

"Yeah, I'll be there," I finally say, earning a smile from Dollar for my answer.

"Cool. I'll wait for you guys outside," Dollar says before he takes off, Nico, Coop, and I watching until the door slams behind him.

"He still hot for your roomie?" I ask no one in particular.

Nico literally growls, and I assume that's his answer. Coop just laughs, slapping his meaty thigh and shaking his head.

"Nico, baby, just admit that you're halfway in love with her," Coop says.

"Hell to the no. Love? You've gotta be kidding me." Nico slams his locker shut and slings his bag over his shoulder before he stalks off, exiting the locker room and letting the door slam extra hard.

Coop and I share a look. "Nico, baby?" I ask.

He shrugs. "Anything to get under his skin."

"Halfway in love with her?"

"It might not be love, but he likes her. He can deny it all he wants, but I see the way he watches her. The way they watch each other. It's subtle, but I notice. I don't know how anyone can't see it."

Nah, he's right. I saw it. I think that's why I called her wifey material in front of Nico. Just to give him shit like the rest of the guys do. And in the end, I offended Sienna more than anyone else.

I'm such an idiot. Not like I can talk about it with Coop either. That would mean I'd have to confess my feelings for his sister—and are they really feelings? Yes, yes, they are, but I don't know what the fuck to do with them. Definitely not talk about them with Sienna's brother, that's for damn sure. Telling him about her sweet pussy and sexy moans and juicy ass is not the way to go about it.

Not that I want to tell anyone about her sweet pussy, sexy moans, and juicy ass. I want to keep Sienna all to myself. And that's a first.

"What about Dollar?" I ask.

"Pretty sure Everleigh spoke to Dollar and told him they could only be friends." Coop grabs his bag and shuts his locker, turning to face me. "But that was a while ago. I thought we already discussed this."

"Maybe we did." I shrug. He's probably right, but I don't remember. I'm too wrapped up in my own shit to worry about anyone else, save for Sienna.

If I'm not thinking about football or school, I'm thinking about her. I pushed her away by calling her a distraction, and she still is. Maybe an even bigger one now.

Sienna's beautiful face floats through my thoughts at this very moment, and I mentally shove the image away.

"No one is coming clean with their feelings around here, except for Ever with Frank. But when it comes to her and Nico? Forget it. They're doing a little dance around each other, and neither of them is willing to take the lead," Coop continues.

Huh. Coop nailed it.

"Nico has never been one to want a committed relationship," I remind him, thinking of myself. Thinking of all of us, with the exception of Dollar.

"Yeah same. But from everything I see, Everleigh is a good girl. Sweet and quiet and patient with all of our asses, which says a lot. She doesn't complain about living with us, either, and she has ample reason to complain because we're annoying as fuck. Plus she's been making us meals every night."

"I thought you gave her reduced rent for the meals," I point out.

"We do, but lately she's making them every night when our original agreement was for three. She even got on Frank about that when we first talked about it, but now she's just . . . taking care of us all the time." Coop rubs his cheek, the sound like sandpaper thanks to his stubble-covered face. "Nico would be an idiot to let that girl slip out of his hands. She's practically perfect."

I wonder if he would say the same thing about me and Sienna. Probably not. If he found out, he'd want to kick my ass.

"You sound like you have a crush on her too." I'm teasing him, and I hope he realizes it.

"Nah. She's great. Pretty. Smart. But I'm not interested in her like that. She's not the girl for me." Coop shakes his head. "We out of here or what?"

"Let's go." I grab my duffel, and we start to exit the locker room. "Who is the girl for you, my friend?"

"No one. I'm too scary." He glances back at me and gives me a fierce scowl as he pushes open the door.

I laugh. "Oh, come on. You're the nicest guy I know."

"No one sticks around long enough to find that out. The girls I try to talk to are legit scared of me. Maybe someday I'll find someone." His tone is wistful, and it hits me.

Coop definitely wants to find someone. He might even have a particular someone in mind. But he sounds so damn defeated, I have a feeling he's given up.

That's kind of sad.

Nico drives all of us back to their house, and just as promised, Ever is in the backyard already setting up the yoga mats. Music is playing from a tiny pink speaker that's sitting on the table on the patio, and the breeze ruffles the fronds of the two massive palm trees that are in the yard, giving off a peaceful vibe. Helps that we can hear the sound of the surf crashing onto the sand from the nearby ocean.

No wonder we all enjoy this. It's the definition of tranquility.

"Hey, guys!" Everleigh's face brightens when she spots us. She enjoys these yoga sessions, that's for sure. "How was practice?"

"Rough," Coop grumbles.

"I'm gonna go shower," Nico calls from the sliding glass door, where he's currently standing with half his body hanging out.

"Why are you wasting your time? You're just gonna work up a sweat doing this," I remind him.

"I stink enough already." He glares at me and I almost laugh. This guy wants to smell good for his pretty little yoga instructor.

"I don't think Everleigh cares. Do you?" I ask her.

She shakes her head, the single braid she has whipping with the movement. "Nope."

"You're an asshole," Nico mutters as he steps out onto the patio and shuts the sliding glass door.

I'm grinning. It feels good to take the heat off me and aim it at someone else. After my little encounter a couple of years ago with Sienna, Nico lived for giving me endless grief because he saw us at the bar together. Saw us leave the bar together too. I've never given him too many details, but I have a feeling Sienna might've filled him in on what happened.

And the jackass didn't let up on me for months about it either.

Doesn't help that he mentioned Sienna has a crush on me a few nights ago when Ever made us dinner. Coop was shocked and questioned me a little bit about it, but I blew him off. Made it seem like it was more of a Sienna problem than my problem, which is total bullshit.

Denying my feelings as usual. I don't know why I do this. Why I run away from emotions, especially when it comes to Sienna. I'm a complete dickhead.

"Come on, boys." Ever claps her hands together. "Let's get into position."

I'm in the front row with Dollar, who watches everything Everleigh does with his rapt gaze. I glance over at the spot where Sienna was last time, remembering yet again how spectacular she looked in that tight pink set she was wearing. How big her tits were and the perfect curve of her ass.

"I'm surprised you'd show up," Everleigh murmurs when she's standing close to me at one point.

I frown. "What are you talking about? I've been here for your yoga classes all week."

"And I'm still shocked you're showing up when you should be talking to a *certain someone* and telling her you're sorry." The pointed look she sends me has my balls clenching up.

Great. She's been talking to Sienna too. Makes sense. The girls have been spending a lot of time together. I wonder how much she's told Ever.

"What is she saying about me?"

"I'm not going to tell you." Ever glances around, that braid smacking her cheek, her head moves so fast. "But you need to apologize to her."

"Says who?"

"Me." She jabs her thumb at her chest. "You were a clueless jerk a few nights ago, and you hurt her feelings. She has a crush on you, and you know it. I think you like having her as your fangirl, but if you're not interested, you should let her know. She needs to move on from you, Gavin, especially if you're not going to do anything about it."

Everleigh's words make me feel like shit. But they also make me realize that she doesn't know *everything*. Meaning Sienna didn't tell her about us having sex.

Huh.

"And I know you were just playing dumb. Seems like you always are. You're not that oblivious, are you?" She lifts her brows, and she doesn't even have to say what she's referring to. Her unspoken words are loud and clear.

"No." I sigh, stretching my arms above my head and making my spine crack. "No, I'm not."

"Then stop being such a jerk and tell her you're sorry, okay?" She sends me an imploring look. "And after that, tell her to stop wasting her time, because that's what it looks like she's doing, you know?"

I'm not about to say any of that to Sienna. "And when am I supposed to talk to her?"

"How about after our yoga session?" Ever rests her hands on her hips. "If you don't go tell her you're sorry, I'm not going to allow you to come to the next class."

"Are you fucking for real right now?" I keep my tone light so I don't sound too hostile, but damn. This woman is basically blackmailing me to apologize to Sienna.

"I am." She lifts her chin, glaring at me. "And don't you forget it."

Women. They're terrifying when they stick together.

Chapter Seventeen

Sienna

I'm sitting at our rickety old dining table with my laptop, trying to write an essay when the front door swings open so hard, I'm afraid it's going to fall off the hinges.

"Hey," Destiny mutters as she stomps inside and slams the door behind her.

I watch as she tosses her backpack on the floor and flops onto our equally rickety couch, which makes a loud creaking sound, thanks to the force of her body.

"Hello to you too," I say slowly, almost afraid to ask, but I do it anyway. "What's going on with you?"

"I broke up with Lizzie just now." She crosses her arms in front of her, her entire face like a pout.

Carefully I shut my laptop because this declaration calls for my undivided attention. We might not talk a lot, but she's been much more cheerful since getting with Lizzie. And now look at her. She's obviously miserable. "Do you want to talk about it? What happened?"

She doesn't say much at first, but I can tell by the way her face nearly crumples that she's upset and on the verge of crying. Something I don't think I've ever seen Destiny do, and we've lived together going on three years. "She told me I'm too stubborn."

Oh, that is 100 percent accurate.

When Destiny doesn't say anything else, I realize I'm going to need to pull the issues out of her. She's not going to offer them voluntarily. "And what else did she say?"

Destiny shakes her head, a single tear streaking down her cheek, and I leap from my chair, go to her, and wrap my arms around her. It hurts my heart to see her cry because she's so, *so* tough all the time.

"She said I don't ever share my feelings with her. That I'm always throwing up walls, and she wants me to be real with her for once." Destiny is full-on crying now, little sobs sounding in her throat as she shakes in my arms. "I don't think she realizes that I'm always trying to be strong because she's the emotional one in the relationship."

"Aw." I press my hand against the side of her head so she has no choice but to rest her cheek against my shoulder. The girl is rigid in my arms, and I wish she could relax. "Maybe you should be crying to Lizzie right now, not me."

"No," she spits out, pressing her face into my shoulder and soaking my T-shirt with her tears. "I can't look weak in front of her."

"Why not?"

"Because I'm not supposed to. I'm the tough one. I've been the tough one my entire life. I'm the oldest of three, and we all had different dads who bailed on us. My mom was constantly scrambling between a variety of jobs, trying to put food on the table and keep a roof over our heads. Right before I turned sixteen, she was asking me to get a job to help out, and I did. I didn't even hesitate, because I wanted to help. I was always there for her, no matter what. Working endless odd jobs to help pay our bills or leaving class early so I could pick up my brother and sister from school and watch them while she was working," Destiny explains, hiccuping.

I wish she would've told me her backstory before. "I had no idea."

"I don't tell anyone, that's why. I don't need any sympathy. I can handle myself." Her voice quakes when she speaks, and I don't say anything. There's no point. She believes she's strong, and she won't let down that wall. Not even to her girlfriend.

But then my thoughts get the best of me, and I have to say something.

"Have you ever thought of just . . . explaining yourself to her? You don't have to tell her every detail about your past, but it might show Lizzie that you're willing to be vulnerable with her, and that's . . . huge." I think of my own issues. Gavin Maddox and how vulnerable he was with me last Saturday night, how vulnerable we were with each other, only to ruin everything the next morning with his glib attitude after fucking me deliciously—and without a condom.

Then he ruined it further when we both were at Everleigh's yoga session a few days ago. Yes, I can admit I was flaunting myself in the cute pink outfit I found on Amazon for a steal. Yes, I was trying to get his attention, and I probably made a fool of myself. But when he called Ever wifey material right in front of me? That burned my ass like nothing else, and I had to leave. Not that he got it.

A deep sigh escapes me, and Destiny lifts her head, her tearstained face breaking my heart—which is a weird feeling for me because most of the time all Destiny does is annoy me.

Huh. Am I the problem here?

"I'm scared to tell her about my past," Destiny whispers. "What if I do, and she doesn't love me anymore?"

"Aw, D." I smile at her, brushing the stray strands of hair away from her face. "I think Lizzie loves you, and you're being so stubborn that you can't even see it."

"She was really upset when she kicked me out of her apartment." Destiny sucks on her lower lip.

"She kicked you out?"

"Well. More like she said, 'There's the door. If you want to go, do it,' and so I did."

That's a big difference. "Go back to her place and tell her you were wrong. Apologize to her."

Destiny makes a face. "I hate saying sorry."

"Right. Because you're so stubborn," I remind her.

She pulls away from me completely, wiping at her face and getting rid of her tears. "Fine. You're proving your point. Lizzie wasn't wrong."

"She really wasn't."

"And I'm a stubborn ass who won't ever give in."

"No, you really don't."

"You don't even like me much, huh?" Before I can answer her—and God, I really don't want to answer her—she keeps talking. "I know I'm an asshole sometimes. I'm not as warm and fuzzy as you, Sienna."

"Warm and fuzzy?" I laugh. "I am not that way."

"People gravitate toward you because you're so open and welcoming."

"I am?" I frown at her. "I thought the only reason people are drawn to me is because of who my brother is."

Destiny makes another face. More like a grimace. "Those people are around for sure, but you can stand on your own two feet. You just never allow yourself to."

Her words feel like a revelation, and I gape at her for a moment before snapping my lips shut and averting my gaze so I can stare at a blank wall. I don't know if I believe her, just like I'm sure she's having a rough time believing me too. But she might be telling the truth.

I just can't see it.

"Like that dude you went to high school with. The one who keeps texting you," Destiny points out.

I might've told Destiny about Ryland and how he's been texting me. And while I think he's nice and he seems really into me, I don't know. He's not Gavin. And now that I've had sex with Gavin multiple times? How can I try to date Ryland? That's not cool. I shouldn't use him.

Besides, Ryland is too short for me—or I'm too tall for him. And if that's the only thing that I'm hung up on, then how superficial am I? He's a nice guy. Smart and funny. I keep brushing him off, telling him

I have to work when he tries to ask me to get together with him, which I do. I'm just . . .

"You're scared to go out with him, aren't you?" Destiny plucks my fears right out of my head and voices them into existence. "And is this because you keep waiting around for stupid Gavin Maddox to get his head out of his ass and realize that you're pretty much in love with him?"

I am full-blown gaping again, and this time, I don't shut my mouth. I stare at her, hating how on point she is. Why am I like this? "How did you know?"

"We're not the closest of roommates, but you've told me some things. Hinted at other things. And I go to the bars just like you do. I see the way you watch him. And sometimes, I notice the way he watches you."

"He watches me?"

Destiny rolls her eyes. "Duh."

I didn't think anyone noticed. For so long I've felt invisible to everyone, but maybe I'm not.

"I'll never forget catching him on top of you in our dorm room our freshman year." Destiny actually shudders. "Ew, men."

This time around I burst out laughing at what she says. "I completely agree. Ew, men for real."

"You two were really going at it. He had his hands all over you."

"Don't remind me." My tone turns melancholy, and I sigh. "I made a fool of myself that night."

"Um, he was the one all over you, remember? I don't think there was anyone making a fool of themselves. Just two people who were hot for each other, kissing on a bed until I rudely interrupted you." She offers me a small smile. "Sorry I did that."

She has never once apologized for that moment, not that I expected an apology. It was an accident, not something she did on purpose. "It's okay. Really. You didn't mean to."

"Actually . . ." Her voice drifts and she drops her head. "I saw you two leave together that night, and I suspected you took him to our dorm room. I sort of went back to see if you were hooking up. Truly? I was a little worried about you and wanted to make sure you were okay. You were pretty drunk."

"Destiny," I breathe, shocked all over again. "You interrupted us on purpose?"

"I wasn't trying to ruin your night, but I guess I sort of did." She looks up, her gaze on mine. "I feel bad."

I decide to be honest. "I wasn't that drunk. You should feel bad. But . . . I appreciate you watching out for me."

"I was shittier back then. Lizzie makes me nicer, huh."

"Definitely," I retort, though I'm smiling because how can I fault her for making sure I was okay?

Destiny jumps to her feet, tugging on the hem of her T-shirt. "I'm going over to Lizzie's right now and apologizing to her."

"That sounds like a good idea."

"And I'm sorry again for what I did. I hope I didn't ruin whatever chance you might've had with Gavin, not that he deserves you. If he can't see your worth, then why are you wasting your time on that guy? Seriously, Sienna."

And with that, Destiny marches out of our apartment, shutting the door gently behind her.

Well. I guess she told me. And maybe she's right. Gavin doesn't see my worth, so why am I wasting my time on him? We had sex. And it was amazing. He said so himself, using all sorts of adjectives to describe how good it was between us.

Only to tell me to be patient and wait for him. I am tired of waiting for everyone. Waiting for someone to notice me. Waiting for something to happen to me. I need to take control of my own life and make things happen. Make friends. Make a man notice me and want me.

My phone buzzes with a text from where I left it on the dining table, and I get up to go check who it's from.

Ryland: Hey. I have a question for you.

Speaking of a man noticing me . . .

Me: What's up?

I watch as he types, my gaze focused on the gray bubble and the dots moving inside. Women's intuition is kicking in big time, and I know, I just *know* he's going to ask me out again.

Ryland: Are you busy tonight?

He's asked me this question a couple of times before, and I always blow him off. Yet he keeps coming back for more, which is surprising.

I should say yes. I don't want to lead him on, but who am I waiting around for again? Nothing is ever going to happen with Gavin. I could continue down the same path we started, but he's just using me. And now that I've had sex with him? My feelings are even more invested. He says he doesn't want any distractions, but at this moment, I'm desperate for one.

And Ryland might be it. I don't have romantic feelings toward him, but that's only because I haven't let myself have them. He might be short, but he's not so bad.

Oh my God, I sound awful even in my own thoughts.

Me: I'm free. What do you have in mind?

Ryland: I was hoping I could take you to dinner. What do you say?

A dinner date. That sounds serious. We need to go somewhere casual. I need his entire interaction to remain casual because I am merely testing the waters.

Me: Okay! What time and where do you want to meet?

See? Casual. Meet him somewhere. Don't let him pick you up.

Ryland: I was thinking I could come pick you up and take you there.

Me: It would be easier if I just met you. Do you like Mexican food?

Ryland: It's my favorite.

Me: How about Hector's? I could meet you there at seven.

Ryland: That sounds perfect. See you then.

I set my phone on the table, digging my teeth into my lower lip. I shouldn't do this. Shouldn't lead this guy on when I'm not interested in him, but who says that I'm not? I need to expand my horizons. Get out of the Gavin-induced haze I've been in. He can't have sex with me and then expect me to wait around for him to get his act together. That's not fair.

Life isn't fair. I know this. The only way I can get over someone is to get under someone else. Isn't that the saying?

My stomach literally lurches at the thought. No way am I going to have sex with some other guy so soon after being with Gavin. That is not my style. But can I go out to dinner with a male friend and see if there's a spark?

I don't think there's a crime in that.

Chapter Eighteen

GAVIN

It's Friday night, and none of us have any plans beyond the usual. It's a bye week, which means no game on Saturday, and it sucks that we've been run so hard during practice this week. But Coach and everyone else on staff wanted to prove to us that they mean serious business. They've dropped a few guys from the team who couldn't cut it. Mostly younger players who don't have the stamina or mental capacity to play at this level.

It's a test. Like a gauntlet to get rid of the riffraff, as Porter described the ones they cut. We all have to suffer along with everyone else during this time period, and quite frankly, it sucks. This is why I think Nico and Coop are putting together an epic party tomorrow night. We need to blow off a little steam.

I wouldn't mind blowing off a little steam tonight, either, but no one seems into it.

"We're going to get hammered tomorrow," Nico gripes at me when I suggest we should go out. "Let's save it up."

"Sounds like a good plan," Coop chimes in. "I'm fucking exhausted after this week."

"Wimps," I mutter, shaking my head. "We can't party a couple of nights in a row?"

"Nope. I'm too tired for that shit. Plus, I wanna save money," Coop says.

"Same. And we're supposed to be watching our caloric intake," Nico adds, sounding like a goddamn nutritionist. Meaning he's been spending a lot of time with Everleigh, since that's her major.

Just a hunch, but I would bet money on it being why he's talking like this.

"Too tired? Save money?" Since when did they become responsible human beings? "Give me a break."

"You never want to party lately, and now suddenly you do. What's your deal?" Nico asks, his brows drawn together. Like I'm confusing his ass.

I glance at my phone. It's almost seven thirty and I'm starving. I decide to change the subject. "Let's grab something to eat. Maybe have a beer?"

I need something to take the edge off. I don't know what's wrong with me lately, but I'm tense as fuck. And it's not all the team shit that's going on either. I've been through that before, and while it's exhausting like Coop said, I'm confident in my position and how I'm doing.

Actually, I do know what's wrong. I haven't seen Sienna in almost a week, and I feel like shit over . . . all our recent interactions. Telling her to be patient was a huge mistake, and I handled it all wrong. I already have a plan formed, and I'm going to apologize to her tomorrow at the party. If she'll even hear me out.

"How about Hector's?" Nico suggests.

"You're addicted to that place," Coop grumbles.

"Sounds good," I tell Nico, eager to go anywhere as long as they're both on board. "Let's go."

We decide to walk over to Hector's since it's so close to their house, like everything else in this town. The place is busy as usual, and we get in line, chatting up everyone who approaches, which is a lot of people. We have a crowd surrounding us, everyone wanting to talk about the season and the upcoming game next week, though it dissipates as we get closer to the order window.

"Hey, isn't that Sienna?" Nico asks.

My head whips in the direction Nico's looking so fast I probably strained a muscle in my neck, but I don't spot her.

"Yep. It sure is," Coop says, pausing. "Who's the dude?"

His tone is suspicious, which is natural, considering that's his sister he's talking about.

Wait a minute.

"*Dude?*" I repeat, scanning the area almost frantically. Hector's has a massive patio, which is full of tables and chairs, and there are so many people out there, I still can't see her.

Until I do. I spot her dark-red hair spilling down her back in loose waves. That bright smile on her pretty face. The way she's watching the guy sitting across from her with undivided interest, and holy shit . . .

I see red.

"I don't recognize him," Nico says, his knowing gaze landing on me. He's even smirking, the bastard. "Do you recognize him, Gav?"

"No," I bite out, working my jaw from side to side. I realize I'm flexing my fingers straight, splaying them out before curling them into tight fists. Over and over again, and I tell myself to fucking relax.

"I don't either," Coop says, keeping his attention on his sister. "Not that she tells me anything."

"You're too overprotective," Nico protests. "That's why she doesn't tell you shit. She's afraid you're going to go ham on some poor dude's ass when you find out she's dating him or whatever."

"I would never do that," Coop mutters, and Nico and I share a look. We both very much doubt it, but we don't challenge him.

And this is just one reason why I keep my feelings for Sienna to myself. I don't need Coop's wrath if he ever found out his sister and I have a—thing. I need to keep him on my side, not make him an enemy.

But shit. I'm in so deep with Sienna, I feel closer to her than I do to her brother. And she's out with some random on a Friday night?

Though what did I expect? She was furious when I asked her to be patient with me. I said everything wrong and fucked everything up. She's already moved on, going out with another guy a week after we were together.

I did this to myself. I should've tried to talk to her days ago, but I didn't. I didn't prioritize her, and maybe this guy will. Maybe he's the better man for her. A better man than me.

That realization is like a swift kick in the dick.

We eventually order our food, and I pay for all of us, sending Nico to grab a table, which he does. Only a few away from where Sienna is sitting with this . . . stranger who seems entranced with her. The dumb fuck can't look away from her, and I get it. He's practically got big red hearts shining in his eyes with the way he's staring at her.

It's fucking infuriating.

Coop and I settle in at the picnic table, and I choose the side that allows me to spy on Sienna unabashedly. She's right in my line of vision, and my gaze roams over her, taking in what she's wearing. A hot-pink strapless dress that's pretty simple. And long, thank God. It covers her legs, which I think are her best asset besides her ass and face and breasts and everything else, and it makes me wonder if she's really into this guy or what.

But then I notice the way the dude's eyes drop to her chest every few minutes. It's subtle and quick, not enough to offend, and I know he's checking out her tits. She's got some cleavage showing, but not too much. Just enough to entice.

Damn it, it's working. On the both of us.

Her hair is piled on top of her head in an artfully messy bun, and she's got thin gold hoops hanging from her ears that swing every time she moves her head. Her freckled skin is on display, and I rest my fisted hands in my lap, hating how bad I want to touch her. March over to her table and grab her, swing her over my shoulder and tell that puny asshole he needs to back the fuck off.

I have no right to do any of that. I don't own her, and I could've. She was willing to give herself to me totally if I'd said the word. I had her in my bed. Naked. I had my mouth on her pussy. I had my dick inside her. Multiple times. I came all over her ass, for the love of God. Talk about a claiming. Only to push her away. I deserve this. All of it.

Dropping my head, I reach for my beer and slug it back, draining almost half my glass in one go.

"Easy there, partner. You don't want to have to go back to that line, do you?" Nico inclines his head, and I glance over my shoulder to check out the line, which is now even longer than when we were in it.

"Right." I push the glass away from me, fighting the instinct to look at Sienna, but it's no use. I can't stop watching her, unable to tear my attention away from her, and it's like she senses it. Senses *me*.

Sienna lifts her head, turning slowly until our gazes meet. I see the surprise flare in her dark eyes, and her expression hardens, becoming unreadable. Without even an inkling of hesitation, she returns her focus to the guy sitting across from her and starts talking, that pretty smile back on her face as she becomes more animated.

Jesus. I'm jealous. Who is this guy? How did she meet him? Has he kissed her yet? Have they fucked? The image fills my head, and I can't stop it from happening. Sienna naked, rolling around on a bed, this—stranger on top of her.

I close my eyes and shake my head, willing the image to disappear, and I breathe deep, opening my eyes to find Nico and Coop watching me with matching perplexed expressions on their faces.

"You okay there, bro?" Nico asks, and just from the tone of his voice, I know that fucker realizes what's going on.

"Fine." I smile. More like I grimace, but I keep it going, pretending that everything is A-OK. Just fucking great. Life couldn't be better. "Hungry."

"Me too. Feels like I could eat two burritos. I should've ordered an extra one," Coop says, oblivious as ever.

"You don't need two burritos. You'll be fine." Nico slaps Coop on the shoulder, his gaze coming back to me. "You, though? I'm a little worried, QB. You're not acting right."

"I'm fine." Even to my own ears, I don't sound fine—which I've already said twice. I sound pissed as hell.

Nico chuckles. Coop is too busy watching the order window, ready to leap when they call our number. Eventually they do, and Coop is off like a shot, moving fast for such a big dude. "I'll get the food."

"Grab napkins," I remind him.

"Sure, Dad," he mutters as he stalks off.

The moment we're alone, Nico goes in. "Not liking what you're seeing, are you?" His smug tone is irritating as hell.

"It doesn't matter what she's doing. I don't own her." The moment the words leave my mouth, they feel like a lie. I wish I owned her. It would sound fucking fantastic if I was able to call her mine. But I don't have the right, and I need to remember that.

"Who is that guy, anyway?" Nico turns and blatantly watches them. Even holds his hand up in a wave when they catch him. Jesus, he just doesn't give a damn, does he? He turns to face me once again. "I don't recognize him."

"Me either."

"She hasn't dated anyone in a while," Nico muses.

I fucked her last weekend is on the tip of my tongue, but I don't say it. Talk about stirring up the drama.

"How do you know so much about her love life?" is what I say instead.

"You'd be surprised at all the details I know. About you. And her." He smirks, the sight of it striking alarm inside me.

I've told him a few things, but I rarely go into detail. I know he and Sienna are close—friendship close. She might've told him something about our recent encounter, which means the secret I share with Sienna might not be so secret anymore.

"You haven't said anything to Coop, have you?" I can hear the edge of panic in my voice, and I swallow hard, trying to calm myself. "I don't need him knowing anything in regard to me and his sister."

"What exactly happened between you two, anyway? She's hinted at stuff but has never come out and said anything concrete." Nico frowns. "I take that back. I do know the two of you went at each other in her dorm her freshman year, but you were interrupted."

Relief fills me, and I take another sip of my beer. If that's all Nico knows, then that's not a big deal. Though I don't want Coop to know about it. "Never mention that again."

Nico chuckles. "Bad memory?"

Great memory is what I want to say, but I don't. We've made even better memories since then. My fingers remember the silky feeling of her soft skin, and my lips recall the taste of her plump, sweet mouth, and that is just . . . not good.

Not good at all.

"You don't need to deny your feelings, Gavin. Allowing them to build up inside of you is bound to push you to your breaking point," Nico says.

Too late. I'm already at my breaking point.

"Dinner is served." Coop drops the tray full of food in the middle of the table, settling into the space he just vacated right beside Nico, who reaches for a burrito at the same time Coop does.

I'm the one who wanted to go out to eat. I'm the one who declared he was starving, but my appetite has fled thanks to what I'm currently witnessing. I grab my burrito almost reluctantly, unwrapping the foil about halfway down, and stare at the top—it looks like it could burst, it's so full. I glance up to see Nico and Coop already eating, our table silent, and my gaze shifts to Sienna. How she reaches across the table at that exact moment to lightly tap the guy's hand with her fingers, and my silent rage rises inside me, settling in my throat. Leaving me in a choke hold.

I drop the burrito back in the plastic basket it came in, disgusted. She touched him and I hate it.

Hate it.

Coop and Nico start talking between taking bites, and eventually I join in on the conversation, needing the distraction. I start eating, polish off half my burrito, and wrap the foil back around it so I can save it for later. I finish off my beer, too, tempted to grab another, and I check the line to see there's only a couple of people in it.

"Want another beer?" I ask my friends as I stand. "My treat."

"Sure," they both say.

I head over to stand in line, keeping a glower on my face on purpose so no one approaches me. I'm not in the mood for idle chitchat, and I definitely don't want a woman trying to flirt with me either. I'd rather be alone, wallowing in my misery.

Something I'm really fucking good at.

Of course, Sienna chooses the moment I'm not at the table to bring her new friend over to meet her brother and Nico. I blatantly stare them down as I watch them chat, grateful the line moves fast so I can order our beers. Within two minutes, I'm headed back to our table clutching our drinks, walking carefully so I don't spill as I hold them in a triangle formation. Sienna and the dude are still standing by our table talking with Coop while Nico watches it all unfold, an amused expression on his face.

Looks like he's enjoying every second of it, too, the jackass.

His gaze cuts to mine, and he's grinning, calling out my name as I approach the table. Sienna's head jerks up, her expression turning almost defiant as she watches me settle the three glasses of beer on our table.

"Gav," she mutters, her lips barely moving.

"Sienna," I throw back at her, equally hostile. I sort of hate it when she calls me by my nickname.

Nico has the nerve to crack up at our little exchange.

"Gav, this is Ryland Hartwig. We went to high school with him," Coop says, indicating the guy Sienna is with.

"Hey." Ryland thrusts his hand toward me, and I have no choice but to take it. "Nice to meet you."

"Likewise." I give his hand a firm squeeze before I let go. "High school, huh?"

"We were on the wrestling team together," Coop adds. "Though I quit after my freshman year."

I eye Ryland up and down, not impressed. He doesn't seem big enough to be on the wrestling team, but then again, the short, stocky guys tend to do pretty well competing in the sport, so what do I know?

"I was heavier then," Ryland doesn't hesitate to add. "After I graduated from high school, I worked on shedding all that extra weight."

"Good for you," Nico says encouragingly, reminding me of a meddling little gremlin. I send him a look, and his eyes go wide. Playing Mr. Innocent—such a crock of shit. "You look great, man."

"Thanks." Ryland dips his head in acknowledgment, and I really look at him, realizing that he's . . . oh shit. He's shorter than Sienna.

And how does she feel about that, hmm? I've even heard her say over the years that she could never date a guy who's shorter than her. Around five ten, I believe? The three of us tower over her. But this guy? Nope.

"We should get going," Sienna says, not even looking in my direction. "Have a good night, guys!"

"Nice meeting you," Nico tells Ryland while Coop calls out his goodbyes.

Me? I remain silent, settling onto the bench seat and reaching for my beer, taking a big swallow.

I'd love to get drunk and forget this night ever happened.

Chapter Nineteen

SIENNA

I hightail it out of Hector's, Ryland keeping up with me and talking nonstop about how great it was to see my brother again, while my only goal is to get away from Gavin as quickly as possible.

Oh, he looked freaking *pissed* seeing me with another guy. He wouldn't stop watching us. I could feel his heated gaze on me practically the entire time once they arrived. I was watching him, too, as covertly as possible, and the moment he got up to order more beer—figures—I took my shot and brought Ryland over to talk to Coop and meet Nico. I knew if I didn't, I'd never hear the end of it from my brother.

Ugh, Nico. He was grinning like a loon and loving every minute of me standing there with Ryland because I'm sure Gavin had some sort of reaction and Nico picked up on it.

But my brother? Nope. He's clueless. He didn't seem to mind seeing me with Ryland, but I don't know if he figured out it was a date. I was trying to keep it casual, but come on. It was totally a date. With a guy we went to high school with, and I was having a nice time until Gavin had to appear and screw it all up.

I think of what Destiny said earlier. *Ew men.* And while I'm thinking of Destiny . . .

Reaching into my bag, I pull out my phone and send her a quick text.

Me: You doing okay? Just checking on you.

No quick response, and I try to take that as a good sign as I stash my phone back in my purse.

"Everything okay?" Ryland asks as we stroll along the sidewalk, headed in the direction of my apartment. At least I'm not running anymore.

"Oh yeah. My roommate had a moment of crisis earlier, and I'm checking up on her," I explain.

"Are you two close? You and your roommate?"

"Um, not really? But I think we're getting closer. We've been roommates since freshman year. She can be a little grouchy." I launch into a modified story about Destiny and her potential breakup with Lizzie. And I call it a potential breakup because I'm hoping the two of them are able to get over their argument and are already back together again.

"I hope they can work it out," Ryland says once I finish explaining Destiny's predicament. He's always positive and I appreciate that. He's a nice guy. Attractive. Ambitious. And he seems totally into me.

Why am I not into him?

Gavin. That's why. I don't want this guy. I want Gavin.

I touched Ryland a couple of times during dinner—on purpose. Trying to elicit some sort of spark between us, but I felt nothing. I kept my focus on him as much as possible throughout dinner, though I got distracted by Gavin's appearance. That incredibly sexy scowl on his face and the way his gaze roamed over me. Possessive. I felt claimed, just by him looking at me.

I'm just not that attracted to Ryland. Not even close, though I should be. My stupid hormones have failed me. It's like they only want one person, and that is so frustrating.

Ryland walks me all the way to my doorstep, and he turns to face me when we come to a stop, his lips parting. He's about to say something when I feel my phone buzz in my bag. Holding up a finger, I pull it out of my purse to see I have a response from my roomie.

Destiny: We're working on it. Pretty sure we're good.

"Looks like my roommate and her girlfriend are getting back together," I tell Ryland as I tap out a response to Destiny.

Me: Yay! I'm so glad.

Destiny: Don't wait up for me though. I'm thinking I'll be staying the night.

Me: Good. Have fun.

I send her a couple of winky-face emojis and a fire emoji. At least someone is having fun tonight.

"I'm so relieved." I shove my phone back into my bag. "I was worrying about them all night."

"You did seem a little distracted. I thought maybe it was because of your brother making an appearance at Hector's." Ryland smiles at me, but I don't smile back.

I wish it was Coop who was the distraction, but unfortunately, that wasn't the case.

"Right. Coop. He can be extremely overprotective of me." I sound dreadfully serious.

"Oh yeah?" Ryland's smile fades. "He won't mind me going out with you, will he? We go way back."

Come on. They weren't that close.

I shake my head. "It doesn't matter. He's still protective of me. I'm his baby sister and we're close. It's like no man could ever measure up in Coop's eyes."

"That's crazy. You're an adult. You can make your own choices." Ryland actually scoffs, and I wonder if he's a little offended.

How am I going to let this guy down easy? I don't know. I also find it interesting that not a single one of those men mentioned anything about their party tomorrow night, not even Nico. And he's a giant shit-stirrer who probably would've loved seeing me bring Ryland as my date to the party.

I'm glad they didn't mention it. I don't want to bring Ryland. I want to talk to Gavin and have it out with him because he's acting ridiculous. And so am I. We're playing games with each other, and that's not fair to Ryland or ourselves.

"I can definitely make my own choices, but I value my brother's opinion." I offer Ryland a soft smile. "Thank you for dinner. It was great."

"It wasn't anything special. Just Hector's." Ryland shrugs. I notice he downplays practically everything he does. He's hard on himself. "We should've gone somewhere nicer for our first date."

It's the words *first date* that move me into action. I have to end this now. I can't keep stringing this guy along. That would be downright cruel.

"Um, about that." I shuffle my feet and avert my gaze, though I can feel him watching me. "I think we might be better off as friends."

He goes silent, and I return my attention to him just in time to see the disappointment wash over his face. "Was it something I said?"

I slowly shake my head, unsure of how to say this without revealing I'm interested in someone else. "You're a great guy, Ryland. Really. I just—"

"You don't like me like that," he finishes for me, sounding upset. "It's cool. I get it. I can't compete when you hang around football players all the time. Is that what you're saying?"

"What? No. Not at all," I start, but he takes a couple of steps backward, talking right over me.

"Whatever. I think it sucks that you won't even give me another chance, but I guess your mind is already made up." He glares at me. "I thought we had something."

I don't like how angry he is. I fully expected him to be disappointed by my gentle rejection, but his behavior is a bit extreme. I decide to not acknowledge what he said. "Thank you for taking me to dinner, Ryland. I had a nice time."

"Thanks for ruining my night," he retorts before he storms off, never once looking back at me. I watch until he disappears before I hurriedly unlock my door and rush inside the apartment, turning the locks into place immediately.

It's quiet inside. And dark. I turn on the single table lamp we have in the living room, wishing Destiny was home. Then I wouldn't feel so alone.

Ryland's over-the-top reaction has completely freaked me out.

I'm awoken by a steady pounding sound, and at first, I think it's my head. But no. I didn't drink a single drop of alcohol tonight. There is no reason I should feel hungover.

The pounding stops, and I lie in my bed flat on my back, my heart racing, my imagination kicking into overdrive. I've gotten used to being here alone, but Ryland's behavior earlier was unnerving. I had a difficult time falling asleep, but I was sleeping pretty hard before the loud noise woke me. Grabbing my phone, I check the time to see it's a little after one o'clock in the morning.

The pounding starts again, startling me, and it's louder this time. Someone is knocking on my door. Aggressively. Panic flares. What if it's Ryland? Oh God.

I should text Coop. Call 911. But then I swear I hear someone say my name—and the voice is familiar.

"Sienna! Goddamnit, open your door now before I bust it in!"

Oh, holy shit. I'd recognize that voice anywhere.

I leap out of bed and stomp my way toward the front door, undoing the locks and swinging it open without a single ounce of hesitation to find the bane of my existence standing on my front doorstep, looking deliciously furious. His hair is messy, and he's got on a threadbare Dolphins T-shirt that has seen better days. It stretches across his chest, showing off every muscle he's got, and everything inside me warms at seeing him.

He's flexing his fingers, curling them into fists, his arms hanging at his sides, and the misery on his face makes my heart want to sing. Oh, I'm the worst. But this is a jealous, *jealous* man who's arrived at my apartment, and my body stands at attention in the hopes that he's going to unleash all that pent up fury he's got all over me.

But I can't act thrilled that he's here. There is a part of me that's annoyed too.

"Gavin, what are you doing? You're going to wake up the neighbors," I start, but he's not listening.

"I don't give a fuck," he mutters as he barges inside the apartment, and I have no choice but to step out of his way. He grabs hold of my waist at the same time he slams the door shut, pinning me against it with his big, warm body, his fingers curling around my chin and forcing me to look up at him. "Is he in here? Are you fucking him?"

"What? No, he's not—"

His lips land on mine. The kiss is almost feral. Rough. *Delicious.* The possessive thrust of his tongue in my mouth sends a scattering of tingles all over my body, and the next thing I know he's lifting me as if I weigh nothing, my back braced against the door, my legs winding around his hips as he presses himself against me. He's hard as a rock, thrusting that thick cock against me where I want him the most, and

I give in. There was no thought of not giving in either. I wanted this. Needed this.

Needed him.

We kiss like we haven't seen each other in months. Years. His greedy mouth never lets up, and his hands are everywhere. Sliding down to my ass, his fingers slipping beneath the thin fabric of my panties, which is all I'm wearing along with an oversize pale-pink tank top. It's so big I have to be careful or else my tit slips out every so often, and Gavin discovers that fun little fact when he skims his fingers across my chest, his fingertips touching my exposed nipple.

"Jesus," he mutters as he pulls away from my still-seeking mouth. "Your body drives me out of my fucking mind."

I can't speak. All I can do is moan when he dips his head and wraps his lips around my nipple, sucking deep, his tongue lashing at my sensitive flesh. I cup the back of his head, holding him to me, and he tugs extra hard on my flimsy panties like he's trying to rip them off my body.

"I hated seeing you with that fucker," he murmurs against my chest, then teases my other nipple with his flickering tongue. "Were you trying to prove a point, Freckles? Because it fucking worked."

"N-no." That was never my intention. I didn't purposely try to run into Gavin tonight, but a small subconscious part of me probably had an evil plan. I'm more than aware that the guys go to Hector's all the time. It's one of their favorite places to eat.

Hmm, maybe I'm more devious than I realized.

But I definitely didn't think this would happen. It's as if a dam broke inside Gavin and he's unleashing everything he's kept locked up all over me. When he drops me to my feet, a wave of disappointment washes over me, only to disappear when he falls to his knees in front of me and grips the sides of my panties in his fists as he presses his face to my pussy and breathes deep.

The back of my head hits the door, and I close my eyes, melting as he nuzzles my pussy with his face. Teasing me. My panties are soaked, my pussy flooding with wetness at having him so close, and I want him to not only pull the barrier away and touch my actual flesh but also keep it there. The way he teases me, holds me, on his knees in front of me.

Like he's worshipping me.

"Fuck, I missed this pussy." His lips move against my sensitive skin, making my body jerk, and he glances up, his eyes blazing with an unfamiliar emotion. "I found your red panties under my bed."

I bite my lower lip, not about to admit I left them behind by accident / on purpose.

"I've jerked off to thoughts of you every night since we last fucked. I can't stop thinking about you, Sienna. You're fucking with my head. Seeing you out on a—*date* with that fucking guy just about destroyed me." The way he stares at me makes it hard for me to breathe, and I watch as he gently pushes my panties aside, exposing me. My scant pubic hair glistens with my juices, and he splays me wide open with his fingers, staring at me. I can feel myself drip, coating the inside of my thighs, and I close my eyes, focusing on the gentle heat of his breath touching my skin. His calloused fingers keeping me open to his searing gaze.

"Such a pretty fucking pussy, Sienna. I can't get enough of it." He licks at my clit once. Twice. Swirling his tongue, slipping a finger inside me at the same time. Filling me up, driving me out of my mind, and when he grabs hold of my thigh and drapes it over his shoulder to give him better access, my legs almost give out.

"Oh God." I'm moaning, my head swiveling back and forth against the door, my fingers clutching at the ends of his hair, tugging hard. He doesn't seem to mind. Just keeps licking and sucking and fucking me until I'm practically crying. He's brought me so close to orgasm only to pull away every single time I'm about to go over the edge.

"I shouldn't let you come," he murmurs, and I open my eyes, looking down to find he's already watching me. "I should punish you."

"F-for wh-what?"

"Going out with someone else." He slides two fingers inside me, holding them there. "This pussy belongs to me."

"Prove it," I whisper, worry clenching my gut when I see the gleam appear in his eyes.

The man loves a challenge. I'm sure he's going to have me screaming that my pussy belongs to him by the end of the night. I might even start screaming that right now.

He dives in, focusing all his attention on my clit, his fingers thrusting inside me again and again until my body is shaking and I'm moaning. Crying out his name as the orgasm sweeps over me, leaving me a near-sobbing, shaky mess.

There is no hesitation. He rises to his feet, grabs me, and slings me over his shoulder so I'm hanging upside down, my hair almost dragging on the floor, I'm so tall. He carries me with ease to the bedroom while I curse him a hundred different ways, irritated that he would haul me around like this. Secretly impressed, too, because I am a solid girl and he acts like I weigh nothing.

Lord, this man is going to be my undoing.

"Put me down." I smack his ass because that's the only thing I can reach, and it's as hard as rock. I tug at the waistband of his athletic shorts and slip my fingers beneath it to find he's not wearing anything underneath, and oh my God, my pussy just got wetter.

We enter my bedroom, and he drops me on the bed, ridding himself of his T-shirt and shorts until he's gloriously naked. "Take off your clothes," he demands, and I do it, shedding my stretched-out panties and oversize tank in record time. I almost choke myself with the tank when it gets caught around my neck, but he doesn't notice.

No, he's too focused on my body and starts at my calves, running his mouth along one leg, then the other. Drops hot little kisses over my knees before moving up to my thighs. Spreading them wide so he can kiss the sensitive skin inside before he settles that mouth once again on my pussy, far too briefly.

I'm breathless. I can't speak or think as he runs that magical mouth of his all over my body like he's trying to claim every part of me. Maybe he is. And when he flips me over and I'm on my stomach, his low command sends a fresh spiral of heat through my body.

"On your knees, Freckles."

I comply, eager to see what he might do. He palms my ass as he kisses the back of my thighs, shifting up until his mouth is on my ass, licking at the underside of one cheek, then the other. Driving me out of my mind with lust because I want his mouth back on my clit.

"Dripping for me." He runs a finger through my folds, gathering up my juices, and I can hear him lick at his finger. Like he's savoring my taste, and oh God, I buck against him, wanting more. More, more, more.

He spanks my ass, the sharp sound ringing in my quiet room, and I go still, the pain and shock of it shooting straight to my core. I've been craving exactly this sort of treatment, and if I'm being real with myself, I'm up for anything. As long as it's Gavin doing it to me.

Chapter Twenty

GAVIN

This sexy, dirty woman is going to be the absolute death of me. She liked it when I barged into her apartment like an asshole—I saw it in the look on her beautiful face. The flash of surprise followed immediately by hunger in her dark eyes. And when I shoved her against the door and kissed her? She liked that too. Fucking loved it when I tried to tear her panties off, and when I went on my knees for her—something I never ever fucking do because what woman is worth getting on my knees for?—she about fell apart. All for me.

She's in this just as deep as I am. Loves this rough, uninhibited moment we're having as much as I do. The more I push her, the more she seems to enjoy it, and I decide to push her a little harder.

I press my hands against her ass, spreading her cheeks, staring at her tiny little hole. She's whimpering, her body shaking, and she rears back against my palms, like she wants me to do it.

So I do. I stroke her there, a light brush of my index finger, tracing the ridges. My touch is tentative at first, then firmer. At the same time, I slide two fingers inside her sopping cunt with my other hand, thrusting once. Twice. That's all it takes. Her inner walls clench around my fingers, and she's coming. Moaning my name, her entire body shaking with the ferocity of her orgasm, and I keep fucking her pussy with my fingers, riding out that orgasm with her until she's pulling away from me, her knees giving out as she collapses on the mattress.

"Oh. My. God." Her voice trembles, and she takes a deep breath. "What did you just do to me?"

"Anybody ever touch you there before?" I drift my fingers across her pale ass cheeks, teasing the line of her crack. Why am I so damn fascinated with her ass?

"N-no."

I love how rattled she sounds. I did that to her, and it fills me with pride. I'm also thrilled by the fact that her ass is now mine and no one has touched it like that. "This ass belongs to me."

I give it a light smack, just hard enough to leave a red mark.

A shuddery laugh escapes her, and she buries her face against the mattress. "Gavin, are you serious?"

I rise and push at her shoulder so she's lying on her back and I can hover above her, my face in hers. "As a fucking heart attack, Sienna."

She blinks up at me, her lips parting, and I can practically hear the argument she's about to unleash on me. And I don't want to deal with it. Before she can say a word, I press my lips to hers in a punishing kiss that turns gentle in a matter of seconds thanks to her. Her lush mouth is persuasive. Delicious. Her hands in my hair, fingernails trailing lightly down the back of my neck, skimming across my shoulders, easing the tension that's been boiling inside me since I saw her with that asshole. Since the last time I had her naked in my bed, if I'm being honest.

I should apologize for being such a dumbass, but I can't find my voice. Don't know the right words to say to her. All I can do is concentrate on kissing her, our tongues lazily sliding against each other. Until my heart slows and my muscles feel warm and languid and her legs are wound around my hips, our bodies perfectly aligned.

"Did you bring a condom?" she whispers against my lips at one point.

"Yeah," I admit, not about to tell her I shoved three in my pocket before I left my apartment.

She smiles against my lips, infinitely amused at my expense as usual. "Go wash your hands and get that condom on, Gavin. I want to feel you inside of me."

I fucking growl when she tries to push me off her, but I go anyway, glancing around in confusion because I've never been in her bedroom before.

"The bathroom is connected. Right there." She points at the door, and I rush inside, shutting the door and turning on the light, wincing against the harshness that almost blinds me.

I wash my hands, staring at my reflection. I look fucking crazed. My hair is sticking up everywhere, and my eyes are wild. Wide and unblinking, the pupils all blown out. She might've calmed me down just now, but I'm amped up again. Eager to get my hands back on her and my dick inside her.

After we left Hector's, I turned down the invite to Nico and Coop's house, opting to go back to my place so I could stew in my emotions for the rest of the night. Until I couldn't take the image of her writhing around in a bed with that little guy any longer—I had to seek her out. Threw on some clothes and went out into the night, barging past all the drunk college students wandering the streets, some of them even shouting my name.

I ignored all of them, too intent on getting to my girl because, goddamnit, that's what she's become. My girl.

Mine.

All mine.

Rubbing the stubble coating my jaw, I give myself a mental pep talk. I've unleashed on her enough tonight. My cock throbs with the need for release, but I'll take it easy on her. No need to scare her.

But the moment I turn and open the door, I find she's sitting in the middle of the bed propped against a pile of pillows, her feet braced on the mattress and her long legs spread as wide as possible. Offering me a glimpse of all that pink, glistening flesh I'm dying to slide into.

I go still, my hand automatically going to my dick. She pouts, her lower lip sticking out, and I panic for a second. How the hell did I disappoint her that fast?

"Where's the condom, Gavin? I'm ready for you."

Her sweet voice washes over me, and I launch into action, grabbing my shorts off the floor and tugging out the three condoms I brought with me, showing them to her before I deposit them on the nightstand. She laughs, the sound curling through me, and I pause. Savoring how happy she sounds, and when she eagerly reaches for me, pulling me down on top of her, I go willingly. Wrapping her up in my arms, cradling her close as I find her mouth and kiss her with everything I've got.

She rests her hands on my shoulders, gently pushing, and I break the kiss. "What?"

"I want—" She pauses, sinking her teeth into her swollen lower lip, and I groan at the sight of it.

"Spit it out, baby. What do you want from me?"

Sienna blinks those pretty dark eyes at me. "I want your cock in my mouth."

Aw, fuck. Who am I to deny her?

Within seconds I'm sprawled in the middle of the bed and she's lying between my spread legs, playing with my dick. Don't know how else to describe what she's doing as she streaks her fingers down my shaft, tracing the veins. Studying it for a moment like she's awestruck.

Or maybe that's my ego talking. Yeah, that's probably it.

Eventually she curls her fingers around the base, loosening her grip to slide up and then down, finding a steady rhythm fairly quickly.

"Oh yeah, baby. That feels good." I watch her from beneath lowered lids as she increases her pace, dipping her head and sticking out her tongue to swipe at the tip of my cock.

That first contact of her tongue on my dick sends a jolt through me, leaving my entire body sizzling, and I break into a sweat, desperate to stay in control. I stare in utter fascination as she wraps her lips around the head, sucking hard enough to hollow out her cheeks. When she lowers her head, taking me almost all the way in, I throw my head back and groan, my hand going to her hair. Tangling in the strands before I push them away from her face so I can see her fully.

Her gaze lifts, meeting mine, and she doesn't look away as she pulls me out of her mouth, her tongue tracing the flared head of my dick. She is the hottest thing alive. Seriously how did I get so fucking lucky? Why did I deny myself this for so long? I'm an idiot.

But we already knew that—especially Sienna.

She continues torturing me with her mouth for long, blissful minutes until I can't take it anymore. I'm reaching for one of the condoms, never taking my eyes away from her while I tear the wrapper open and she continues to work over my cock with her mouth.

"You need to stop," I say once the condom is free from the wrapper. She glances up, her gaze going to the condom clutched in my fingers, and she pulls my dick out of her mouth, wiping at her face with her fingers.

"So bossy," she murmurs.

I reach for her, then pull her down on top of me, and she goes willingly. "So fucking sexy," I tell her in return, and she smiles.

Every time I compliment her, she lights up. I can see it in her eyes. That smile on her pretty face. All I want to do is lavish praise on her, spend all my time with her, but how are we going to manage that with my intense schedule? With the mental stress I'm under? I need to handle this carefully. I don't want to lose her.

But I don't think I'm ready to tell the world about us either.

All those thoughts leave my brain when she rises, her hands braced on my chest as she rubs that soaking wet pussy all over my cock. My eyes cross, it feels so fucking good, and I shove the condom in her face. "Put it on me, baby."

She plucks it from my fingers, slides down my body, and presses the ring over the head of my dick, slowly rolling it on. Her fingers keep brushing my hard flesh, and I grit my teeth. Think about the formations in the playbook our team hasn't used much yet so I don't concentrate on how good everything feels and blow before I even get inside her.

Sienna makes me feel like an out-of-control teenager who can't help but come at the mere brush of a girl's fingers. That's how much she affects me. I need to get my shit together. Make it good for her. Make it good for the both of us.

"I get to be on top?" she asks.

I rear up and take her mouth, hungry for her always. "If that's what you want, cowgirl."

Smiling, she sits up, lifts her hips, and grabs hold of my dick before she lowers herself on top of me. A groan leaves me at all that soft, wet heat gripping my cock, and I rest my hands on her hips, closing my eyes. Breathing deep as I count to five.

When she still hasn't moved, I crack open my eyes to find her watching me, her brows drawn together. "Are you okay?" she asks.

Swallowing hard, I nod. "I'm worried if either of us moves, I'm gonna come."

The slow smile that curves her lush lips is almost my undoing. "Out of control for once in your life, are you, Gav?"

I frown. "I sort of hate it when you call me that."

More of that sweet laughter rains down on me. "Why?"

"You make it sound like an insult."

"Haven't you ever noticed the way girls always say it?" She leans over me, my cock almost sliding out of her, and she works her hips, sinking back down on me, and fuck, that is too good. "They don't even know you and they call you Gav. Gav this, Gav that. I think the nickname makes them feel like they're closer to you."

"You're close to me, and you only call me Gav when you're mad at me." My frown deepens, and I grip her hips, stopping her from moving. "Are you mad at me?"

"Not at all." She kisses me, her tongue doing a thorough search of my mouth before she pulls away. "Why would I be mad at you when you just gave me the best orgasm of my life?"

Pride fills me, making me want to give her another one of those stellar orgasms, and I lift my hips, pushing inside her so deep that both of us moan. She begins to ride me, my hands on her hips guiding her, keeping the rhythm steady. She's not what I would call a little thing, but she doesn't weigh as much as she thinks, and it's easy to lift her, hold her down, shift her hips into the position where I can thrust as far as I can get.

We keep the slow and steady pace until I get impatient. Greedy. I increase my thrusts, fucking her hard, and she just takes it. Throwing her head back, her eyes falling closed, giving me a beautiful view of her body. Her perfect breasts. I reach for them and play with her distended nipples with my fingers, massaging them in my hands while she bucks against me. She hisses out a breath, her inner walls strangling my cock, and oh fuck.

I'm gonna come.

Dropping one hand, I brush my fingers against her clit, spinning tiny circles around it with my thumb, and she gasps. Breathy little moans sound low in her throat, and she rocks her hips forward, her body instinctively seeking my touch, and I press hard. Faster. Fuck her harder. Faster.

Until she comes undone, her entire body shaking, my name falling from her lips with a whimper. That tight pussy squeezes and pulsates around my shaft, pushing me into my own orgasm, and the second her climax winds down, I'm coming, too, my orgasm so strong it rattles my fucking brain.

She collapses on top of me, her hair in my face, her cheek pressed against my sweaty chest, though she doesn't seem to mind. She lies there for a moment, completely still, and I wrap my arms around her soft, damp body, my dick still inside her. I am completely content, and I don't think I've ever felt this way before.

Shit. This girl is starting to mean more to me than I thought was possible. And that's a scary fucking thought.

Chapter Twenty-One

SIENNA

I just had the best night of my life. Like hands down, that was the most earth-shattering sexual experience I've ever had, and of course it was with Gavin.

I knew it would continue to be good between us. Our first time together wasn't a one-off, lucky moment. He is just . . . oh my God.

I don't have words to describe how he makes me feel.

He didn't stay after he gave me my second orgasm. Or was that my third? My third. He pulled on his clothes while I watched him from my bed, sleepy and barely able to keep my eyes open. He kissed me before he left, murmuring, "See you tomorrow."

And then he was gone.

I fell into a deep, dreamless sleep and woke up more invigorated than I've felt in a long time. I have to work at Back Yard Bowl this morning, and I show up promptly at ten o'clock, grateful I at least didn't get the closing shift. The moment I'm finished, I'm heading over to Everleigh's and we're getting ready for the party together. I have a dress already planned out and everything, and I fully expect Everleigh to bring it tonight too. My original plan was to show these dumb men— Gavin and Nico—what they're missing.

But Gavin isn't missing anything. He was so mad when he showed up at my apartment last night. Jealous, thinking I was still with Ryland. I didn't mean to provoke him by having dinner with Ryland, but that entire night worked in my favor. And while I feel bad for using Ryland, I really was trying to move on.

Gavin's proved that's impossible. He can't move on either. How are we going to navigate this situation now? We didn't really discuss next steps, but I'm guessing he doesn't want to tell anyone else, and for once . . .

For once I agree with him. Going public will open us up to all sorts of things. Plenty of speculation and opinions that I don't want to hear. Gavin is a celebrity on campus—and in Santa Mira in general. The moment they find out he's steadily seeing someone, the little sister of one of his best friends who's also on the team? The rumors are going to run rampant. They already do when it comes to Gavin. People are wondering about his love life all the time. Do I want all eyes on me?

Not yet. That sounds way too intimidating.

Maybe it won't be so bad, having a secret relationship with him for a while. He can concentrate on football and having a successful season, and I can cheer him on as a supportive "friend" who allows him to fuck her endlessly whenever he wants. And once the season is over, we can make our relationship public. If we make it that long.

What am I saying? If I've been this patient for as long as I have, we are going the distance. The poor man doesn't have a chance of getting away from me, not that I think he wants to. I saw the way he looked at me, touched me. His growly "this ass belongs to me" comment after he made me come so hard; I saw stars.

Talk about possessive. I never thought I wanted to be owned, but when it comes to Gavin, I guess I do. He can own me all night long.

Sigh. I need to get all thoughts of dirty, delicious sex out of my brain and concentrate on work. At least my shift is only for five hours.

The moment I clock in, I get straight to work, tossing all the trash left behind on the tables and wiping them down. There's eventually a lull in customers coming in around ten thirty, and I go behind the counter to help clean up, wishing I could work the register. It's the easiest task and the least messy. The only issue that could come up is disgruntled customers, but everyone's generally content when they come in here, and I think it's the atmosphere. No one who works at Back Yard Bowl is tense or in a frantic rush. We're all mellow and friendly, and I love it.

"I'm taking a break," Matty announces to me after he rings up the last customer and we're all alone. Our general manager and the owner's son, Matty is twenty-five and a lifelong Santa Mira resident and university graduate too. He's also the typical surfer dude, with his long wavy dirty-blond hair that's prettier than mine and a never-ending positive attitude. "You missed out, Sienna. It was even busier when we first opened this morning."

"I'm glad I missed it," I say with a laugh, wiping down the counter with a fresh, hot rinsed rag. "Though I'm hoping the lunch rush will keep us going."

I prefer to be busy while I'm here. Time flies by faster that way.

"Don't worry. It'll get busy again soon," he reassures me.

"Maybe I can pick your brain a little more," I suggest. The last few shifts we've worked together, I asked Matty endless questions about running a business. Specifically a business that deals with serving food. Back Yard Bowl isn't a traditional restaurant, but it's not necessarily close to being an ice cream stand either.

My parents have been encouraging my dream. To the point that my mother helped me choose a few business courses I'm going to take next quarter. My dad has been searching on the internet for cheap freezers, and while they're all out of my price range—we're not made of money—it does help me to see what I'll need to save up for.

This dream might seem silly to some, but I'm truly excited about it. I'm grateful for Matty's advice, too, because he's got a lot of insightful information about the restaurant and food scene in Santa Mira.

"Sure—" Matty starts, the little bell hanging above the door ringing, indicating someone is coming inside.

A woman enters the shop, carrying a massive floral arrangement that's so tall, we don't even see her face. I watch as she carefully maneuvers her way through the tables and chairs until she's at the front counter and carefully setting the vase down.

"Can I help you?" Matty asks, sounding amused.

"Delivery for Sienna Cooper," the woman announces, glancing over at me. "You Sienna?"

I nod, stunned. Giddy with excitement because no one has sent me flowers before. "Those are for me?"

"Sure are." She smiles brightly. "Have a nice day!"

I don't move until the woman has left the store, and when I glance over at Matty, I find him watching me, curiosity written all over his face.

"Flowers, Sienna? I didn't know you had a boyfriend. Or girlfriend, or . . . whatever. I'm not one to judge someone for whatever their sexual preference is." Matty holds his hands up in front of himself in a defensive gesture.

His dismay at potentially offending me knocks me out of the shock that came over me, and I laugh. "I don't have a boyfriend, Matty. I don't have a clue who these flowers are from."

Okay, I'm lying. I have a sneaking suspicion they're from Gavin. A thank-you for blowing his mind last night? I know he enjoyed that blow job I gave him. I'm eager to do it again as soon as I can. I'm just surprised he would be so obvious, sending me flowers at work. Did I even tell him where I was working?

I don't think so, but I can't remember.

"There's a card included," Matty points out, and for a moment, I don't want to open it, almost afraid to read what's inside. What if Gavin says something stupid, like *Thanks for the friendship? Thanks for the friendly fuck; that was amazing!*

I wouldn't put it past him to say something dumb like that. He's not the best with his words, but would he really send me flowers and write a message like that? God, I hope not.

Or . . . maybe he sent me flowers after realizing last night that he's madly in love with me. Once he saw Ryland and me together, that sealed the deal. Now he's proclaiming his undying love for me, and we'll live together in blissful contentment for the rest of our lives.

Ha! I sound absurd even in my thoughts.

Plucking the card from the plastic holder that's nestled among the flowers, I open the tiny envelope and read what's written inside.

> I know how you feel, but Sienna, I can't stop thinking about you. I hope you'll give me another chance. It would mean the world to me if you did.—Ryland

Disappointment crushes my good mood, and I sigh, hanging my head. Ryland sent the flowers? He wants another chance? The man doesn't get the hint, and I wasn't even hinting. I'm not interested in him like that. Especially after everything that happened between me and Gavin.

"That bad, huh?" Matty asks after I'm silent for way too long.

I glance up at him to find he's studying me, concern in his gaze. "Kind of?" I wince, dropping the card onto the counter.

"You could've fooled me from the expression on your face just now. I worried maybe your cat died and someone was sending their condolences." He frowns. "You don't have a cat, do you?"

"I have no pets. Definitely no dead ones." Matty always mentions random things. His mind must be a wild place to be.

"Good." His relief is obvious. "You just looked . . . really disappointed when you read that card."

"I did?" That's because I was.

"Yeah, definitely." Matty nods. "Did an ex send you those or what?"

"No. I went on a date last night with a guy I went to high school with, but when he asked if we could do it again, I told him I didn't see him beyond a friend. He's the one who sent them."

"Even after you told him you wanted to stay friends?" Matty whistles low. "Dang, he must have it bad."

"You think so?"

"Why else would he send you flowers?" He studies the arrangement, his eyes going wide. "I'm not one to send flowers a lot, but that right there is impressive." He waves a hand at the bouquet. "And expensive," he adds.

A sigh leaves me, and I study the flowers. Matty's right. It's a gorgeous bouquet. So colorful and with a variety of flowers—and it definitely looks expensive. "It's too bad. He's a nice guy—just not the guy for me."

"Nice guys always finish last," Matty mutters, shaking his head. "I should know. I always find myself in last place."

"Aw, Matty." I feel bad, and I push the vase of flowers closer to him. "You want my flowers?"

"What? No way. They're yours, even if you're not into the guy." Matty levels his serious gaze upon me. "Maybe you need to tell him that again, Sienna. Don't string this guy along. Trust me, it hurts."

"I'm not stringing him along—more like he's doing this to himself. But you're right. I should probably talk to him again about this because clearly my words didn't sink in." I study Matty. "Have you been strung along by someone before?"

"Multiple times. Girls. Guys. I don't discriminate. I fall in love with a person's soul, not their gender, but I get trampled on time and again." He grimaces. "Everyone says I'm too nice, but I can't help it."

"You probably are too nice, but that's a great quality to have." I give him a hug because I can't resist, and while I know this probably isn't something I should be doing with my boss, he hugs me back, albeit briefly.

We spring away from each other when the bell that hangs over the door tinkles, announcing someone has walked in, and Matty waves a hand at the flowers. "Take them to the back, please?"

"Will do, sir." I salute him, making him laugh, and grab the flowers so I can rush them into the back room, setting the vase on Matty's desk. Grabbing my phone from the back pocket of my jeans, I tap out a quick text to Ryland.

It's best to get this over and done with. I feel like a shit for doing it after he sent me something so beautiful, but I have to.

> Me: Thank you for the flowers. You didn't have to do that.

Like, he really didn't. It would've been best if he'd left me alone completely, but here we are.

> Ryland: You're welcome. And I know I didn't have to, but I wanted to. I hope you like them.

> Me: They're beautiful.

I press my lips together, contemplating how I should word this. It's a delicate situation, and I don't want to be a complete bitch toward him. Maybe I'm channeling my inner Matty and being too nice.

> Me: I really appreciate them, but I did tell you how I felt about you last night. I hope you understand.

He responds quickly.

> Ryland: You can't blame a guy for trying, can you?

I release an irritated breath before I send him a reply.

> Me: Let's just keep this friendly.

Ryland: Define friendly.

Is he for real right now?

"Sienna! Can you come out and help, please?" Matty pops his head through the doorway, and I glance up from my phone, feeling bad.

"Sorry. I was texting the guy who sent me the flowers, and he keeps talking to me." I set my phone down. "I'm coming."

"Thanks."

I follow Matty back out and wash my hands before I help a customer at the register—go me. I stay there for the next couple of hours since the customers stream in at a steady pace, taking my mind off my little problem with Ryland. But I'm going to have to deal with it again.

Hopefully he won't be too difficult.

Chapter Twenty-Two

GAVIN

The party is starting at Nico, Coop, and Dollar's house, and I'm in a foul mood. And for once, it's not my father who put me there. There are a multitude of factors contributing to my shitty attitude, but a new one to add to the list popped up earlier this afternoon, and it sent me right over the edge.

I saw a sports report on ESPN where they were talking about serious contenders for the national title, and they mentioned the Dolphins. The reporter tore me apart, critiquing my game play so far this season and speculating that I might not "measure up" despite my recent statistics. Then he went on to discuss other teams and had nothing but glowing reviews for every single one of them. I was the only one called out for shit game play, and that put me in an immediate funk.

I regret ever turning on the TV to check game scores earlier. Fucking brand-new reporters who are barely out of college and have zero experience playing football, having the balls to tear apart my abilities and claim I probably don't have what it takes to lead our team all the way. Like it's all on me and no one else.

Fuck you, too, ESPN.

Walking into the house, I'm tense for other reasons. Knowing that Sienna will be here tonight and I won't be able to touch her in public when my thoughts have been rampant with images of mauling her in the best way. Tearing off her clothes and fucking her hard against a wall. Over a chair. In the backyard on one of those yoga mats Everleigh uses. Can't make a public spectacle of our sexual escapades, though, so I'll have to remain calm and in control.

That's difficult, considering whenever I'm around her, I'm overcome with the need to touch her and it's only getting worse. I thought I might get her out of my system after fucking her multiple times, but nope. It just made me crave her more. An incessant need is building inside me as every hour passes, and I'm already scanning the house in search of her. She's most likely already here with Everleigh.

It's probably best if I avoid all women and get shit faced tonight. Forget my troubles for once and drown them in alcohol. Probably not the right approach in handling my issues—football and women; well, make that a specific woman—but screw it. This is the team's only weekend during the season where we allow ourselves to party our asses off and get truly fucked up. Come Monday morning, we're back on the grind. Working toward our goal to win a national championship.

But I can't get that stupid ESPN report out of my head. Why does it feel like the season is already slipping out of my fingers when we've only played a few games? Games we've actually won, I might add. But other teams are doing just as well and even better, stats-wise. The competition is fierce this year, and it's intimidating as hell.

Kind of like the women in my life—well, two of them. Nothing much scares me, but that little Everleigh is a terror when she wants to be, trying to boss me around and tell me I need to apologize to Sienna—which I did, but I'm not about to mention that to her tonight. That's a conversation I don't want to have. She'll just start harping on me and giving me a hard time when all I want to do is relax.

And then there's Sienna. What happened between us last night rocked my fucking world, and I don't know what to do about it. Or how to handle it—handle her. She haunts my fucking dreams on a regular basis, and now it's even worse, knowing that she'll let me do whatever

I want to her. I didn't hold back, and she gave as good as she got. Took everything I did to her with a smile and a moan.

She's like my every dream woman come true.

Funny how I've been fighting my feelings for so long. I've been waking up to thoughts of her in the middle of the night for months. Hot and sweaty and with an aching erection, my body strung tight with need. Need for her. Before our encounters, I'd become overly acquainted with my hand, and I was worried I'd develop calluses on my palm that have nothing to do with a football.

Not any longer. No more jerking off unless she wants to be the one who does it—and damn, does she do it well.

I pause in the living room, faintly amused that no one greets me, which isn't normal. I'm blending in to the wall while everyone who lives in this house is running around, finishing setting up for the party that's about to happen.

My amusement evaporates when I lock eyes with Everleigh, her disappointment in me written all over her face as she walks past. And I don't want to make things right by telling her I made up with Sienna. That'll only lead to more questions I don't feel like answering.

Instead, I go sit and sulk on the couch, turning up the volume on the TV so I can watch the game currently on. One of our biggest rivals is playing, and they're demolishing their opponents, taking great pleasure in destroying them, from what I see on the television screen every time they gain an advantage. Smiling and giving each other high fives. Doing ridiculous dances on the sidelines—and in the end zone when they score.

Every single guy on that team is an asshole. I can't wait to wipe their faces in our victory in a couple of weeks. That's what I tell myself at least because I'm not about to let the doubt come in too strong. Not tonight. There's no place for it.

There is never any place for it, and I need to cling tight to that for the next few months and get through this season on top.

Nico comes to a stop when he passes through the living room for about the fiftieth time, finally spotting me on the couch. "What the hell is your problem?"

Great. I must still look pissed. I try to even out my expression, but it's no use.

"ESPN" is my answer.

"Well, whatever the hell that means, forget about it. I need your help." He inclines his head. "Come on."

I haul myself off the couch and follow him, hoping whatever task he needs my assistance with will distract me enough that I forget everything and relax. I'm almost desperate with the need to have a good time tonight. Whether or not that involves Sienna is up to her. I'm not about to push myself on her.

Even though she seems to like it.

"Ever wants these lights strung up here," Nico says once he's outside, pointing at the top of the patio's overhang. There's already a stepladder set up, the package of opened lights sitting on the top step. "Will you help me?"

"Sure. Anything for your girl, right?" I'm teasing, and Nico doesn't even react, which is hella disappointing. Though I suppose I should lay off. Why poke the bear?

Working together, we string the lights along the edge of the overhang, and I run an extension cord down one of the pillars and plug it into the outlet nearby. The lights come on, and Nico hops off the stepladder, admiring his work. "Looks good. Thanks, bro."

"You're welcome." I scan the area, taking everything in. "Backyard looks great."

There are chairs set up and a couple of tables. A keg is in the far corner of the yard, and there's even one of those outdoor firepits in the center of the yard, a stack of wood sitting next to it.

"It's all thanks to Dollar. He set up most of it," Nico explains.

"Coop around?" I keep my voice casual. We've never mentioned Sienna to each other since the big reveal, and it's making me anxious.

Like the unspoken elephant in the room that just grows bigger and bigger every time we're around each other.

"Yeah, he's here. Sienna is too. She's with Ever in her room. They're getting ready for the party." Nico grins.

I scowl. Guess it's his turn to give me shit.

I think of what happened last night before I went over to Sienna's apartment, and a horrible feeling washes over me. No, she wouldn't . . . would she? Though if she's in the mood to provoke me, that would be one way to do it.

"Do you know if she's bringing a . . . date?" I think of the wimp we all met last night. Ryan? No, his name is a variation of Ryan, but I can't remember it. And that's because I don't really care enough to remember it.

Fuck that guy. He doesn't stand a chance. Can he make Sienna come like I do? I'd guess not.

"Who? Everleigh?" Nico's fierce tone reeks of jealousy.

"No, dumbass. Sienna."

"I doubt it, but you never know. We didn't tell that guy she was with about the party. But I have no idea if Sienna invited him here or not. She might've."

My stupid heart is crushed into a thousand tiny little pieces at the thought of that asshole showing up here and hanging out with Sienna all night. I stand up straighter, pretending I am just fine. "Cool."

"You can admit to me if you're into her, Gav. I'm not her brother. I won't kick your ass for having thoughts of defiling Sienna," Nico reminds me, and I duck my head. Hating that Nico knows me so well.

You'd think Coop would know me just as well, considering the three of us have spent plenty of time together over the years, but then again, Coop is not one to share his feelings. Some would call him emotionless, but I think it's more that he keeps it all locked up tight. And when he explodes?

Watch the hell out.

"I don't know how I feel about her," I finally say, which is a lie. I know I want to have sex with her again. I want to make her smile and hear her laugh and watch her come apart in my arms. I like talking to her. I like it when she tells me things that she doesn't say to anyone else. It shows that she trusts me, and I want to keep earning that trust, but shit.

I don't know how to come clean about us with everyone else. Her brother and the team and the fans and the general public. I'm a Santa Mira celebrity, and I've seen what happens when some of my teammates get steady girlfriends. People on social media turn into stalkers, reporting on our every move. Following us wherever we go. And if they found out it was Sienna, who's already tied to us? They'd go wild.

That sounds like a lot of extra drama I don't have time to deal with.

Nico shakes his head at my answer, his disappointment clear. "Come on, Gavin. I think you're totally into her. You've been totally into her for years, yet you pretend you don't have a single clue about the fact that she feels the same way. The oblivious act has been working for you, and for whatever dumb reason, Sienna seems to fall for it, but I'm not letting you off the hook anymore. You need to do something about that girl. Either go all in or cut her off completely," Nico says, his tone firm.

"You been talking to Ever lately or what?" I scratch the back of my neck, hating how uncomfortable I feel at talking about Sienna. Maybe I shouldn't have come to this party. It's been unpleasant since the moment I set foot in the house.

Nico grimaces. "No. I'm just tired of watching you two pretend you don't have feelings for each other, when those feelings practically fill up the room to the point of suffocation every damn time that you're together."

"That's a pretty—descriptive way to put it." I'm still scrubbing the back of my neck. Something I do when I get anxious, and the moment the realization hits, I drop my hand.

"And pretty accurate too. But hey, it's just a suggestion on my part. If you want to keep up this charade, go for it." Nico offers me a smile, and it feels genuine. "I'm dealing with my own shit, and it makes me snappy. Sorry."

"Hey, it's cool." I incline my head toward him, and his smile fades, though his eyes are still friendly. "Let's forget all about women tonight and keep the peace. What do you say?"

"I say that's a great idea." Nico holds out his hand, and I slap it, then perform the intricate handshake we invented our freshman year. When we were young and full of hope. Not that my hope has died, but I'm a much more realistic person nowadays. "To getting drunk."

"To getting drunk," I repeat in agreement.

"And possibly getting laid," Nico adds.

I drop his hand, taking a step back. "I said we were going to forget women, asshole."

Not like I can, but it sounds good, right?

"Yeah, well, a man can still want some pussy, am I right?" Nico laughs, and I see right through him.

He's playing this all off, and while I'm laughing, too, there is only one pussy I want—and damn, that is such a crude way to think of Sienna.

Chapter Twenty-Three

SIENNA

I am ready to party, and the black dress that I'm wearing feels like armor, save for the fact that my boobs keep threatening to fall out of it. Not wanting my brother to see me with so much cleavage exposed, I've got an oversize denim jacket on, which is coming in handy since the air has turned chilly once the sun went down.

Everleigh and I have been locked away in her room for hours, preparing for this party, and not once, not a single time, did I mention what happened between Gavin and me last night. Haven't mentioned Ryland to her either. I'm almost afraid to. I know if I tell her I had sex with Gavin, she'd probably lecture me about how he's using me—after she asks that I give her all the dirty details.

And if I tell her that I also went on a date with Ryland? Oh, forget it. She'll encourage me to keep seeing him. I can hear her now, telling me to let go of Gavin and move on once and for all. But now that we've had sex so many times, it's going to be near impossible to let Gavin walk out of my life. No way. I'm pretty sure he feels the same way. That man is into me.

He was jealous of Ryland. Jealous. That still blows my mind. He couldn't bear the thought of me being with Ryland and barged his way into my house—and further into my soul.

Yeah. I'm so gone over Gavin. And while I am in a tight predicament when it comes to Ryland not wanting to give up on me and sending me flowers, I can't tell Everleigh about that either. I'm so used to doing things on my own without anyone's input, I know I can handle this little situation I got myself into. I'm positive Ryland will leave me alone. Eventually.

It's wild how I had zero men showing any interest in me and now I've got two wanting their shot. Poor Ryland. If Gavin wasn't around, I would totally go for him, though I would be doing it just to see what could happen. I didn't feel much chemistry between us.

But the heart wants what it wants—and so does the body. My heart and body are dead set on Gavin Maddox. Doesn't matter how foolish that seems or that I could be wasting my time.

I want him. Still. Badly. And I'm pretty sure he wants me.

That's why my makeup is perfect and my hair looks great, thanks to Ever's help. The strapless dress is sexy, and I'm sort of ruining it with the denim jacket, but whatever. The moment I take it off in front of Gavin—oh, a girl can dream—I can only imagine his reaction. His eyes will pop out of his head, and he'll start to sweat before he drops to his knees and proclaims his undying love and devotion to me.

See? I have it all planned out. Oh, and I'm also completely delusional. Undying love and devotion? I'm exaggerating.

The moment we exited Everleigh's room and ventured out into the living room, we separated and lost each other. There are so many people already here, and the music is loud. Conversations are happening all around me, people shouting and screaming as they try to be heard over the loud bass throbbing, and I push my way through the crowd in an attempt to get to the kitchen. It takes a little longer than it should, but I finally make it, heading straight for the fridge, where I stashed a bunch of seltzer drinks. I pull out a High Noon and crack it open, not bothering to check the flavor because I love all of them.

"Where's Everleigh?" I turn to find Frank smiling at me, a familiar blonde trailing behind him, her nose wrinkling in disgust when he mentions the name Everleigh.

The blonde's name is Portia, and she's Nico's ex . . . I don't even know how to define what they had. Were they actually boyfriend and girlfriend? Sort of, but not really? They went out for a few months, and she was a nightmare. Clingy toward Nico and mean to all the guys and especially to me. Like I was after her man or whatever.

Dumb.

And now she's here tonight and hanging out with Dollar? That's odd.

"I don't know. I lost her," I tell him, keeping my tone light. I don't even bother looking at Portia or acknowledging her, and she does the same to me. She's so rude. But I'm being rude, too, so whatever.

"I'll go look for her outside." Frank turns away from me, and Portia trails after him, both of them headed outside while I watch them go, perplexed by this turn of events.

Chaos always reigns at big parties.

I move about the house and talk to people I know, saying hi to familiar faces. Getting pulled into hugs by various Dolphins team members who all know who I am. I feel like their little mascot, the sister of Coop who's at every game and party, and while I love talking to them, I'm constantly on the search for someone else.

The only one I really want to see. But he's nowhere to be found.

I end up outside and search for Everleigh, or Gavin. Preferably Everleigh first, because I need her to talk me down off the anxiety-ridden ledge I suddenly find myself on. Why am I so nervous to stumble across Gavin again?

The memory hits me out of nowhere. We were at a party last year, and I got really drunk. It was at Coop and Nico's apartment, and I was going to crash out in my brother's room because my head was spinning so bad, and when I opened his bedroom door, I got the shock of my life.

Gavin and some random woman going at it on Coop's bed. Just like he went at it with me on my bed. I ducked out of there quick, before either of them could see me, and I darted into the bathroom, where I proceeded to barf in the sink.

Not my best moment. I refuse to get that trashed tonight. I want to get a little drunky but not too drunky . . .

I don't spot Gavin anywhere, and it looks like I can't find Ever, either, which is bringing down my good time. The crowd around the outdoor firepit is growing, and I check everyone standing there before I decide to give up and head back into the house.

The moment I do, I spot my brother sitting at the kitchen table, where the makeshift bar is set up, Everleigh standing right next to him. They're in deep conversation, Everleigh sipping from her cup every few seconds, and I make my way over to them and tap Ever on the shoulder.

She whirls around, a big smile on her face. "What's up, homie?"

I wrap her up in a bone-crushing hug, relieved to find her. "Someone's feeling herself."

"At least someone is feeling me, even if it's only you." Ever pulls away from me, finishing her drink in one long swallow before she smacks her lips together. "Another round, bartender!" while shoving her cup into Coop's broad chest.

I share a concerned look with my brother. The girl is drunker than I thought, and the night is still young.

"There you are," Coop says to me as he takes Ever's drink and sets it on the table. "I haven't seen you all night."

"There's a reason for that." I tuck the front of my jacket together, hiding the dress from his judgmental gaze. "Are you corrupting my friend with copious amounts of alcohol?"

"She's the one who asked for a double." He prepares another drink for Ever, who is jumping up and down as she waits. "And that's my roommate you're referring to."

"Whatever, she likes me most." I swing my arm around her shoulders and press my cheek to hers. "Right, snookums?"

"You know it, babycakes." Ever kisses my cheek, making me laugh, though it dies when I hear a few random dudes start chanting "Kiss her! Kiss her!"

Jeez. A little sign of affection between women and men have to make it sexual.

"Do not kiss her," Coop says with a grimace as he hands Ever a fresh drink.

"I would never," Ever says, wincing after she takes a sip. I bet Coop loaded that drink with alcohol. "I'm not here to put on a show for the guys."

"I want what she's having," I tell him, and he immediately starts making me a drink.

"Coming right up."

"And besides, we would never do that," I remind Coop, rolling my eyes. "We don't need to egg them on."

"Good, because they're all assholes." He glares at the group of chanters, silencing them with a firm look. Typical Coop. "There. They'll leave you alone. Now go about your business."

He hands me my drink, Ever and I look at each other, and then we're out of there, ready to check out the crowd. She tells me how she went outside and talked to some random drunk girl who wanted to trade places with her, and then gripes about how Nico is surrounded by women and he won't even look in her direction.

"Did you happen to see Gavin?" I ask, my voice as innocent as I can make it, but from the look she's giving me, I know she's not falling for it.

"No. I didn't see him, and Sienna?"

"Yes?" I ask, scared to hear what she's going to say.

"Forget that guy." She taps her chest with her fingers. "Just like I need to forget my guy."

Hmm. Love how she referred to Nico as hers. I can tell she's trying to convince herself. She's just as gone over him as I am over Gavin.

Actually, I'm probably worse since I had sex with him. Multiple times. And I'd like to do it again. Multiple times.

But I go along with Everleigh's idea. Pretty sure she's looking for support.

"Deal." I hook my arm through hers and steer her through the throng of people, stopping to talk to the ones I know, which are quite a few. I introduce Ever to everyone, and she chats them up, the friendliest I've ever seen her. I'm sure the alcohol has something to do with that.

The drink Coop made me is mega strong, and it's going down fast, making me wish I had another. Ever has also finished her drink, meaning she's really feeling good now, and we're just about to go out on the front porch and see what's up when Ever comes to a stop, forcing me to go still as well since our arms are linked. She's staring at the couple by the front door. Frank and Portia.

Oops. I forgot to mention that Portia came to the party.

"Oh no." Panic flares in Ever's gaze as she glances over at me. "I need to warn Nico that she's here."

"Seriously? Forget that guy, remember? We made a deal with each other."

"But Nico hates Portia." Ever lowers her voice, tilting her head toward me. "I have to tell him."

And with those final words, Everleigh takes off, abandoning me completely so she can go run to her man and warn him his ex is at the party.

Figures. Though I would do the same for Gavin if the situation was reversed, so who am I to judge?

Taking a deep drink from my cup, I head for the front door, ignoring the guys calling out my name, and I laugh and smile and wave, not about to stop and chat with them. Sometimes they get a little handsy once they've had a few drinks, and I'm not in the mood to push them off me. I can only imagine what would happen if Coop caught them doing that, or worse?

Gavin.

Needing some fresh air, I open the door, coming to a stop when I see who's standing directly in front of me, his expression one of pure shock, and I'm positive my face looks the same.

It's Ryland.

Chapter Twenty-Four

SIENNA

Ryland's expression switches up, a big smile appearing on his face. "Hey, Sienna! I was hoping I'd run into you here." Ryland enters the house accompanied by two other men I don't recognize; his gaze is only for me.

"Hi, Ryland." I offer a weak wave, wiggling my fingers before taking a fortifying sip from my drink because I'm gonna need it. I immediately wish it was even stronger. "Wow, um . . . I didn't know you were coming to the party."

"Just found out about it. My buddies—" He glances to the left, then the right, realizing that his friends have already ditched him. That was quick. "They told me about it, and I thought I'd come check it out, since it's at your brother's house."

Guilt swamps me when it shouldn't. I told Ryland straight up that I just wanted to be friends, and here he is. I don't want to think I'm the only reason he's here, but come on. I think that might be the case.

Or maybe not. I prefer to believe I'm *not* the reason he's here, and I try to play it off that we've run into each other.

"Yeah. The team always has a big party on their bye weekend. This is a traditional thing." I shed the denim jacket thanks to me starting to sweat over Ryland's unexpected appearance. After opening the hall-closet door, I shove my jacket inside and pull the door closed, then turn to smile at him. The guilt still lingering, I decide to confront the issue head on. "I'm sorry I didn't mention the party to you yesterday."

"No worries." His voice doesn't raise. He doesn't seem mad at all, and I admire that about him. I'd be hurt and even a little angry if I was in his position, but he doesn't seem bothered by any of this whatsoever. "How are the flowers?"

"They're beautiful." It's a little annoying that he would bring them up again. Didn't I thank him enough? But here I go. "Thank you for sending them."

It hits me that I'm unsure if I ever told him where I worked either. Did I? I might've mentioned it in casual conversation, but when? During dinner last night? I can't remember.

"Good. I spent a lot of money on them. I wanted to impress you." He tips his head to the side, contemplating me. "But I guess it didn't work."

Did he just admit he wanted to impress me? That's so . . . odd. "It's a gorgeous bouquet, but you know how I feel, Ryland." I don't know how else to answer him.

"Oh, I know. Guess I got carried away, but I wanted everyone at your work to see that you've potentially got someone new in your life." His smile grows, his focus dropping to my chest and lingering there for a beat too long. Considering I'm wearing two-inch platform black sandals tonight, I tower over him even more than usual, and he's practically at chest level.

Unease slips through me, and I take a step back, wishing I'd never gotten rid of the jacket. I am fully exposed, and he's taking advantage of it. "The only one who saw the flowers was my boss, Matty. And he's not interested in me like that."

"Matty, huh? How old is that guy, anyway?" His tone is vaguely hostile, and I'm thrown.

What's his problem? And what's up with him wanting everyone to know that I have someone new in my life when—joke's on him—I don't? How does it matter what anyone else thinks, anyway? I don't like how he's talking to me.

At all.

"He's just my boss," I finally say with a little shrug. "It was no big deal."

The tension seems to ease from his shoulders, and he nods once, muttering, "Okay. Okay, cool. Cool."

What the hell? Is this guy on drugs? I feel like I'm witnessing a complete personality transformation. "Are you okay, Ryland?"

His gaze jerks to mine, and I swear there's a spark of guilt shining in his eyes. "What do you mean, am I okay? I'm great, now that I'm here and you're with me. I was hoping I'd get another chance."

Did I say guilt? I think that spark is more like defensiveness. And he's hoping he'd get another chance with me? After I told him I wasn't interested multiple times? This guy is freaking me out. I need to get away from him for a minute and gather my thoughts. I'm struggling even being in his presence, and I need some distance.

"Excuse me for a moment. Need to grab a refill." I shake my cup at him to indicate it's empty before I turn to head for the temporary bar— and my brother. But Ryland locks his fingers around my wrist, stopping me. Glancing over my shoulder, I focus on where he's touching me for a moment before lifting my head, narrowing my eyes. Frustration fills me, and I let it fly, all my earlier politeness forgotten. "Let go of me."

His fingers spring away from my wrist as if he unlocked them, and he takes a step back, chuckling. "Now, now. No need to get so defensive."

"You're being really weird right now," I tell him, deciding I'm not going to hold back any longer. This guy is overstepping my boundaries. "And you're making me uncomfortable."

"Making you uncomfortable? Aren't you the one who went out with me last night and didn't bother to mention that your brother is having a giant party the next day? What, did you conveniently forget? Or maybe you were hoping to ditch me completely and hook up with someone else when I just sent you flowers?" Ryland's cheeks are red and his eyes are blown. He looks ready to full-on rage at me, and I'm not standing for it.

"Who the hell do you think you are? I've already told you how I felt. Multiple times. It's like I go on one date with you and now you're acting territorial because you sent me flowers? We never even kissed." This man. I am shocked he'd act this way.

"I'll take care of that." He storms toward me, and I take a step back, my butt hitting the wall behind me. I'm trapped with nowhere else to go, and I part my lips, ready to yell at him when he settles his mouth on mine instead.

I feel nothing. Not a single thing. Just Ryland's too-wet lips on mine, trying to persuade me to get into it. He settles his hands on my waist, and I shove them off me. My nonreaction proves that he is not the one for me. All Gavin has to do is look at me and I'm about to go up in flames.

"Stop." I push Ryland away with all my might, and he goes staggering backward, nearly falling into a group of partygoers behind him. We stare at each other, my breathing coming a little fast, but not in a good way. No, more like in a totally freaked-out way because I can't believe he tried to kiss me.

He basically forced himself on me, and that is just—it's not cool. At all.

"You should leave," I say, my voice cold. "And don't ever contact me again."

Ryland takes a step closer to me, working his jaw, his eyes icy. I don't back down, nor do I look away, and he takes a deep breath before he says, "We'll talk another time."

He goes to the front door and exits the house, leaving me a shaky, disturbed mess. I bang the back of my head against the wall and close my eyes, counting to five before I crack them open again. The group of people I shoved Ryland into were mostly girls, and they're all watching me with a mix of surprise and concern.

"Are you all right?" one of the women asks me.

"Was that guy harassing you?" another one of them adds.

"I'm fine. I handled it." I push away from the wall and approach them, grateful that they seem to care when I don't even know them. "But thank you for checking on me."

"I'll say you handled it," the one who originally asked if I was okay retorts. "You shoved that guy hard."

"So sorry he ran into you. That was partially my fault." I make an apologetic face, wincing.

"You don't need to apologize. It was badass, how you took care of him." The woman lifts her hand into the air. "You're my hero."

I slap my palm against hers, my laughter soft. I'm still shaken up, but it's getting better, especially thanks to these girls. "Aw, thanks. I didn't really do anything."

"He seemed a little—intense," the girl adds, and I nod my agreement, still confused by Ryland's behavior.

It's like he doesn't even listen to me. I tell him I want to stay friends—he sends me flowers. He shows up at this party and acts like he owns me, and when I call him out on it and say that he has no reason? Then he tries to kiss me.

And I thought I was delusional. Ryland is even more so.

I don't like that he said we'll talk later either. It almost sounded like a threat, which is freaking scary.

Holding on to that flicker of fear, I pull my phone out of my pocket—I love it when a dress has pockets—and block Ryland's number immediately. Then I go and unfollow him on social media, blocking him there too. I don't need that guy trying to contact me again and apologizing. I wouldn't accept it anyway, but blocking him should solve all my problems. Now he won't be able to contact me at all.

Screw that guy. He's a creep.

I chat for a little bit more with my newfound friends before I take off in search of Everleigh. But I can't find her anywhere. My brother is still at the kitchen table playing bartender, and the people surrounding him are about thirty deep. Not deterred, I push my way through them until I'm standing directly beside Coop.

"Hey, you need to take a break," I tell him.

He rises to his feet, towering over me. "Great idea. I'm out, everyone. There's plenty to drink around here."

They all groan their disappointment, but Jonesie magically appears, eager to take over Coop's position.

"Let me make you a drink, Sienna," Jonesie says, and I'm not about to turn him down. I also appreciate that he let me cut in front of everyone too. Coop keeps chatting Jonesie up, telling him how to handle things while Jonesie makes my drink. When Jonesie's finished, he hands it to me. "There you go, hottie."

I laugh, taking the drink from him. "Thank you." I make a cheers gesture and take a sip, impressed. It's delicious.

After giving Jonesie a few more instructions, my brother grabs hold of my arm and steers me out of the house and into the backyard. "Okay, you need to spill," he says the moment we're alone.

Panic filters through me, leaving me shaky. Taking a deep breath, I ask, "What do you mean?"

If he's talking about Gavin, I'm going to confess all my sins. Every single one of them.

"I heard some guy was harassing you earlier. Who was it?" Coop's nostrils actually flare as he glances around the yard. "You better tell me who it was, Sienna. Don't bother protecting him either."

"Oh jeez. I can handle it." I roll my eyes, but Coop swings his furious expression back on me, and I give in. "It was Ryland."

He frowns. "Who?"

"The guy you saw me with at Hector's. We went to high school together. He was on the wrestling team with you."

His frown eases and he nods. "Right. What happened? Did he touch you? I'm gonna fuck that guy up if he so much as laid a hand on you."

There is no way in hell I'm going to tell Coop that Ryland did touch me. "Well, I sort of . . . rejected him when he walked me home after dinner, and he's not taking it very well."

I don't bother telling him about the flowers or what Ryland said to me earlier. It's none of Coop's business, and I don't need to make this worse. I keep my lips shut and watch him, bracing myself for his reaction.

"That little wimp?" He makes a dismissive noise and waves his hand. Everyone is little compared to my brother. "Is he still here? I'm gonna take him out. Remind him he needs to respect women, especially my fucking baby sister."

"Coop. No." I shake my head, keeping my tone calm. There is no need to rile him up further. My brother is currently flexing his fingers and curling them into fists, like he has every intention to beat Ryland up. "Don't worry about it. I can handle him."

His shoulders visibly relax. "You can?"

"Definitely." I nod. "But I appreciate your eagerness to fight him."

"Fight him? It wouldn't be a fair fight. I'd demolish him with one punch." He literally blows on his knuckles like they're what? Weapons? Oh boy.

"Okayyy." I roll my eyes.

"But if he gives you any more shit, tell me right away. I'll fuck him up." Coop's tone is fierce, and I know he means every word he says, which I love. He's taking my feelings seriously instead of always running to my defense—with his fists. My brother truly always has my back.

"Thank you." I give him a hug. "I appreciate you."

"No prob." He pulls away, keeping his hands on my arms as his gaze sweeps over my dress. "Damn, sis. You need to cover yourself up."

I roll my eyes, taking another step backward, and his hands fall away from me. "Give me a break, Coop. You act like I'm five. I can wear what I want."

"Mom would flip if she saw you in that dress."

"Mom would probably tell me I look fabulous." And that's the truth. My brother is way too overprotective, and he needs to get over himself.

"Hey, guys!"

We both turn to find Everleigh approaching us, a cup in her hand and a big smile on her face. "I thought you were trying to find Nico," I tell her.

"I just did. He's right over there." She indicates with the flick of her head where Nico is standing.

With Gavin.

My heart in my throat, I remain mute while my brother and Everleigh chat. I can't look away from Gavin now that I've finally found him. He's wearing jeans and a black crewneck sweatshirt. Nothing special, but to me, he's the handsomest man I've ever seen. His hair is neatly in place—a rarity—and his face is freshly shaven, his expression gravely serious as he talks with Nico.

God, I want to throw myself at him, rub my body all over his, and beg him to take me somewhere more private. After having sex with him multiple times, it's not enough. I want more. Pretty sure I'm now completely addicted to him, and I don't mind. Not one bit.

But I can't throw myself at him. Instead, I stand there and listen with my brother as my friend babbles at us. And when Coop suggests we should go talk to Gavin and Nico, I remain composed as we make our way closer to them. It doesn't take long for Gavin to spot me, his eyes warming and his lips tilting up in the tiniest smile. Feels like a private, intimate smile just for me.

Feeling brave, I walk right up to him and wrap him up in a hug, savoring the feel of his big warm body pressed into mine. "Gavin. I haven't seen you in forever."

His hands linger on my hips, making me tingle. "Figured you were avoiding me."

I pull away, and it feels like he's sending me secret messages via his eyes. Asking me to play along, which I do. He knows I wasn't avoiding him, but everyone else thinks I have been.

"Looking good, Sienna." His gaze sweeps over me, settling on my chest, and I stand up a little straighter. It doesn't feel gross for him to look at me this way like it did with Ryland. No, I want Gavin to see me like this. Appreciate the view, so to speak.

"Why thank you." My cheeks are hot from his compliment. More than that, from the way he's watching me. Like he's a starving man and I'm a juicy steak. Didn't he call my ass juicy once? Ah, this man has such a way with words. "You're looking good yourself."

If he's starving, I'm positively famished. I know what he's got going on under those jeans and the sweatshirt, and my hands start to itch with the need to touch him.

"What are you ladies up to, hanging out with Coop?" Gavin's question is more directed at Everleigh.

"We dragged him away from his bartending duties," Everleigh says. "And got someone else to take over."

"Who?" Nico asks Everleigh.

She won't even look at him, keeping her head averted and aiming it right at me. I'm impressed. And how much did she drink when we got separated? "I don't know his name."

"It was Jonesie," Coop answers for her. "He wanted to do it. Supposedly he has skills."

"He made me a special concoction, and it's delicious." I lift my cup in a cheers gesture yet again before I take a healthy drink, wincing at the strength of the liquor.

Everleigh giggles, tapping her cup against mine before she takes a sip. Nico watches her like he's never seen anything better in his life, and when he finally looks away with a big smile on his face, he catches me staring at him. That smile fades, and I shake my head slightly.

These men. They're ridiculous. Always hiding their feelings.

"I was talking to our coaches about your yoga class," Gavin tells Everleigh, catching my interest.

Her eyes go wide. "Why would you do that?"

Gavin proceeds to explain how he suggested Ever should come to some of their practices and lead some yoga sessions. Everleigh can't stop beaming, her entire body wiggling with excitement, and it makes me feel like a proud mother at how happy Gavin is making her feel. How he thought about her and wants to help her—and the team too.

Okay, not a proud mother. That's a stretch. More like a proud . . . fuck buddy? Secret lover? Nah, I don't like how any of those sound.

A proud . . . girlfriend?

Yep. That's it. That's exactly how I feel.

Gavin eventually stops talking, and he grins at me and Everleigh, and oh wow the sight of his smile does things to me. Makes me feel all squirmy and needy when I see that glow in his eyes. The way he shifts closer like he wants to be near me. I don't know if anyone notices, but I do.

I notice every single thing the man does when he's in my presence.

His focus is only for me, his lids lowering in that sexy way, and I'm reminded of the last time we were together in my bed. A blast of heat surges through me, settling between my thighs, and I part my lips, ready to say something vaguely suggestive to him . . .

But then Nico starts talking, distracting Gavin completely, and I clamp my lips shut. I'll get him alone tonight.

I know I will.

Chapter Twenty-Five

GAVIN

I might've accused her of trying to avoid me, but I'm the one who's been staying away from Sienna all night, knowing the moment I saw her, I'd want to chase after her and get the hell out of here. I need to remain at this party as long as possible, hanging out with my friends. My team. But the later the hour, the rowdier everyone gets, and there are so many people here, most of them I don't even recognize.

The guys live in a neighborhood that basically turns into party central over the weekend, and it seems like everyone who wanders the streets seeking a place to hang out and get drunk has shown up.

That's my cue to get the hell out of here.

Everleigh leaves our little group first, and within minutes, Nico is trailing after her. Coop takes off after receiving a text from Jonesie that he needs help at the bar, and Sienna follows him, though she did grab my hand and give a squeeze before she took off.

She's getting bolder, but no one notices. Would they even care if we ended up together? Our friends might approve—eventually. Her brother, though? I'm not sure.

And I'm not ready to risk it.

Sienna always stays in my line of vision, though, not straying too far from where I stand in the backyard with a few of my teammates, all of them discussing our chances this season. I worry enough about that and don't want to talk about it anymore, so I tune them out and concentrate on Sienna instead.

She's looking hot as fuck in that little black dress that barely covers her delicious body and those sexy black high-heeled sandals that make her legs look extra long. The image of me pushing inside her while she's wearing nothing but those shoes flits through my brain, and that's all it takes. I'm chasing.

On the hunt for my girl.

She realizes quickly that I'm coming for her, and she starts walking. Wandering toward the side of the house, and I follow her, remaining at a healthy distance. No one is paying attention to us, anyway. As the crowd gets drunker, they get more focused on their own thing. In search of more alcohol; in search of that girl or guy they're into; in search of an empty bedroom or bathroom so they can fuck around.

Glancing over my shoulder, I check to make sure no one is following me before I round the side of the house to find Sienna leaning against the wall, her hands behind her back, her feet kicked out, one ankle crossed over the other.

I come to a skidding stop, taking her in. The dress molds to her delectable body, and I curl my fingers into fists so I don't do something stupid. Like rip the dress off her.

"Hey, Gav." Her naughty smile makes my dick twitch.

"Hey, Freckles." I don't come any closer, enjoying the view for a little while longer. Damn, she's sexy. Confident. Beautiful.

"Think they caught on?" Her voice is soft, and it takes me a second to understand what she said.

I take a step closer, checking over my shoulder one last time before I turn and face her. "Caught on to what? Us?"

"Yes. I think we played our usual roles rather well." She smiles, and I can't help but smile back.

"Is that what we're doing? Maintaining our usual roles?" I may play dumb in front of our friends, but I know what's up. Nico said I'm pretending not to notice her, and he's right. How can I miss this girl? This gorgeous, beautiful girl.

More like I'm dumbstruck by Sienna and how she makes me feel.

She nods. "We can't let them know what's really going on, can we?"

I take a couple of steps closer to her, her scent hitting me. Spicy-sweet and making my mouth water. "Are you telling me you want to keep up the pretense that you're crushing on me and I have no idea?"

Her dark eyes are wide when they meet mine, her lips pursed in a sexy pout. "Wouldn't that be easier for you? I know you're currently under tremendous pressure, Gavin."

I love it when she says my full name. Love it more when she looks at me like that, innocent yet sultry. A total contradiction. And what she's saying is true. I'm under a lot of pressure, and I wasn't lying when I told her I didn't need a distraction. And that she was my biggest distraction.

She is. The biggest one I've got. One I welcome with open arms, but only under certain conditions.

And damn, that sucks.

"I am," I finally say, closing in on her, my hands landing on the curve of her waist. Pinning her to the wall. "Think anyone would find us back here?"

It's a dark and narrow spot in this part of the house, and I can hear people on the other side of the fence, in the front yard. There are people in the backyard not too far away from where we're at too.

Yet all I can think about is fucking her right here. Shrouded in the dark yet surrounded by all kinds of people—some that we know. Including her brother.

That's pretty messed up. But when it comes to Sienna, I lose all sense of reason. She's all I can focus on. All I can think about.

See? The ultimate distraction.

"No. No one could find us." She slowly shakes her head. "They can't even see anything back here, it's so dark."

My eyes have adjusted to the dark, and I can definitely see her. I press my body to hers, let her feel what she's doing to me. I've already got an erection, and I've barely touched her. "Where the hell did you get that dress, anyway?"

My voice is a growl, and it makes her giggle. I squeeze her hips, dipping my head so I can inhale the delicious scent of her shampoo. God, her hair is soft.

"At a store." She tilts her head back at the same time I pull away slightly, her gaze meeting mine. "Do you like it?"

"I like this." I draw my index finger across the top of her breasts, pleased when I see the goose bumps rise on her flesh. "Fucking sexy."

"Thank you." She sounds pleased, a gasp of surprise leaving her when I dip my finger in between her cleavage.

"Such soft skin." I tug a little on the front of her dress to find it'll give easily, and I take my time while I continue touching her, amping up the anticipation between the two of us. "Aren't you cold?"

A shiver steals through her. "A little."

I lean my head against hers, my mouth at her ear. "Want me to warm you up?"

She nods, exhaling sharply when I jerk the front of her dress down, her breasts popping out. "That's not the way to warm me up, Gavin."

Sienna sounds amused. She has no idea what I have planned.

"Be patient, baby. This might work." I duck, drawing a hard little nipple into my mouth and sucking it deep. Her hands automatically clasp the back of my head, holding me to her, and I reach for the hem of her dress, shoving it up her thighs to find she's not wearing panties underneath.

Aw fuck. How can I resist that?

"Gavin." She whispers my name so softly I almost don't hear her. I pull away from her breasts, and she spreads her legs when I brush my fingers along her slit and press them deeper, encountering nothing but hot, wet flesh. I stroke her there, pushing my thumb against her clit, keeping my gaze on her beautiful face. Entranced with her every gasp and shift, her eyes widening, her lips parting. The shuddery breaths that leave her.

Voices draw closer, and we both go still, my head turning toward the front yard. There's a couple standing on the other side of the fence, talking in low tones, and damn, they are mere feet away from us.

"Baby," I murmur, and she opens her eyes, her gaze hazy with lust. "I need you to be quiet."

She nods, seemingly in a trance, and I remove my hand from her pussy, then press my wet fingers against her lips. She licks at them, making my dick surge, and I'm suddenly moving at a frantic pace. Grabbing my wallet, plucking the single wrapped condom I stashed in there, and tearing the wrapper open. I undo the button fly of my jeans, grateful I didn't wear boxers because I had a feeling something like this would happen between us.

Glad my instincts were correct.

Her gaze drops to my crotch as I pull my cock out, her lips still parted, and she licks them, making me groan. The couple in front of the fence go quiet for a moment, and we stare at each other, panic fluttering in my chest.

But then they start talking again, and I grab hold of Sienna's hips and flip her around, pressing my front against her back, my mouth at her ear once more. She molds her body into mine, her head tilting back, her hair brushing my face.

"Brace your hands on the wall, baby. And spread your legs."

She does as I ask, looking like she's about to get frisked by the cops, though her tits are hanging out the top of her dress and the skirt is bunched around her waist, the sight of her bare ass making me eager to get my dick inside her. She's shivering—from the cold or from what we're about to do; I'm not sure—and I roll the condom on, rest my hand on her hip, and slip inside her, never stopping until I'm completely wrapped up in her tight heat.

I fuck her steadily, trying my best to keep myself under control, but damn, it's difficult. She feels so good. Too good. I bump against her perfect ass every time I thrust, and she's slightly bent, her hands clawing at the wall, her pussy dripping all over my cock. This girl gets so wet for me, and I can't get over it. I want to clean her up with my tongue. Feel her cream all over my face, but that's not happening out here. We've got to make this quick.

More voices join the others, these ones all male and extremely loud, which is just the cover we need. I grip Sienna's hips tighter, pounding, grunting with every thrust, and she tilts her head back with a moan. I grab hold of her hair with my fist and pull, making her whimper, and I lean in, running my tongue down the length of her neck, nibbling her there.

She comes mere seconds later, her pussy clenching in a rhythmic motion around my dick, sucking my own orgasm right out of me. I hold my body against hers as it sweeps over me, gritting my teeth and swallowing down the loud groan that wants to escape. I lose all sense of time and place, focused only on the sensations racing through me, and when I finally come to, I find that I'm draped over the top of her, my hands clasping her breasts, my mouth on her neck, breathing heavily.

Kissing the spot where her shoulder and neck connect, I carefully pull out of her pussy, wondering what the hell I'm going to do with the damn condom.

Sienna tugs her dress into place while I remove the condom and stash it in a stack of plastic planters that someone must've left back here. Fuck it.

I turn to face her, impressed by how put together she looks. The dress is back in place, and her hair is smooth, hanging down her back in soft waves. It definitely doesn't look like I was just tugging on it only moments before. The only giveaway that she's had sex is the rosy flush on her chest and neck. The way her eyes sparkle when they meet mine. That's the giveaway she's been fucked by someone.

Fucked by me. Pride fills my chest, and I start to reach for her when she speaks.

"I should probably go," she starts, but I cut her off.

"Where?"

She glances toward the outdoor firepit, where lots of people have gathered. "I need to find Everleigh."

"She's probably with Nico."

Sienna looks back at me, her expression hopeful. "You think so?"

"I'm guessing, but come on. He's in denial over how he feels about her." *Just like I am with you.*

A faint smile curls her swollen lips. "I hope he finally realizes how great she is."

Her words strike me right in the damn heart, and for a second, I'm tempted to clutch it. Because in this very moment I'm realizing how great Sienna truly is. I've been feeling that way for a while, but the force of my emotions for her are coming at me one after the other, and I can't speak. There's a lump in my throat that feels like the size of a football, and when I finally swallow past it, my voice comes out like a croak.

"Come home with me."

She presses her lips together, doubt flooding her gaze, and I worry she's going to reject me. Bracing myself, I prepare for her to come up with a list of excuses and tell me no. I even briefly close my eyes, desperate to calm my suddenly racing heart.

"Okay," she murmurs.

I crack my eyes open to find her watching me, her brows lowered like I confuse her, and yeah, I probably do. I confuse myself. "Let's go."

I hold out my hand, and she takes it, interlocking our fingers. We leave the party together, sneaking through the house and walking out the front door. Not a single person even notices that we're holding hands, and I wonder why the hell I'm so stressed about the potential relationship with Sienna in the first place.

Seems to me, no one really gives a damn what we're doing anyway.

Chapter Twenty-Six

GAVIN

November

I'm in my own personal hell: at dinner with my parents. Slowly but surely dying inside as I sit at a table in a fancy restaurant with a fancy meal in front of me and an equally fancy and incredibly overpriced cocktail to my right. I reach for it and take a fortifying gulp as I listen to my father drone on about what a disappointment I am. After I just played a great fucking game. My entire team played great. And that's because we *are* great.

What the fuck does my old man know about it?

Apparently plenty if you based it on the way he's going on. Criticizing my every move.

"You shouldn't drink so much during the season," Dad snaps when I bring the cocktail to my lips yet again.

I suck it down, then set the glass on the table with a thump. Spotting the server, I lift my hand, pointing at the drink once I get his attention, and he nods his answer before heading for the bar.

Thank God. At least someone is listening to me tonight.

"Did you even hear me?"

I level my gaze at my father, dread coating my stomach when I see the anger in his eyes. Why is this man so pissed off all the time? I don't get it. "I heard you."

"You're in season. Training every single damn day," he reminds me.

"A couple of drinks to celebrate our victory isn't going to make me gain weight." I lean back and pat my stomach, studying my father's midsection. He's gotten a little thick over the last couple of years, meaning he's one to talk.

Dad snorts and takes a drink from his own glass. I shift my focus to my mother, who's sitting next to him, her expression impassive. She never rushes to my defense. Never says a damn word, really, and I wonder—not for the first time—if my father has threatened her if she ever speaks up. Or he's just got her so well trained, she doesn't dare say a word to cross him.

Miserable son of a bitch. Can't imagine my mother is happy either. They've been married for almost twenty-five years. That's a big deal. A long-ass time. But why do they bother? I don't even think they like each other.

Who likes my father? No one I know. Definitely not any of his employees. He leads by fear, and that is the last thing I want to do. My teammates like me. Respect me. I like and respect them. I am nothing without them, and I let them know that on a regular basis.

We haven't had one of these family dinners after a game the entire season, and I was perfectly okay with never doing it again. They haven't been around as much since he's been so busy with work.

Dad starts rambling about our playoff chances yet again, and I cut him off, desperate to change it up. "Mom, what's going on with you?" I ask her.

She blinks at me, seemingly startled that I'd acknowledge her. She even rests her hand against her chest for the briefest moment, like I surprised her. "What's going on with me?"

I nod. "Uh-huh. Tell me what's new."

"Well . . . I've found a new group to play bunco with. We meet on the first Thursday night of the month. They're a great group of women. We have a lot of fun."

"That's nice," I say, and I mean it. My poor mother. At least she has some friends. "You told me last time we talked that you were getting your closet redone?"

"Oh yes. And that's coming along nicely too. Well, we've only got the plans drawn up, but they're going to start working on it soon—"

"Why are we talking about this shit again?" Dad asks, sounding bored. He even yawns for good measure.

"Because I wanted to know what's going on with Mom," I remind him, my voice tight. My gaze shifts to hers, and I try to ignore the flare of fear I see in her eyes. "What else?"

"Oh, not much." She waves a hand, like she's dismissing herself, and damn, I hate that. "What about you, Gavin? How's school?"

"Great. Doing well." I can feel my father seething in his chair, but I don't give a shit. Making small talk might be painful sometimes, but it's better than listening to my dad talk shit and tell me how pathetic I am.

"You're still on track to graduate?" she asks.

"Definitely." The server appears with a fresh drink, and I take it gratefully, already sipping from it as he removes the empty glass from the table and rushes away. "Hopefully going to get drafted."

Dad makes a harrumphing noise of disbelief, but I choose to ignore it. Ignore *him*.

"Have you met anyone?" I return my gaze to my mother's, and I see the hope there. "Dating someone steadily?"

I think of Sienna and what we've been doing the last couple of months. Sneaking around and pretending we're not into each other when we're around our friends. Her brother. They have no idea I'm balls deep inside Sienna pretty much every night I get the chance to see her, which is often, thank God.

Though that's such a crude way to put it. Balls deep. I care about her. She makes me smile. She makes me laugh. She makes me want to try harder and do better, and I am doing all those things for her. This woman who's embedded herself into my life so deep, I don't think I'll ever be able to get her out of it.

And I'm okay with that. I really am.

"I have," I finally answer, my words coming slow. Hesitant. "We've been seeing each other for a couple of months now."

"Haven't heard a single word about that," Dad says, like he's trying to call me out on a lie.

"That's because I haven't told you." I send him a withering look, sick of him. Sick of everything.

And missing Sienna with every fiber of my being. I'd give anything to have her here with me tonight. Sitting by my side and sending me those sweet smiles. The ones that remind me everything is going to be all right. She'd pat my thigh when she'd feel me growing tense, and I'd appreciate her watching out for me because the two people who brought me into this world never seem eager to do that.

My parents showed up at the game unexpectedly, and I didn't get the chance to invite Sienna to come with us. And I'm glad I didn't subject her to this painful dinner. My dad doesn't deserve to be in that woman's presence. She's too good for him. Sienna is too good for me, as well, but I somehow got lucky and she seems totally into me.

"What's her name?" Mom asks, sounding genuinely interested. Maybe I don't give her enough of a chance. Maybe it's wrong of me to lump her in with Dad when it comes to everything he does, but I can't help it. They're a team, and they always have been.

What's weird is it's always been a team of two versus . . . me. Their own kid. I never understood that. I still don't.

"Sienna," I say, my heart growing lighter at just saying her name out loud. I rub at my chest, missing her like crazy.

"Coop's sister?" My father *would* know exactly who she is. Great. "You think that's smart, son?"

I take a big chug of my drink before I answer him, needing the alcohol to give me strength. "What are you talking about?"

"She's your teammate's sister. You aren't going to last, so why piss that guy off when he's on your side? Though I suppose it doesn't matter much, considering your season is almost over." Dad leans back in his chair, contemplating me. "Women are a distraction, son."

As my mother sits next to him. Such a stand-up guy. "Having her brother on the team means Sienna understands what I'm going through. She gets it."

"A woman could never understand. They don't know what it's like." He lightly swats Mom on the arm with his fingertips, making her flinch. "Right, hon?"

"Right," Mom echoes, her voice faint.

I sit up, reach for my drink, and finish it off completely before I speak. "My woman understands."

Oh fuck. I sound like I'm growling, which I suppose I am. I hate how he just said that about her. How he dismissed my mother completely and made her agree with him. He doesn't even know Sienna. God, he's such an asshole.

"As a matter of fact, I'm in love with Sienna Cooper." The moment I say the words out loud, I know I'm speaking the truth. I love her.

I do.

She's got a good heart. An ambitious mind—she's going to become the ice cream queen of Santa Mira; I just know it. And she's got a great body.

Oh, and the most beautiful heart of any human being I've ever known. That woman—my woman—she gets me. I need her like I need air.

"That's just your dick talking." Dad grimaces, and Mom drops her head as if she's embarrassed.

"No, it's not." I jump to my feet, eager to get the hell out of this restaurant and away from my dad. "I love her. I'm in love with her. And hopefully she's in love with me."

Is she? She acts like she is, but we've never said that to each other. I need to tell her. Right now. Tonight.

"She's probably in love with your money," Dad mutters, shaking his head. "You can't trust this girl, Gavin. I know the Coopers. They're flat-ass broke. Don't have a pot to piss in, and I'm sure she's latched on to you because she takes one look at you and has stars in her eyes. Well. More like moneybags."

I'm seething, my hands curled into fists, my vision nothing but hazy red. "Fuck you for saying that about her. You don't know her. She's smart and ambitious and sweet. She's fucking beautiful, and I'm a lucky bastard that she even wants to be with me. I don't deserve her."

Dad's expression and his voice are both ice cold. "You better watch what you say, son. I'd have no qualms smacking you across the face for what you just said to me."

I don't even care. He doesn't scare me. He hasn't for years, but the man does know how to get into my head, and damn it, I let him every time. I need to stop.

I need to grow up and be my own man. Fuck this guy.

Glancing around the busy restaurant, I return my gaze to my father, seeing him for exactly what he is. A small miserable man who's nothing but a bully.

"I dare you to try." My voice is deceptively soft. "Come on, Dad. Smack me. I know you want to."

He doesn't move from his chair. Just glares at me, his nostrils flaring. If I'd followed in his footsteps, if I'd allowed his resentment and his anger to seep into me, I'd be a walking, talking, identical version of him, and I refuse to carry on the cycle.

"That's what I thought," I say after he doesn't respond, nodding. I go around the table and give my mother a quick kiss on the cheek. "Text me, Mom. I'd like to get together with you soon. Just the two of us."

I don't bother saying anything to my father, and he doesn't utter a peep either. Though I can feel his icy glare following my every step as I make my way out of the restaurant. I'm staggering a little, drunk off three expensive cocktails, and I push through the front entrance, shivering when the cold air washes over me. The restaurant we're at is right on the water, not too far from the harbor, and I take a deep breath, the salty scent of the ocean filling my lungs.

No one chases after me, least of all my father. No apologies, no *I didn't mean what I said.* I'm alone. A feeling I've been familiar with for years.

But then I remember I'm not alone at all. I have my friends and my teammates and my coaching staff and my girl.

Sienna.

I whip my phone out of my pocket, bring up the Uber app, and order a car, typing in that I want it to drop me off at Charley's. The team will be there, and if I'm lucky, so will Sienna. And even if she hasn't arrived yet, that's okay. I can get even more drunk before she shows up. I know having her by my side will make me feel better, but I need to forget this entire dinner ever happened. And alcohol is the only answer.

Chapter Twenty-Seven

SIENNA

Two months.

Gavin and I have kept up the pretense of not being into each other for two long months, and let me tell you, it's pure torture. But there's also a sense of freedom to it, as weird as that sounds. Before, I would stress about Gavin and worry that he was out screwing around with other women. Always lamenting to myself *Why not me?*

Now I don't have to worry about it. The only person that man is screwing around with is me, and oh my God, when we're finally together during those late nights and stolen moments, he uses and abuses my body in the most thrilling ways possible. I didn't think it could be like this. Sex. A relationship. Even though it's a secret and no one really knows about us, that's exactly what it is.

A relationship. The very best one I've ever been in.

Keeping our distance in public allows Gavin to fully concentrate on football and school. The two top priorities in his life, which I completely understand. I do. And truly, I'm able to prioritize things in my life as well. School, work, and myself, though not necessarily in that order. I'm even taking an extra course because I've pretty much stopped going to the parties and get-togethers at my brother's house all the time. There's no point anymore. I mean, yeah, I'll go there and hang out with Ever, who's now in a full-fledged relationship with Nico, and he's occupying most of her time, which I totally get. But otherwise, I stay away from the house—oh, and my brother because I feel guilty over my secret. They all think I've been avoiding Gavin, but they're wrong.

There's no need for me to always hang around the team and wait for Gavin to pay attention to me anymore, and that's where the freedom comes in. I'm liberated from my own self-defeating thoughts. I've never felt more sure of myself in my life, and it's wild to contemplate.

I thought having a secret relationship with Gavin would annoy me. Devastate me. Make me feel like I'm not good enough for him, believing he's not willing to share me—*us*—with everyone in his life. That's not the case. He told me recently that once they're deep in playoff season, he thinks we should reveal ourselves as a couple. Just hearing him say those words made me nervous, but he's right that we have to come clean sometime. But does it make sense to do it during the playoffs? That's when the stress ramps up for everyone, especially Gavin. Nico and Ever are out in the open now, and no one gives them too much grief, from what I can see. Oh, women still have something to say to Nico because he's sickeningly attractive, but Ever is so confident that man is hers, she has nothing to worry about.

I don't know what it's going to be like if and when Gavin and I become public. He gets far more attention than Nico does. Or any of the other players on the team for that matter. Will people freak out or be supportive of us as a couple?

But I'm starting to think he's getting sick of pretending too. When we are in public together, he gets a little grabbier when I'm close. Looks at me with this tender glow in his eyes, like I'm the best thing that's ever happened to him. I can tell Nico's noticed, but he's not saying anything. My brother, though?

Still hopelessly clueless.

That's why I gave in to Gavin's pleading last night and decided to go to Charley's to hang out with the team after today's game. And what a game it was. Downright magical—and the day was too. I was screaming my head off in the stands with Everleigh when they sent Frank in during the last quarter of the game since he's been benched most of the season thanks to a shoulder injury. And when he intercepted the ball and scored a touchdown? I about lost my mind.

The only bummer was that Nico got hurt and was out of the game, but according to everyone, he's fine, thank goodness. He got a concussion, but it's a minor one, and he's feeling okay, according to Everleigh's recent text. Talk about relief. I adore that man, even though he can drive me crazy sometimes, but he's always been a good friend to me. They all are, especially Everleigh. She's been so supportive and makes time to hang out with me, even though she's so busy with everything going on in her life.

The guilt is getting to me, though. I feel bad, lying to everyone about Gavin and I being together. Will they be mad at us when they find out the truth? Probably. We're pretty convincing, pretending that we don't want to be near each other. They all think I hate him and that he avoids me.

And while I don't regret what we're doing, I hope everyone will understand why we did this. Our reasoning might be dumb to them, but we understand each other, Gavin and I. And that's all that counts.

When I get to Charley's I wander around the bar, surprised by all the friendly greetings I get from the various football players when they first spot me. When I go up to them, every single one mentions that they've missed having me around. I get a lot of hugs too. It's kind of shocking because I didn't realize they noticed me when I was there. I swear, I felt like I blended in to the furniture most of the time, and now they're all acting like I'm their long-lost, much-missed friend.

Life is so weird.

"Is Nico here with Everleigh?" I ask once we're all seated at the usual tables the staff at Charley's keeps reserved for the team.

"No. Once the docs cleared him, they went out to dinner with his mom." Coop lifts his brows, sending me a meaningful look.

"I'm glad he got cleared." Coop is still sending me that same look. "And I'm not surprised they went out with his mom. She seemed to get along great with Everleigh."

"Don't you think it's a big deal that Nico took Everleigh to go out with his mom? They're close. He runs everything by his mama, and he's never had a girl meet her," Coop explains. "I think they're getting serious."

From the way Ever talks about Nico, I don't doubt for an instant that they're serious. "I think it's great. They're good for each other."

"I agree with you. And I see the way he acts around Ever. He's fallen for her. Hard. He's definitely in it with this girl." Coop brings his beer bottle to his lips, tipping his head back and taking a long swig.

"In what?" I stare at my glass of water, sort of wishing I had a fruity cocktail to drink instead. Since I rarely go out to the bars anymore, I've been focusing more on my health. It helps having Everleigh guiding me since she's studying to be a nutritionist and she has great advice. I've cut back on my alcohol intake, as well as sugar and carbs, and I've been working out more. Everleigh and I have private yoga sessions a couple of times a week, and I've been running around the track at school. I've even lost some weight, though that wasn't my goal when I started this endeavor. I wanted to be healthier and have a clearer mind.

Instead of worrying about everything I can't control, I gained some clarity about my life and my goals. I feel better and look better, and I'm more confident.

"Nico is in it for the long run with Everleigh. He's in love with her." Coop sets his beer bottle on the table, then reaches for the damp label and shreds it with his fingers.

"Did he tell you that?"

"No, but it's obvious. We can all see it."

He's right. We can. Can people see it between Gavin and me? I haven't said it out loud to him, but I'm in love with Gavin. I've crushed on him for what feels like forever, and now that we spend time together, my feelings have only intensified. It has to be love. What else could it be?

And that's serious. I'm in love with Gavin Maddox. Is he in love with me? I think so. I hope so. He acts like he is, but who knows? Maybe it's just raging lust. He does want to have sex with me all the time, but I feel the same way. It only gets better between us every time. I let him do whatever he wants to me, and trust when I say he wants to do a lot of things to me. With me. It's wonderful. He's wonderful.

A soft sigh escapes me. I've got it so tremendously bad for that man. Maybe that's why he wants to tell everyone. He feels the same way about me.

Coop and I end up being the only ones at our table, and it's weird, how Gavin hasn't shown up yet. Dollar is standing in front of the other table nearby, retelling his game story for about the millionth time. He's animated, his arms gesturing everywhere, and I'm sure the story gets wilder the more he repeats it, but everyone is humoring him because after being benched for the whole season, to get that chance to make such an epic play . . .

His teammates understand. They get it. Dollar is now a bit of a legend, and they're letting him revel in it.

"You dating anyone?" Coop asks me seemingly out of nowhere.

I freeze, shocked by his question, and I tell myself to relax.

"What? No, not at all." I shake my head, still a little thrown and trying to play it off. I probably sound too defensive, but he caught me off guard. "Lately I'm in bed by nine every night."

With Gavin most of the time, but I don't say that out loud. Coop would probably freak out.

"Boring." He nudges me with his elbow, and I slide away from his reach, sending him a glare, though I'm not mad. "When did you turn into such an old maid?"

"I've taken these last few months to work on myself," I remind him, always on the defensive with Coop. I don't know why he picks on me about it. Oh, maybe because he's my older brother?

Yeah, I'm sure that's it.

"I'm proud of you, Sisi." He takes another drink of his beer, not even paying any attention to me while I sit next to him, suddenly choked up.

Coop hasn't called me Sisi in years. It's a nickname he gave me a long time ago when I was a baby, and it stuck until high school. By that time, I would get mad at him for calling me that, and he eventually stopped.

But right now, hearing him say he's proud of me and calling me Sisi? I sort of want to cry.

"Thank you," I manage to choke out, clearing my throat. He sends me an odd look, and I flash him a closed-mouth smile, not wanting him to notice that I'm all teary eyed. Thankfully he isn't paying attention, and Dollar chooses that moment to approach our table, grinning so widely I wouldn't doubt that his face will hurt later.

"Guys, I am on top of the world tonight," Frank announces, spreading his arms out wide. "Best game of my life."

"It was amazing, bro," Coop says, his praise genuine. I can hear it in his voice. They all pick on Frank because he always has a reaction, but there is genuine affection between the roommates, and I love how supportive they are of each other when it matters.

I give Frank the accolades he's seeking. "You were great today, Frank. The best catch of the game, maybe even the season."

My brother gives me a look that says *Laying it on thick much?* but I just smile serenely at him in return.

"Thanks, Coop. Sienna." Frank smiles at me and scoots onto the booth seat, sitting next to me. He leans in and kisses my cheek, pulling away with a smile. "You're looking good."

"Don't get any weird ideas." I thrust my index finger in his face, and he laughs, pulling away from me but still staying in the booth with us. Other teammates eventually join us at the table, and we're all making small talk, mostly predictions about their playoff future and where they think they might end up.

I remain quiet, simply absorbing their good vibes as they chat. Everyone's in a positive mood, still riding the high from their win. They've lost only one game the entire season, and they are well on their way to that national championship they want so badly.

But there's one person who hasn't shown up yet, and while I'm supposed to act like I don't care, I can't take it any longer. And I'm not about to risk texting him right now. What if Coop sees me?

"Hey." I tap Frank's shoulder, and he turns to look at me, his brows lowered in question. "Where's Gav tonight?"

Ugh, I still hate calling him that, but I'm trying to keep our conversation casual. Like I don't really care where he might be, which is a total lie.

"His parents showed up unexpectedly, and he went to dinner with them after the game," Frank explains before he turns away from me, resuming his conversation with the guy sitting next to him.

My heart drops. He never told me his parents were coming, but maybe he really didn't know. And he's with them still tonight, having dinner together? Is he ready to fling himself off a bridge yet or what? I don't mean to sound dramatic in my own head, but I remember what he said to me that night when we first had sex. What he's shared with me when he does talk about his parents, which isn't often. I get the sense he'd rather pretend they don't exist most of the time.

He admitted to me recently that he has a horrible relationship with his father and they've never been close. Which makes me feel sad because Coop and I are so close to our parents. I appreciate having them in my life and will text my mom about anything and everything just to show I'm thinking about her, which I always am.

Someday soon when we reveal our relationship to everyone, I'm going to bring Gavin over to my mom and dad's, and they're going to make him feel so welcome. They both adore him and think he's a great friend to Coop. Just wait until they find out he's their daughter's boyfriend.

Mom is probably going to faint. She's said to me more than once she thinks Gavin is handsome and charming.

Same, Mom. Same.

After approximately thirty minutes of sitting in silence and growing increasingly worried while everyone around me is having a great time chatting and drinking, I eventually make my way out of the booth so I can leave Charley's. I can't concentrate or pretend to have a good time when I know Gavin is out there suffering through what I'm sure is a tension-filled dinner. I hope his father isn't being too terrible toward him.

Though he probably is.

I make my way through Charley's, my gaze snagging on the back of a man who's sitting at the bar, his head dipped, his shoulders hunched. There are women flanking either side of him, and I know without a doubt who it is. How long has he been here, anyway?

Operating on pure instinct, I march right up to him and tap him on the shoulder, not saying a word. Gavin turns to his left, his eyes widening in surprise, and his relief at seeing me is obvious.

"Ladies, the love of my life just showed up. Whatever you had planned is definitely not happening tonight. Sorry," he announces as he bobs and weaves from his position on the barstool.

Oh dear. This man is stinking drunk. Why else would he call me the love of his life? Talk about blowing our cover.

"Gavin." I lower my voice, my gaze locking with his. "Are you okay?"

"Why wouldn't I be? Played the best game ever tonight. Did you see it?" He sounds like a little kid, eager and hopeful.

"You know I did." I send a scathing look to both women who are still sitting there, waiting for a sign from Gavin that they're all going to leave together—goodbye, ladies. It's never going to happen.

They get the hint and scurry away, but not without sending me rude glares of their own as they walk past.

Gavin laughs as he watches them go, his gaze returning to mine. "Always scaring them off, aren't you, baby?"

I want to melt at the nickname, but I tell myself to stay strong—for Gavin. It's clear that he's hurting. He doesn't get shit-faced drunk often, and that's exactly how I would describe him. He's got a goofy grin on his face, but his eyes are weary. Even a little sad.

"Since you won't, someone has to," I tell him, my voice light. "Ready to go home?"

"No way. I just got here!" He's shouting, drawing some attention, and I keep the smile pasted on my face.

"How long have you been here, Gavin?"

"How long, Sam?" he asks the bartender.

"An hour at least," Sam answers.

I'm shocked. How did we not notice him? Were we all too preoccupied with Frank's storytelling? Normally I can even sense Gavin's presence when he enters the room, but not this time around.

"You should at the very least stop drinking," I warn him softly, letting my concern show on my face. "Bad night?"

"The fucking worst," he says without hesitation. "You volunteering to take me home, Freckles? Want to slip into my bed and cuddle? Stay the night?"

He is blowing our cover left and right this evening. "I'm going to call you an Uber."

"Don't bother. I can walk home. I'm fine." Gavin tries to stand and wobbles on his feet, plopping back onto the stool. "Fuck. Maybe not."

I pull my phone out of my jeans pocket and pull up the Uber app, ordering us a car in seconds. "Come on. Let's go outside."

I grab at Gavin's arm, but he's resistant, pointing at the bartender. "Hold on. I owe Sam here some money. I can't leave without paying him."

"I put it on your tab, Gav. Pay us next time. We know you're good for it," Sam reassures him.

Gavin tumbles off the stool, straightening his body and offering Sam a salute. "You're a good man, Sam. Unless you're creeping on Freckles here. Then I get pissed."

I'm mortified, but Sam doesn't seem affected by his remarks. He deals with drunk people all the time.

Grabbing hold of Gavin's arm, I steer him toward the front door, ignoring the way my skin tingles where it makes contact with Gavin's muscles. Ugh, his biceps are sexy. Everything about him is sexy, and I'm doing my best to act like he's only my friend, but it's like my body can't resist.

It gravitates toward him until I'm leaning against his chest and he's got his arm slung over my shoulders, the two of us wrapped around each other as we stand outside and wait for the Uber to show up.

"Did you really just help me walk out of the bar?" He seems confused.

I nod. "Someone had to get you out of there."

His smile is soft. Sweet. "You're the best, Freckles. I love you."

Chapter Twenty-Eight

Sienna

He did not just say what I think he said . . . did he?

That dopey grin is still on his face. I've always believed a person's true feelings come out when they're drunk.

Maybe, just maybe, Gavin *is* in love with me.

Hmmm. That might be hopeful thinking on my part.

A car fitting the description of our Uber pulls up to the curb, and I change the subject, desperate to get us out of here and somewhere more private. "Here's our ride."

"Thank God." He lurches out of my hold and staggers over to the car, bending down to peek through the open passenger-side window. "Hey, dude."

The guy is watching Gavin with shock and awe written all over his face. "Gavin Maddox?"

"That's me." He slaps the edge of the open window with both hands and shifts toward the rear passenger door, opening it for me. "My lady."

I almost laugh at the way Gavin gestures gallantly toward the open door, and I send an apologetic glance to the Uber driver.

"Hey, uh. This car is for Sienna, not Gavin," he says, sounding confused.

"I'm Sienna," I tell him as I get into the car, Gavin sliding in after me. He's nestled close, his side pressed into mine, and he slips his arm around my shoulders, hauling me even closer.

"You smell fucking delicious," he tells me as loud as possible.

I meet the driver's gaze in the overhead mirror, and he looks away guiltily.

"Gavin. You need to stop," I whisper.

"He doesn't care." Gavin's voice remains just as loud as he waves his hand at the driver. "Do you care that I'm in love with Sienna Cooper?"

"Not at all," the driver says, shifting so he sits lower in his seat, like that might help him disappear. "You can love whoever you want."

"That's exactly what I'm saying." Gavin exhales loudly, that smile still on his face. "It shouldn't matter. I don't know why we're keeping this a secret, baby. Everyone deserves to know how we feel about each other."

I want to die of mortification, and I also want to sing from the rooftops because is Gavin declaring his love for me to our Uber driver? Apparently so.

"I told my parents that I'm in love. Want me to tell you what my dad said?" He pauses but doesn't give me a chance to speak. "Nah. You don't want to know. It was mean. He's a mean son of a bitch, and I'm sick of his shit."

"Gavin . . ."

"Don't. The tone of your voice—you sound like my mom." He leans his head against the back of the seat, closing his eyes, his expression agonized. This poor man. He must've gone through it with his parents during dinner. "Always making excuses for my dad. Always trying to get me to go along with the plan. Whatever that is."

I remain quiet, glancing out the window to see how much longer we have in this car. Thankfully his apartment complex is close by, but we're stuck at a red light that seems to go on forever, and Gavin can't stop talking.

"I have my own plan. To take this season all the way and win it all. Graduate. Get drafted by the NFL. Take you with me wherever I end up. I know you have a year left, Freckles, but you don't need to finish if you don't want to. You can travel the country with me." He's still got his head slung back against the seat, and he turns it in my direction, his expression oh-so serious. "I'll buy you a ring, and we'll get married. What do you say?"

Is he now *proposing* to me in the Uber? He cannot be serious. The man has clearly drunk way too much alcohol tonight. "I should probably finish school first."

He frowns. "That's a little disappointing, baby. You mean you'll stay here and finish while I leave?"

"Um . . ." My voice drifts, and I'm beyond grateful when the car pulls into the parking lot of his complex. I immediately change the subject. "I think we've arrived."

"Oh shit." Gavin lifts his head, staring straight ahead. "I live here."

I almost laugh at his surprise.

"Straight ahead, dude. My building's all the way in the back." He leans forward, thrusting his head between the seats. "Yeah, drop us off right there."

The car jerks to a stop, and I'm reaching for the door handle, escaping the car quickly. Gavin stumbles out of it right after me, and I grab his hand, holding on to it as tight as I can, though I know he'll take me down with him if he falls.

Gavin waves at the driver as he leaves before turning to me, that silly smile still on his handsome face. "I'm glad you came home with me, baby. I can't wait to get you naked in my bed."

His brutal honesty is . . . shocking to say the least. He's been sweet toward me the last couple of months, and I haven't felt uneasy with him the entire time we've been together, but in this moment?

I'm thrown by his behavior. It's not normal for Gavin to speak so freely, and I'm blaming the alcohol.

"How much did you drink tonight, anyway?"

"Not enough," he says as he starts for his building. Somehow, he makes it to his front door, though he's not walking in a straight line. I follow him, apprehensive until the moment he walks inside his apartment, and only then can I breathe again. If he would've fallen outside, there's no way I would've been able to get him off the ground. He's way too heavy. I would've had to call my brother for help, and that would've brought a lot of questions that I don't know how to answer.

I shut and lock the door, then turn to find Gavin has already left the living room, leaving a trail of clothing behind him. His shirt. His belt. His shoes. He kicked off his jeans in the doorway of his bedroom, and I grab everything, clutching the pile of clothing and accessories to my chest when I enter his room to find him falling forward on the bed in just his boxer briefs.

"Maybe I did drink too much," he says, his voice muffled by the mattress.

I dump his clothes on top of his dresser. "Were you drinking at dinner?"

"Oh yeah." He rolls over on his side, resting his elbow on the bed and propping his head up with his hand. "It was the only way I could get through that nightmare."

"It was that bad?" I wince, bracing myself.

"You don't even know the half of it." His voice lowers. "Come closer, future wife."

I go still at his words, shocked all over again. I can't get used to him saying these sorts of things. Will I ever?

I edge closer to the bed, gasping when he lurches forward and grabs my hand, pulling me onto the mattress with him. He wraps me up in his arms and rolls us over so I'm lying beneath him, his gaze locked on my face. "You're wearing too much clothing."

"I didn't strip like you did."

"I was hot." He bends his head, kissing my neck. "*You're* hot. So fucking hot, Freckles. I need you naked."

I close my eyes as he makes his way down my body, kissing the parts of me he exposes. He lifts my sweater and kisses my stomach. Undoes the snap of my jeans, slowly lowering the zipper. The moment my panties are revealed, he's kissing them, making me tremble.

"I can smell you. You want me." He lifts his head, grinning at me. "You always want me, huh?"

There's no point in denying it because he's right. When do I not want him?

"I always want you too," he continues, his voice gruff as he starts tugging on my jeans. "Lift your hips, love of my life."

The nicknames are adorable. The way he's touching me? Sets my skin on fire and leaves me a shaky, needy mess. I lift my hips for him as he requests, and he slowly pulls my jeans down, nearly falling off the bed when he gets them all the way off. He yanks off my socks next, his gaze lifting to find me watching him.

"Take off the sweater," he demands, and I do as he says, revealing that I have no bra on underneath. I went and changed after the game, wanting to look prettier for him, and I don't even think he got a chance to appreciate my outfit.

Oh well.

"You're beautiful, baby," he murmurs as his gaze rakes over me, and I forget all about feeling sad that he didn't appreciate what I wore. The way he's looking at me more than makes up for it. "And I'm not just saying that because I'm drunk."

He always compliments me when I'm with him, and he's remained sober the last couple of months, avoiding alcohol because he didn't want to consume the extra calories. "You're beautiful too," I tell him because he is. His body is absolute perfection, and he works hard to maintain his physique.

Gavin laughs, shaking his head. "If my dad heard you right now, he'd be so pissed. He'd say you're trying to feminize me or whatever. Calling me beautiful like that."

"You *are* beautiful." I grab hold of his arm and pull, and he collapses onto the mattress with ease. I crawl on top of him, straddling his hips, my face in his. "You've not only got a beautiful body, but you're beautiful on the inside, too, Gavin. You're kind. Smart. A natural-born leader who cares about those who are important to you."

"You're important to me." His hand comes up, fingers threading through my hair. "You're the most important person in my life."

My heart starts thumping wildly at his declaration. I know he's drunk. He might not remember saying any of this to me tomorrow, but the sincerity glowing in his eyes tells me he means it.

And I believe him. That's not wishful thinking on my part either. This man is for real. He's all mine and he loves me.

"I'm tired of hiding our relationship from everyone. I know I wanted this, and you did, too, but it's getting so fucking hard to keep my feelings to myself. When all I wanna do is unleash them all over you." He cups my face, a gesture he knows I love, and I lean down, brushing his lips with mine. "I meant what I said earlier. I'm in love with you."

"Are you sure?" I whisper, my heart now firmly lodged in my throat. I swallow past it, noting the flicker of irritation in his eyes. "I don't doubt you, I just . . . you're drunk. And emotional after a rough night with your dad."

"That rough night, as you call it, opened my eyes and made me realize I don't treat you like I should. Hiding you like a secret when I should put you on a goddamn pedestal like you deserve."

He kisses me again, his mouth soft and persuasive, and just as I'm about to part my lips for his tongue, he ends it, the glimmer in his gaze fierce. "I'm not like my father. I never will be. I love you, Sienna. I want a life for you. With you. And I will never stifle you or tell you what to do. That's how my father treats my mom, and it's so fucking unfair. She barely has a life. He dictates her every little move, and there is no freedom for her. He controls her in all the ways, and that's fucked up. I would never do that to you."

"I know you wouldn't." I smile, trying to ease the mood that's suddenly come over him, but he continues.

"We're telling everyone we're together. I can't take it any longer. And I don't care what my dad said. I deserve love. I do. And I love you." His mouth is on mine once more, the way he's kissing me feeling almost desperate. I press my hands against his face this time, trying to gentle the kiss with my lips.

His mood is all over the place. He's laughing, he's in love, he's mad, he's upset. I wrap my arms around his neck and cling to him, our mouths moving against each other, tongues sliding, circling. I still haven't told him I love him, and I don't know why. Maybe because this doesn't feel real? Like he's going to wake up in the morning and deny he ever said any of this? That's my fear, and it might be irrational, but then again . . .

It might not.

He rolls me over until I'm underneath him, my legs spreading to accommodate him nestled between my hips. I don't stop kissing him, loving how he's almost frantic with need, and it takes us only a few minutes to shed the last of our clothing and for him to somehow slip on a condom before he's buried deep within me.

Gavin holds me close, his mouth on my neck, his hands on my hips as he lifts me up, plunging deep. I run my hands up and down his back, trying to soothe him and calm myself. This night, this moment, is unlike any other we've shared before, and we've shared a lot. This feels like a turning point. A new beginning. And I'm ready for it.

Hopefully he is too.

Chapter Twenty-Nine

GAVIN

I wake up with a throbbing headache and a soft woman in my arms, wound all around me. Like a dumbass, I left the blinds open in my bedroom yesterday, and there is all sorts of sunlight streaming into the room, blinding me to the point that I don't want to open my eyes. It hurts too fucking much.

That's probably also my head.

Shifting, I rear back and squint at the bundle lying halfway on top of me. Sienna is out, her eyes shut and lips parted in sleep. I stare at the smattering of freckles across the bridge of her nose. At her thick eyelashes and her rosy cheeks. We had sex twice last night, but I think I made her come three times. I was drunk and horny and pissed at the world.

No, pissed at my dad. He can go fuck himself for showing up at my game and ruining my mood. Taking me to dinner and ruining it further. I probably would've had a much better time if Sienna had gone with me, though there's a part of me that's glad she didn't have to hear the things my father said. Knowing Sienna, she would've stood up for me, because that's what she does. She believes in me like no one else I know.

I'm over pretending we don't matter to each other. I know this was a mutual idea and we've made it work for quite a while, but I'm done. I needed her last night, and when she swooped in and rescued me at the bar, I'd never been happier to see someone. By the time she showed up, I was pretty drunk.

Maybe a mistake, but as I lie here, I remember everything that happened. Everything I said. The booze worked like truth serum on me, and I said some . . . things that were definitely a choice. Whether that choice was good or bad, I'm still not sure yet. Guess all that depends on how Sienna is going to react toward me when she finally wakes up.

I slip out of bed and shuffle into the bathroom, taking a piss before I wash my hands and check my reflection in the mirror. Damn, I look like I went on a bender, which I did. There are bags under my eyes, which are tinged red, and my face looks haggard. Tired. I take some ibuprofen, splash some water on my cheeks, and dry off quickly before I stagger back into the bedroom. Only to find Sienna is awake and sitting up in the middle of my bed, the sheet tucked around her chest like she doesn't want to be naked in front of me.

Well, fuck that. Not a good sign.

"Morning." I clear my throat, trying to get rid of the roughness in my voice.

"Good morning." She sounds amused. "How are you feeling?"

Hmm, well she's not acting like she hates me.

"I've felt better." I briefly drop my head to find that I'm naked, but I've got no shame, so I remain standing. "How are you feeling?"

"Considering I'm not the one who was a drunk fool in the Uber last night, I'm feeling pretty good." That small smile curling her lips is cute. She probably thinks she's real cute for what she said too.

"I was a drunk fool?" I'm pretending like I don't remember, but I do.

"Oh definitely. You said some . . . wild stuff."

"Wild? Like what?"

Her cheeks turn the faintest shade of pink. Interesting. Does she not want to repeat to me what I said? Because I remember everything. I talked nonstop about how I love her. How I want to buy her a ring and marry her. Take her with me if I get drafted by the NFL, and start my career with her by my side.

And it's all true. I meant every word I said.

Not sure she liked the part about her leaving school to come with me. I didn't mean it. School is important to her, and I'm not going to snatch her personal dreams away like my father did to my mom. That poor woman.

Having dinner with them last night was like torture, and my dad seemed to relish giving me endless shit. Like the old man gets off on being hard on me. I'm pretty sure he believes that attitude is what's made me into who I am today.

I didn't bother telling him I got support from others and that's what kept me on this path of success. My friends and former coaches back at high school. The current coaching staff and everyone else who works for the football team, along with my teammates. My best friends.

This woman right here, watching me with caution in her gaze, like she's afraid I'm going to tell her to get the hell out of my bed and never come back. Like I would ever do that. I need this woman in my life too damn much to ever let her go again.

She's mine. I'm gonna put this woman on lock, and soon. I want forever with her. Does she want me the same way?

God, I hope so.

"I don't know." She shrugs, and my gaze goes to her pretty shoulders. Once the headache clears, I think I'll spend the rest of the day kissing every single one of Sienna's freckles, which is going to take a long-ass time.

Sounds like a great plan.

"Come on, Sienna. Tell me what I said." I go to the bed, slipping beneath the comforter and tugging it over me at the same time I reach for her hand and pull her into me. She gasps, her hands settling on my chest. "Was it that bad, baby? Did I embarrass you?"

"More like you embarrassed yourself a little." She keeps her head dipped so I can't look in her eyes. "You treated the Uber driver like your best friend."

I chuckle. "That poor guy. I remember how big his eyes got when he saw me in his window."

"He freaked a little," she agrees, her head still bent.

I slip my fingers beneath her chin and tilt her face up, our gazes meeting. "Are you scared to tell me?"

She nods. "Kind of."

"Because I said I was in love with you?" I raise my brows.

Her expression shifts into shock. "You remember?"

"I was playing with you." Her face falls, and I rush to correct myself. "Just now, not what I said last night. I remember everything. And I meant every word of it too."

Her eyes fill with tears, and holy shit, I didn't want to make her cry. "You did?"

"Yeah. I did. Shit, Sienna. You're crying." I dab at the tears streaking down her face, and she closes her eyes, a watery laugh escaping her.

"Happy tears, Gavin. You . . . you love me? Really?"

I nod, worried she might not feel the same. She never said it back to me last night. I definitely remember that and try not to focus on it too much. And so far, she hasn't said it today either.

She's making me nervous.

"I love you so much, I can barely think about anything else. Anyone else." I cup her cheek, stroke my thumb over her skin. "You're everything to me."

Sienna stares at me with those big brown eyes, a trembling breath escaping her, and I brace myself. Preparing for the worst. I shouldn't have said that. It's probably too soon, and maybe I'm feeling needy after spending time with my parents last night. I refuse to believe that just because my parents aren't great at showing me love means that I don't know how to do it. But I do. I know I do.

And I know I love this woman.

"I'm in love with you too," she finally whispers, and the ache in my heart eases. "I love you, Ga—"

I cut her off with my mouth, kissing her until the both of us can't breathe. Until our bodies and our breaths and our hearts are so completely intertwined, you can't tell who's who.

Well shit. Who knew I could be so damn sappy once I found love? I sure as hell didn't. I hope I never say this kind of shit out loud in front of my friends.

No. Scratch that. I don't care if I sound sappy and lovesick in front of the guys. I am lovesick, and it might sound terrible, but I feel great. I have the love of my life in my arms, and she feels the same way I do. Life can't get much better than this.

Well . . . a national championship would be a nice way to end the season. But that's coming.

I can feel it.

Sienna eventually pulls away from me, her hand going to her mouth, her eyes wide. "You made me forget I have morning breath."

"How many times have I told you that I don't care?" I reach for her again, but she rolls away from me, getting out of bed. She grabs her phone to check it, her face falling as she scrolls through what seem like endless notifications. She remains silent, continuously scrolling and reading, and unease trickles down my spine.

Worried, I sit up, scratching the back of my neck. "Everything okay?"

"Oh no," she whispers, and my panic ratchets up.

"Sienna." Her head jerks up at the serious tone of my voice. "What is it?"

"I think our Uber driver exposed us."

"What?" I have no idea what she's talking about.

"Look." She holds her phone out, and I take it, frowning at the photo of me and her in the back of a car. I've got my head tilted back against the seat, and she's watching me, concern all over her pretty face. I realize it's a social media post, and the caption below the photo says

Santa Mira QB Gavin Maddox confesses his love for teammate's sister Sienna Cooper.

I lift my head to find Sienna watching me, gnawing on her lower lip. "What the hell is this?"

"It's that one profile that keeps tabs on the university gossip. *Tales of UCSM*—you've heard of it, right?"

I nod. Everyone knows about *Tales of UCSM*. Sometimes it shares serious info, but most of the time it spreads gossip around campus.

Guess the word is out now.

"That photo is from the back of the Uber we took last night. I don't even remember him taking a pic of us." She takes the phone out of my hand and sits heavily onto the mattress, her worry coming off her in waves. "I have all sorts of notifications because this guy tagged us, Gavin. I've got texts from my brother. Nico. Everleigh. Frank. Even Jonesie."

I grab my phone and check it to find I also have a ton of notifications. Mostly social media ones, thanks to the photo tag, but there are plenty of texts, too, including some in the group chat I have with my best friends.

Nico: What the actual FUCK dude? You're in love with Sienna and we're finding it out on a gossip site?

Dollar: Were you drunk QB? Is that why you said it? Fucked up if that's the case.

Coop: WTF

Dread coats my gut at Coop's simple text. That's all he said. *WTF.* Shit.

I bet he's pissed.

There's a text from Everleigh too. Hers almost makes me laugh. Almost.

Everleigh: It's about damn time you got your head out of your ass if what that guy said is true! Sienna is the best thing that will ever happen to you. If you two are actually together, I can't believe you kept this from us.

"I need to call my brother." Sienna hits a button on her screen and brings the phone to her ear. It rings and rings, eventually going to voicemail, and I hear the rumble of Coop's familiar voice asking to leave a message. She ends the call before the beep sounds, her wide eyes meeting mine. "We need to talk to our friends."

"You think they're mad at us?" I wince, scratching the back of my neck again.

"Mad? Um, yeah. From the tone of their various text messages, most definitely." A sigh escapes her, and I haul her into my arms, not wanting this moment to end badly. We confessed our love for each other. We planned to tell everyone anyway; we just got scooped by our rat fink Uber driver. We can't let him ruin everything.

"Some of the comments about us being together, they weren't very nice," she admits, her mouth moving against my neck when she speaks. "I knew this would happen."

"I bet not all of them are awful." She pulls away so her gaze meets mine. "Right?"

"There were a few positive ones." Sienna shrugs. "I guess some people are just going to hate."

I worried about that too—before. Now I don't care what anyone thinks. "Haters gonna hate, baby. Fuck 'em. They don't matter." I touch her cheek. Smile at her, but she doesn't smile back. "Come on, Sienna. It's going to be okay."

"I just don't want our friends to be angry. Or my brother. They all matter to me. They're like my family," she admits, her voice soft.

"They're like my family too. We've got this. They'll understand."
I kiss her forehead. "I know they will. They're our best friends. They'll
be happy for us. I'm sure of it."

She tilts her head back, her gaze imploring. "You really think so?"

Shit, I hope so.

Chapter Thirty

SIENNA

Gavin was wrong. Our friends don't understand why we chose to hide our relationship from them, and they're definitely upset with us. Maybe not quite mad—well, for some reason Frank is all fired up over it—but they're definitely unhappy with our, and I quote, *shady behavior.*

That's how Nico describes it, anyway.

It's Sunday afternoon, and we're currently at the house, pleading our case in front of a jury of our peers, because that's what it feels like. Gavin and I are on trial for keeping our relationship secret, but we're wasting our time since it feels like everyone's minds are already made up. They don't approve of what we did, and they're never going to let us forget it—case closed.

That's according to Nico, who's acting like he's the representative for everyone, while Gavin and I sit together on the love seat, facing our friends. And my brother, who hasn't said a single word since we arrived, and that was twenty minutes ago.

The look on his face makes me uneasy. I don't think Gavin likes it, either, though he hasn't said anything. He keeps glancing over at Coop, waiting for him to speak, but he doesn't. Of course he doesn't. I think he's enjoying seeing us twisting in the wind, waiting for his opinion to drop.

The longer he goes without speaking, the more worried I become. Yes, this is normal for him, but I can't stand the suspense. I'd rather know he hates me than sit here and wonder about it.

Finally, the voice of reason—a.k.a. my new bestie, Everleigh—starts talking.

"Look." She smiles, her gaze dropping to the spot where Gavin and I are clutching each other's hands. "I think it's adorable that you two are together. It's about damn time. But I don't understand why you had to keep it from all of us. We're your friends."

"Your family," Coop finally says, his voice rough as gravel.

I wince. The guilt trip finally worked, as I knew it would. "I'm sorry that I didn't tell you about us, Ever. That we didn't tell any of you. I wanted to, but I have to admit . . . there was something freeing in letting go of all of that worry and stress over wishing Gavin would notice me. Pretending to avoid him was so much easier, and it worked out because you all thought I didn't want to be around him, when really I didn't feel the need anymore because we were together a lot of the time. I know it doesn't make much sense, but it worked for me. For us."

"When did you guys even see each other?" Frank asks, his tone hostile.

"Mostly at night," Gavin says, glancing over at me with a faintly dirty smile. One that makes me blush.

"That's why you stopped coming over on game night," Nico mutters, shaking his head. "You were fucking around with Sienna."

"Hey," Gavin snaps. "Watch your mouth. That's my girlfriend you're talking about."

"Yeah." Coop reaches around Ever and lightly slaps the back of Nico's head. "And that's my *sister* you're talking about."

Nico ducks away from Coop's still-seeking hand. "Come on, Coop. You haven't had much to say. Are you telling us you don't have a problem with the two of them sneaking around for months and not telling us about it? That one of your best friends is now supposedly in love with your little sister?"

Coop goes quiet again, and the entire room fills with tension as we wait for his response. My palms are sweating, and I squeeze Gavin's hand, leaning my head against his shoulder. I don't want to lose my brother's support, but I know we disappointed him. He has every right to feel that way and . . . yeah. We're terrible humans.

"I get why they did it," Coop finally says, shocking all of us. "Gavin is under a lot of pressure. It doesn't matter that we're a team and he's only as good as the rest of us make him, but he's the unspoken leader, and all of the media watches him. Criticizes him. It's actually pretty fucking unfair if you ask me."

"Thanks, Coop," Gavin starts, snapping his lips shut when Coop glares at him.

"I'm not finished."

"Right." Gavin lets go of my hand and starts scratching the back of his neck. He only does that when he's anxious. "Go on."

"Anyway—all the attention is on Gav, and that's a lot for him to deal with. If he wanted to keep the relationship with Sienna secret so there were no prying eyes spying on them, I understand. I'm just glad you guys finally came clean with us."

"Only because they were forced to," Frank reminds us. Gee thanks, friend. "That Uber driver even recorded audio of the two of them together last night."

"Wait, what?" Gavin leaps to his feet, stalking toward Frank and holding out his hand. "I wanna hear it."

Frank fumbles around with his phone and hands it over to Gavin, who turns up the volume. Yep, I can hear him, rambling on drunkenly. Making his declaration.

"He doesn't care." Oh, Gavin's voice on the recording is even louder than I realized last night. "Do you care that I'm in love with Sienna Cooper?"

"Not at all," the driver responds. "You can love whoever you want."

"That's exactly what I'm saying. It shouldn't matter. I don't know why we're keeping this a secret, baby. Everyone deserves to know how we feel about each other."

My heart swells to about three sizes larger than normal when I hear the sincerity in his voice. Those sweet words that threw me for a loop when he originally said them. Unable to stop myself, I reach for him, delivering a kiss to his lips, whispering against them, "I love you too."

He cracks a smile. "I didn't even say it just now. That's a recording."

"And it's the sweetest recording I've ever heard." I touch his cheek, our gazes meeting. His beautiful blue eyes are sparkling, and all his earlier anxiety seems to have melted away. "I love you so much. I'm so glad you're mine."

We kiss, and Gavin of course takes it a little further than he should, causing Coop to clear his throat. We spring apart from each other, Gavin scratching the back of his neck again while Everleigh is clutching her hands in front of her chest, a giant smile on her face.

"Oh my gosh, you two are so cute together! I love it. And from the sounds of that recording, you were going to tell everyone anyway. The Uber driver kind of helped with it? Maybe?"

Ever winces after saying that, and Gavin rolls his eyes while I shrug.

"I'm still pissed at him," Gavin mutters. "If I ever come across that guy again, I'm blasting him."

"We can kick his ass," Nico suggests, his face lighting up at the idea.

"Yeah, most definitely." Frank thrusts his fist into the air.

"No way." Gavin shakes his head. "I'm mad at him, but not that mad."

"I'm so happy for the two of you," Ever says, rising to her feet. "Come here and give me a hug. This is a big deal. Two of my favorite people are together and in love! This is a great day. We should celebrate."

Gavin and I stand and approach her, the three of us moving into a group hug, and slowly but surely, more people join us. Frank. Nico. Even Coop.

My brother inserts himself in between me and Gavin, slinging his arms around our shoulders and glancing down at me. "You really love him?"

"I do," I whisper.

He turns to look at Gavin. "You better take care of her, Gav. She's the sweetest woman on this planet. You don't deserve her."

"I know," Gavin says solemnly.

"You break her heart, I'll break your throwing arm. I mean it."

"Damn, Coop," Nico mutters, but Everleigh slaps him in the chest, shutting him up.

"I won't break her heart. And she owns mine already." Gavin tilts his head so he can look at me. "I'm going to marry her someday."

"Oh wow," Everleigh whispers. "This is so romantic."

"Way to make me look bad," Nico grumbles, earning another light slap from Everleigh.

"Are you okay with that?" Gavin asks Coop.

"I'm okay with it." Coop pauses. "Brother."

I'm crying. Gavin and Coop are hugging each other, and Everleigh runs over to me, gathering me up in a fierce hug.

"I can't stay mad at you," she murmurs before kissing my cheek. "But we're going out to dinner this week. Just the two of us. I need alllll the details about what happened."

"Yes, let's get together. I promise I'll tell you everything," I say, wiping the tears away from my eyes, glancing over my shoulder to find Gavin already watching me, love shining in his gaze.

All that love I see there, it's all for me.

Me.

We go back to my apartment after having dinner with everyone at the house. Everleigh and I made it, and it was so freeing in a different way, being able to show all my love and affection for Gavin and not having to hide my feelings any longer. I could tell he felt the same. At one point he came into the kitchen, his hands settling on my hips when he stood behind me, and he gave me a quick kiss on the neck. Everleigh about lost it over the sweet gesture, and he flashed her a quick smile before he exited the kitchen as fast as he'd entered it.

"That man loves you," she whispered, her excitement for me palpable.

"He really does," I whispered back, just before we started giggling like middle schoolers.

Her enthusiasm about our relationship makes me even happier, and while I understand why they put us through it, I'm grateful they're thrilled for us. I have supportive friends. A supportive brother too.

"Why are we here again?" Gavin asks me as I unlock my front door.

"I wanted to pick up a few things before I go to your place," I tell him as I open the door, coming to a stop when I see who's sitting on the couch.

It's Destiny. And her girlfriend, Lizzie. They're all cuddled up together, their gazes locked on the open laptop sitting on the coffee table. Destiny pulls away from Lizzie to hit the space bar and stop whatever they're watching.

"Oh. Hey." I walk farther into the apartment, and Gavin follows behind me, shutting the door. "I didn't expect you to be home."

"Lizzie's electricity is out, so we came over here to finish the movie we started at her place." Destiny's gaze shifts to Gavin. "What the hell is he doing here?"

"Um . . ." I didn't expect so much hostility coming from Destiny, but she is a bit of a Gavin hater, so I guess I shouldn't be surprised. And didn't she see what happened on her social media? I would've thought she'd already heard about us.

"We're together." Gavin slips his arm around my shoulders.

"For real?" The skepticism in her voice is obvious.

"Definitely. And hey, I'm Gavin." He drops his arm from around me and takes a step toward the couch, offering his hand to Destiny to shake. She takes it, reluctantly. "Sorry for sneaking into your dorm room that one time."

Destiny's mouth drops open, and her girlfriend's expression immediately turns suspicious.

"What exactly is he talking about?" Lizzie asks.

"I was feeling up Sienna, not your girlfriend." Gavin smiles and offers his hand to Lizzie. "I'm Gavin."

"Nice to meet you. I'm Lizzie." She shakes his hand limply, staring at his face, and I don't blame her for having that dazed expression. Gavin is charmingly handsome, and he's just pulled poor Lizzie into his orbit.

"Stop working your magic on my girl," Destiny grumbles, making everyone laugh. Even Lizzie, whose cheeks are bright pink.

I go to my bedroom while Gavin makes small talk with Destiny and Lizzie. After grabbing a duffel bag, I fill it with a few things, then move on to the bathroom, where I shove my toiletry bag inside it. I'm spending the next few days with my man. I even take my backpack with me, my laptop nestled inside. I don't have school until Tuesday, but I work tomorrow afternoon while he's at practice, so that won't be so bad. I'm going to spend the next two nights with him, and I can't wait.

"Ready?" I ask when I return to the living room.

"Yeah." Gavin grabs both bags from me. Such a gentleman. He even opens the door for me. "Nice meeting you both."

"Treat her right, Gavin Maddox!" Destiny shouts as he pulls the door shut.

"Don't worry, I will!" he yells back, making me smile.

Making me melt in a puddle.

How did I get so lucky?

Epilogue

SIENNA

They made it. The Dolphins are playing in the national-championship game, and while I'm thrilled for them, I'm also a nervous wreck. All of us are, and by all of us I'm talking about me, my parents, Everleigh, and Nico's mom, Claudia. We've been on the edge of our seats since we got here. No snacks are being eaten, no drinks beyond water. It's freezing outside, and we're all bundled up—and we're a collective bundle of nervous energy. It's awful.

But also exhilarating. I want this win so badly for both my brother and Gavin. This game is important to them. Feels like the most important game of their careers, and everything is riding on this win. If they lose?

I can barely stomach the thought, but that won't ruin their potential. Quite a few of them are predicted to make it into the NFL draft. Gavin is currently a top pick. So is Coop. Nico and Jonesie too. I want it for all of them, even though I realize they might not all get drafted.

That's a worry for another day. Right now, I need to focus on this game and hope that all the positive vibes we've been casting out into the universe have worked. I have manifested the shit out of this. I visualized them winning. Constantly talk about them winning, though after a while Gavin made me stop. Too worried that my saying they'll win could jinx them.

Athletes are incredibly superstitious.

"I can't take it." Everleigh covers her eyes with her gloved hands, though two fingers are spread so one eye is still visible. She reminds me of that one emoji.

"Drop your hands. It's not that big of a deal." Don't I sound easy breezy? It's a facade because I definitely don't feel that way. My stomach is twisted into knots, and I worry I might throw up.

Ever removes her hands, wringing them constantly, and I avert my head, unable to look at her or the field. Instead, I scan the sea of faces filling the stadium. Sense the excitement filling the air. We're leading on the scoreboard, and there are only five minutes left on the clock. We're in the fourth quarter, but I can't relax. Things can and usually do change at a moment's notice. There will be no reason to celebrate early. I'm waiting until that clock hits zero before I can finally relax.

We just scored a field goal, which means the opposing team comes jogging out onto the field, and I rest my hands under my thighs, hating how agitated I feel. My mother pats me on the arm, and I glance over at her, smiling softly.

"They're going to win," she whispers. "I can feel it. Mother's intuition. It's rarely failed me before."

"It's true," Dad adds, his attention never straying from the field as he shovels popcorn in his mouth. He's the only one who's able to eat during the game. The rest of us just groan when he tries to push whatever it is he's snacking on at us. "Hey, wait a minute. Joy, isn't that the boy who was on the wrestling team with Coop?"

I sit up straighter, focusing on where Dad is looking. Guess he didn't have his eyes trained on the field. Because I see exactly who he's talking about—Ryland walking up the steps toward the top of the stands, holding hands with a very pretty and very tall brunette.

"Who are you talking about?" Mom squints as she looks around.

"It's Ryland," I murmur, relieved he's found someone else to focus on. Obsess over. He left me alone after that night at the party, and I'd even started to think he wasn't that bad. But then I remember that one afternoon a few weeks back when Coop and I were at the store picking up snacks before we headed to his house and we spotted Ryland. He made some snide remark about me and Gavin being together, surprising me that he would be so bold. My brother was ready to tackle him in the middle of the supermarket, and I had to remind him that he couldn't cause a scene. That he could risk his position on the football team if he did something stupid, and that seemed to get through to him. Thank God.

Yeah. Ryland doesn't deserve my sympathy. I don't need to make any excuses for him. I still feel awful for kind of using him, but he also got a little weird on me.

Okay, a lot weird. But now he's someone else's problem, and I can't worry about him, especially not right now.

"I remember that boy!" Mom tries to find him, but he's already gone, most likely in his seat. "I wish we could've talked to him."

I am so glad we weren't able to talk to Ryland. That sounds like my own personal nightmare.

There's a group of girls who look around my age sitting not too far away from where we're at, and when I glance in their direction, I catch a couple of them taking photos of me. This has happened on occasion after everyone found out that Gavin and I are together, and while it made me uneasy at first, I guess I've gotten used to it? Women used to come gawk at me at work, too, and Matty would waste his energy trying to run them off all the time. Until he finally came up with the bright idea of putting up a sign in the window. It says GET A PHOTO AND AUTOGRAPH WITH GAVIN MADDOX'S GIRLFRIEND! ONLY FIFTY BUCKS!

No one really comes in and tries to take my picture or harass me anymore. Not that they harassed me, but they would ask lots of questions. Some of them personal. One time a girl asked for Gavin's dick size. She brought in a ruler and everything.

Embarrassing.

I've been working a lot, though. Saving up my money for my future ice cream empire, as Gavin calls it. He calls me the ice cream queen, and I think that's cute, even though I sometimes think my business idea is silly. Gavin never makes me feel that way, though. That man 100 percent believes in me. Just like I believe in him.

We resume our focus on the game, and I tear off my glove so I can nibble on a hangnail. A gross habit that I seem to fall back into every time I get nervous while watching a game. Gavin isn't even on the field. My gaze drops to where he stands on the sidelines, Nico right beside him. Gavin's got his hands on his hips, and his helmet is off, the cold breeze rushing through the bowl-shaped stadium making his hair ruffle, and I wish I was down there with him, offering him comfort.

But then again, I'm glad I'm not down there because when he's this tense, he's almost impossible to comfort.

"Coop is doing so well, considering he's playing a different position," Mom says after our defensive line, which includes my brother, keeps blocking the opposing team from gaining much yardage. They're barely moving down the field, and I can tell the players are frustrated.

"He is," I agree, and Everleigh nods. Coop filled in for an injured defensive lineman for the last couple of playoff games, and he's playing better than ever.

They settle into position, and the play goes into motion, the players scrambling all over the field, the QB about to get sacked by one of our linemen when he throws the ball. He hits the ground, but the ball soars into the air, landing right in my brother's hands.

"Oh my God!" I leap to my feet first, everyone else following me, and we're jumping up and down as Coop runs down the field, heading for the Dolphins' end zone.

"Look at how fast he is." Pride fills Mom's voice. "That's our boy, Jerry!"

Coop makes it into the end zone despite the two guys on his tail trying to drag him down, which is near impossible, considering how big he is. The referee throws his arms up in the air, signaling it's a touchdown, and half the stadium loses it. The joyous roar of the crowd is impossibly loud, and I'm hugging my mom and dad before turning to Ever, and I hug her and Claudia too. We're smiling and laughing, and some of us are even crying, and during it all, my dad continues to shove popcorn into his mouth.

"Guess we're celebrating tonight" is the only thing he has to say, which has Mom shaking her head.

"Oh, Jerry." She wipes the tears away from her cheeks. "Our boy is a star!"

He is. They all are. And I can't wait to rush the field in a couple of minutes and celebrate with the team. With Gavin. They did it.

And I couldn't be prouder.

I'm on the field and it's absolute mayhem. People are everywhere. Confetti still flutters in the air and is covering most of the field. Everywhere I look I see Dolphins team members celebrating with their family and friends. I got separated from my parents once we came down here, and I haven't seen them or Coop. Haven't found Gavin either. I'm starting to panic, and my head feels like it's on a swivel, looking left, then right. Then left again. Where are they?

"Sienna!"

I jerk my head toward the sound of my brother's voice, and I see him standing there flanked by our parents. I run over to them and give

Coop a hug, clinging to him for a moment before I tip my head back. He has the biggest grin on his face that I've ever seen, and he gives me a little shake.

"We did it."

"You did it," I tell him, beaming with pride. "That play was great."

"The ball just landed in my hands." He shrugs, always modest. "I got lucky."

"You did not. It was an amazing catch. And you ran it into the end zone with those two guys clinging to you, and you looked like you couldn't be bothered."

"They were a nuisance more than anything else."

I start to laugh. Mom and Dad do, too, and when I glance to my right, I do a double take when I see who's standing there.

Mr. QB himself. Gav. I hear women shouting at him right now, his nickname on repeat.

"Gavin." I let go of Coop and head straight for my boyfriend, closing my eyes when he pulls me into his arms and crushes me to him, resting his cheek on top of my head. We hold on to each other and don't speak for a moment, absorbing each other before I finally pull away slightly so I can look into his eyes. "You did it."

"We did it." He's smiling at me, his eyes sparkling with joy and triumph and so much love. "Your brother is the MVP."

"He's acting so nonchalant about it."

"Please. He secured the win." Gavin dips his head, his mouth finding mine in the sweetest, softest kiss. "We won."

"I know." I'm smiling, giddy with excitement and pride. "I'm so happy for you, Gavin. So proud."

"Thanks, baby." His smile is soft. Intimate. I remember wishing he would look at me like this. Just once. And now he does all the time.

"Wait!" I take a step back, his arms falling away, and unzip my jacket to show him the T-shirt I made myself using Destiny's Cricut. My roommate is a fanatical crafter. "Check out my shirt."

His gaze drops to the front of my chest, reading what it says, and I am beaming. Trying my hardest not to laugh.

"Gavin's number one fan." His gaze lifts to mine. "Wait a minute. Didn't I joke with you about being president of my fan club?"

Nodding, I take a step closer to him, grateful he's got his arms back around me. "And I never forgot what you said. Now look at us."

"I love it." His expression turns serious. "I love you, Sienna. I appreciate you so damn much. I can't believe you tolerated my ass for this long."

"I love you too," I tell him, reaching up to touch his face. "Despite what you think and what you've been told in the past, you're easy to love."

He hasn't spoken to his father again since that fateful dinner, but he's been texting with his mom a lot, and they even got together for lunch a few days ago. Just the two of them. He told me after they met up that he wants me to go with him next time. That he wants to introduce the two most important women in his life to each other, and because I'm a giant sap, I cried when he said that.

God, I love this man. So much.

He kisses me again. "You're the best thing that's ever happened to me, baby. And don't you ever forget it."

"So." I'm grinning. "Now we wait for the draft?"

"Yeah." He grimaces. "Don't know if my heart can take it."

"I'll protect it." I rest my hand upon the center of his chest, feeling nothing but his protective gear. "I've got you."

"I've got you, too, Freckles." He delivers another kiss on my lips, lingering for a moment before he finally pulls away. "We're going to do this, huh?"

"Do what?" I'm frowning.

"Us. You and me." He kisses my forehead. "Forever."

"Yes," I breathe, nodding again and again. "We definitely will."

We hear our friends calling our names, and we both turn to find Nico and Everleigh headed toward us. I remain at Gavin's side, absorbing his strength and his love, my heart so full it feels like it could burst. Does life get any better than this?

With Gavin Maddox by my side, I'm thinking yes.

Yes, it does.

Acknowledgments

I love writing in the Kings of Campus world, and I hope you love reading about these characters! Sports romance is one of my favorite subgenres to write, and I adore the found-family vibes in this series. I had the best time with Sienna and Gavin, even though I wrote their story in an extremely short amount of time. Ugh, I love them so much, and after I turned in the edits, I missed them. I still miss them!

I want to acknowledge everyone at Montlake, especially Maria and Mackenzie. Working with you and everyone else is so easy, and I appreciate everything you do for me. Big shout-out to Georgana Grinstead for always having my back and to everyone at Valentine PR. And of course, a giant thank-you to the readers. Without you, I am truly nothing. Thank you for reading my words. It means the world to me, and I am eternally grateful to be able to write books every damn day.

About the Author

Monica Murphy is a *New York Times* and *USA Today* bestselling author of over sixty novels. She writes mostly contemporary, new adult, and young adult romance. Both traditionally and independently published, her work has been translated into more than ten languages.

Murphy lives in central California near Yosemite National Park with her husband, children, one dog, and four cats. When she's not writing, she's thinking about writing. Or reading. Or binge-watching something.